KELLY O'FLAHERTY

CRANTHORPE
MILLNER
PUBLISHERS

First published by Cranthorpe Millner Publishers (2022)

ISBN 978-1-80378-019-1 (Paperback)

www.cranthorpemillner.com

Cranthorpe Millner Publishers

For Ross

For being my rock, my light, my everything
And for being my demon hunting partner

Author's Note

Hi there,

Thank you so much for picking up this book. I set out to write a story with the aim of spreading awareness about mental health, to offer support and understanding to those struggling and to also help their peers to understand what it's like to live with depression.

The story is largely based on my own experiences. I hope you can find support and understanding in these pages, but be aware that it may prove difficult to read at times. So, if you are struggling right now, and choose to read this book (thank you!), please make sure you have someone to talk to, somewhere to go, if it becomes too much.

I've included a list of helplines for UK/Ireland at the back of this book if you need someone to talk to.

At its core, this is a story about hope, friendship and love even though the journey can be dark at times.

Don't let the demons win.

- Kelly.

1.

My heart beat loudly in my chest, reminding me that I was still here, that I was still alive. I tried to focus my attention on the expansion of my lungs, locked safely in the confines of my ribcage. They felt sure to break free at any moment. I dug my nails into my arm, trying to regain control, trying to hold it back. I couldn't let it take over. Not here, not now.

I glanced down at the marks on my skin as the sounds from the classroom swam in my ear. I looked up and tried to focus on the teacher, tried in vain to make sense of the muffled words in my ears. The words on the page in front of me were blurring together into an illegible mess.

I dug my nails deeper into my arm and pulled one of the scabs away. The pain was enough. My heart slowed, my breathing steadied, and slowly the world came back into focus.

I prepared myself for their judgment, for their glares of contempt, but no one turned in my direction, not even the person sitting beside me. Sometimes I wondered if she was truly just oblivious or purposefully ignoring what she'd affectionately call my "drama".

These moments had quickly become all too familiar to me. I felt them coming on like an approaching wave of darkness. I'd see the ripple in the still waters of an otherwise okay day, disturbed by the sudden presence of an invisible force beneath the surface. Then, all too quickly, the wave would wash over me, dragging me further and further down into the depths of the darkness until I was sure I would drown, my stifled cries caught in my throat.

"Are you all right?" Rachel said as the class finally ended.

"Yeah, I'm fine," I answered automatically. I never considered saying anything else. I never considered sharing my thoughts with her either, this girl who had been by my side for years, day in and day out, the girl without whom I couldn't possibly have withstood school.

The art of making conversation and the ability to start friendships were skills I had surely been born without. My parents would quickly use the excuse, "she's just shy" whenever I failed to give a relative an answer longer than two words as they asked me about my life. Soon enough, they learned to stop asking.

Sometimes I'd feel like I couldn't think at all. Spoken words would hit my ears, but my mind would conjure no response, so I would remain silent.

The fact that I had Rachel as a friend really was a miracle in itself. We had first met just before maths class four years ago as we waited for the teacher to arrive. I had become accustomed to keeping to myself at this point and had learned to ignore my growing envy as I watched others gather around, talking loudly and cheerfully amongst themselves. I'd find myself yearning to be a part of that group, only to jump in fear when one of them glanced over at me. I kept my head low as I scrawled nonsensical things into my sketchbook. I brought it with me almost everywhere; it had become something like another arm for me.

I was certain that Rachel must have taken pity on me as she sat down beside me and started casually talking, seemingly unfazed by my delayed response. The pencil in my hand skittered across the page as I forced myself to look up at her. My heart started to pound in my chest and I tried to think of something to say, anything at all, so I wouldn't look like a complete idiot. But, I needn't have worried. It seemed like she could talk enough for the both of us.

She was a plain sort of girl, with big-rimmed glasses that perfectly flattered the shape of her face. She stood a good half-a-foot beneath my towering five foot six inches. Her mousy brown hair hung at the sides of her face, with no real shape or style to it. That didn't really matter though. What mattered was that she was the first person in the school to offer me any kind of friendship, and the only one determined enough to get through the wall I had built around myself.

Somehow she managed to put up with my silences and awkward answers. Our friendship blossomed quickly as she invited me to sit beside her and her friends at lunch. As the days went on, that group steadily grew. It was almost like she was collecting friends; it was all so effortless for her. Pretty soon, I became accustomed to having her by my side and thought that finally I would have the chance to be a normal teenager, with my own friendship group, sharing jokes and gossip, and going to parties. However, it would seem that the demons whispering in my ear were rarely wrong.

"They don't bite, I promise," she said laughingly one day, noticing my hesitation to sit beside these people who were my classmates yet complete strangers.

I forced myself to sit down beside them, barely saying a word for that entire hour.

***

The sound of a knock on the door woke me far too early.

"Samantha, honey, time to wake up," Mum called. I groaned loudly and urged her to leave me alone. "Don't be like that. Time for school! Get up and have some breakfast."

4

I listened to the sounds of her footsteps as she moved away from my room and out of the house. Mum was always up extra early as she worked in the boys primary school. She always managed to sound quite chipper and full of life, too. The morning affected me a little differently.

I had my own alarm set to wake me later again as I inevitably drifted in and out of sleep. The routine was the same every day. The alarm would sound just before eight a.m. and I'd hit the snooze button one too many times until I really did need to get up. I'd silence the alarm and pull my lead-like legs off the bed.

That October morning, I quickly threw on my uniform, pulling the collar of my blouse up over the neckline of the navy jumper. I picked up my hairbrush and struggled to pull it through the mess of hair on my head. Brown strands fell to the floor, forever combined with the fibres of the carpet. I paused for too long, critiquing my face; the premature bags beneath my eyes, the paleness of skin that rarely sees the sun, a new spot on the side of my nose - features I doubted anyone would describe as *pretty*. I pulled a bobble out of my dresser drawer and tried tying my hair up with it, but oh God, no; my ears looked far too big for my face. I quickly pulled my hair down again and smoothed it back into place.

I glanced around my room noting, once again, that it needed to be tidied, but I never had the energy to do anything about it. A bundle of clothes lay in the corner, ready to be transported to a washing machine. Scattered notes and pieces of paper were strewn across the floor - hopefully not important ones. I had attempted to cover up the ghastly pink paint on my walls with an array of posters; some of my favourite artworks ranging from Van Gogh's Impressionism to Georgia O'Keeffe's unique Abstract paintings. Many of them were faded and torn. I really needed new ones.

Deciding to tidy up tomorrow instead, I grabbed the sketchbook from the desk and stuffed my pencils into my bag. That bundle of papers would often be a saving grace to me on the more boring days (i.e. every day).

I hurried downstairs, running a bit late, as usual. I put some bread into the toaster and went to the fridge to collect the lunchbox that I knew would be there.

Sometimes I felt bad that Mum still felt compelled to make lunches for her sixteen-year-old daughter; she'd insist that she was simply taking care of her baby. Truth be told, I would've just grabbed a bunch of snacks instead of bothering to make a sandwich or anything substantial if it wasn't for her.

The lunchbox had a sticky note on the lid. It read, in very neat handwriting, "Don't be late! Love you xoxo."

I quickly made my way down the path towards school, Tíreen Community College, swallowing the last bit of toast. I passed many other students on my way - none of them in any particular hurry - despite the fact that it was almost five minutes until nine o'clock. Many students were lounging about outside shops; some even attempting to take a not-so-sneaky drag of a cigarette. As I passed, one of the girls, whose blonde hair fell down to her waist, exhaled a great cloud of white. Her friends giggled alongside her.

I pushed myself up the remaining length of the path towards the school, practically running through the courtyard and in through the entrance hall of the school as the clock neared nine.

The school building was nothing remarkable, at least not to me, but then who was I to judge in my youthful ignorance? The long corridors seemed to stretch out for miles yet were so narrow there was barely enough room for two people of average size to walk side by side without constantly bumping into each other.

The walls throughout the school were painted a bland beige; clearly not much thought had been put into choosing it. It was as if they had purposefully chosen a colour to enhance the claustrophobic nature of school life even further. The doors embedded along the length of the walls were painted a dull, pale yellow so they would be easy to miss were it not for the cut-out area featuring a pane of glass allowing passers-by to see into the rooms beyond.

I squeezed my way through the crowds of students

littering the corridors and rushed towards the end of the hallway. The sound of dozens of voices talking at once almost drowned out the monotonous tone of the bell sounding over the intercom, yet still the *ding-ding-dinging* fulfilled its purpose of demanding movement.

I almost tripped over someone who was lazily sitting on the floor with their legs stretched out before them. I uttered a swift apology and was gifted a muted grunt in response.

I finally arrived at my maths classroom just as my classmates were going inside. I spotted the familiar head of hair in front of me, shorter than most others but noticeable nonetheless. As we filed into the classroom, I manoeuvred around everyone to catch up with her.

"Morning, sleepyhead," Rachel greeted me.

I stifled a tired yawn. "Morning. Sorry ... just couldn't get out of bed."

"Nothing new there, then."

"You know that I'd much rather be here, learning all about logarithms and quadratic what-ya-ma-call-its," I said.

"It is what it is, Sam," Rachel replied, as we positioned ourselves in our usual seats. Rachel preferred to sit up close to the front of the room to see the board and teacher clearer. It also meant that no taller student would sit in front of her. No one would dare sit in the front row unless they wanted to be mocked forever.

Our classmates continued to chatter amongst

themselves as we waited for our teacher to arrive - Mr. McCarthy wasn't one to hurry.

"I could've slept an extra ten minutes," I mused, as I watched the minute hand on the clock at the front of the room creep towards the figure two.

"I'm sure that would've made all the difference."

"Every second counts, as they say. I'm gonna have a nap." I laid my head down on my crossed arms but was quickly roused again by Rachel lightly swatting the back of my head.

"Get up. I can see him outside, talking to the principal." Just as Rachel finished saying this, the door eased open and Mr. McCarthy shuffled inside. His ageing body made his every movement seem to require complete and utter focus, taking an immense amount of energy. I felt sorry for him as he slumped down into his chair. Maybe *he* could've used those extra ten minutes in bed.

The chatter in the room quickly dulled to a quiet murmur as Mr. McCarthy cleaned his glasses on the edge of his jumper – which surely doesn't help much. *Wouldn't that just get flecks of fabric all over the lenses?* I wondered.

"Quiet down now, class has started. You've had more than enough time to chat." In contrast to his somewhat frail form, Mr. McCarthy's voice seemed especially energetic today. "We'll pick up where we left off. I believe it was—" We waited in silence as he took a moment to glance through his notes. "Ah yes, chapter seven."

As we each opened our books, the sound of the simultaneous turning of pages filled the room. Just as Mr. McCarthy cleared his throat to start the lesson, the door to the classroom creaked open with hesitation.

"Late again, Gallagher?" Mr. McCarthy said to the head peeking around the door. The student mumbled what I assumed was some sort of apology, but I couldn't hear him properly, despite being fairly close. I doubted the teacher could either. "No time now, you're late enough. I'll speak to you later. Get to your seat quickly and quietly. Chapter seven."

"Did you see that?" Rachel whispered beside me.

"See what?" I asked as I scratched a doodle into the side of the textbook. I glanced up again to catch him walking back to his seat with his head hung low. He sat down in a row at the back of the class. His friend beside him gently patted him on the back in greeting.

"The huge bruise on his face," Rachel pointed out, baffled that I didn't notice.

I suppose I hadn't paid much attention to his face. I decided to try to steal a glance now, out of curiosity, and quickly looked back over at him. A sizable bruise was clearly visible across his left cheek. The purple hue stood out against his pale skin and I wondered how I had missed it. He tried - and greatly failed - to smooth his longish dark hair over his face to conceal it. I turned away just before he caught me looking.

"Ouch," I commented under my breath to Rachel, "Wonder who he pissed off." Rachel chuckled, hiding her grin behind her hands as Mr. McCarthy shot us a look that immediately silenced us.

Nine times out of ten, Michael Gallagher would show up late for the first class of the day. He always seemed genuinely apologetic, but after a while, the teachers stopped asking for excuses. I wondered what it was this time. I had the feeling he wasn't just a lazy teenager, there was more to it than that.

Forty minutes later, the bell rang to announce the end of class. I noticed that Michael stayed behind after the last of us had left. I couldn't help but be curious ...

2.

My fifth year in secondary school was in full swing. The number of notches on my calendar grew with each passing day; another day, one step closer to the end. Someday, I'd no longer have to walk through those same doors and walk down those same corridors as I had done day after day after day. Someday everything would change and I'd be set free.

So much of my life had been consumed by school and all the triviality that comes with it. It's true when they say that school life can be likened to prison life - the routine schedule with a tolling bell that threatens expulsion at every sound, the glare of passing eyes as they attempt to bore into your mind and reveal your deepest and darkest secrets, the stale air inadequate for the amount of lungs it has to satiate and the eyes in the walls that watch your every move, waiting eagerly for a moment in which to make your existence unbearable.

As the walls pressed in upon me, I became increasingly aware of myself and the amount of room I occupied. *Shrink, you're taking up too much space. Get out of the way, move, run.*

The air grew heavy in my lungs as I attempted to steady myself. Every day I walked down the same corridors, clutching my sketchbook to my chest as if it could act as body armour. I felt the weight of others' stares upon me. What were they looking at? I repositioned the earbuds in my ears and tried to focus solely on the music and drown everything else out.

Rachel was the opposite. She walked down each corridor with a smile spread across her face, unfazed by the eyes that fell upon her. She seemed to be friends with almost everyone, proffering hellos as easily as breathing. She was impenetrable, a staple of happiness, strong willed and impossible to tear down. She was happy to be here, happy to be alive; just happy.

"It's nearly the end, you know," she said to me one afternoon during lunch.

"The end? The year just started," I replied. It was only just early October. We had barely gotten into the depth of our studies. Word of the dreaded Leaving Certificate had barely been uttered.

"No, that's not what I meant. I meant it's almost over. Two more years and we're out! Scary."

"I feel like it's been an eternity here."

"Just a little bit more ..." She smiled wistfully. "Know what you wanna do yet?"

"I dunno ... college?"

"Oh, of course. You're going to art college.

13

Crawford or something. No buts about it." She said, matter-of-factly, as if it had already been decided.

"Crawford? No way," I laughed.

"Why not?"

"There's no way I'd be able to get in there. Have you seen the stuff they do? It's insane!" I said to her as images of incredible art flashed before my mind's eye. I had visited the students' exhibition on a number of occasions over the past year. I could still see those doors standing enormously tall in front of me, analysing whether I belonged there. The walls were covered in a variety of works and installations, some beyond my wildest dreams.

I saw expressions of movement and emotion littered upon each canvas, pulling me in. I witnessed explosions of colour and vitality and felt overwhelmed by the sheer presence of genius and talent. I felt small and insignificant among them.

"I've seen what *you* do. You just don't know how good you are. You're applying because *I* said so." I couldn't help but smile in response to Rachel's words of encouragement. She would scold me anytime I uttered words of self-doubt and catch me whenever I consumed myself with hesitation and worry. I allowed myself to put faith in her words, holding them tightly as time went on.

I flicked through my sketchbook; it was almost full. I'd have to get a new one soon. Most of the pages

14

had become filled with nonsensical doodles drawn to simply pass the time, simply to keep myself awake and focused during another long and drawn out session in the classroom. Mixed in amongst these ramblings of the mind were creations bursting from my imagination, expressions, feelings and thoughts from my soul.

I'd often take out my pencil and sketch the people around me, noting their posture, their expression and their very being. I'd take care that they didn't notice me studying them; I imagined that they wouldn't take kindly to my persistent glances. The pages quickly filled up with drawings of gestures and expressions, details of hands and eyes, as well as full portraits.

The eyes, in particular, were always fascinating to me. The eyes were powerful – the windows to the soul – where all secrets were revealed. The eyes could never lie. If you looked hard enough and focused deeply enough on them, you could see through anyone.

As I drew, I'd find myself pulled away into another world and for a blissful moment I'd be in control. I could control everything that happened there on the page. I could change anything that I didn't like and make it mine. I could say what I wanted through the stroke of a line and the pull of a brush. I could express my pent-up frustration and show the world who I really was.

However, these drawings were just for me. I could never show these doodles and scribbles to someone else, to someone important. Rachel praised them whenever she saw them over my shoulder, but she was my best friend so she had to support me. My parents would say the same; they would tell me to chase my dream until the very end. Could I actually be good enough to get into a prodigious art school? Could I really do this as a career and make a living from it? I wasn't so sure.

3.

Crimson, vermillion, ruby, scarlet. The word "red" wasn't enough to describe the colour of the blood as it broke free from my skin. I sat transfixed on my bed and watched as the droplets formed and flowed slowly across my arm. I felt no inclination to stop it.

I could barely explain how it all happened; why I let it happen in the first place, that night three years ago, and why I continued to let it happen. None of it made any sense. It felt like I was falling - falling and falling with no sign of stopping. I tried to reach out to grab the precipice of the cliff that had disappeared beneath me. I tried to force air out of my lungs to call for help but only made myself breathless. I tried to push against the forces that were pulling me further and further down into the endless darkness, but I remained helpless.

I could see the question formed on everyone's lips: *why*? I had nothing to complain about; no great trauma, no horrible abuse. I didn't have the right to complain. I had learned to keep my mouth shut. It was better, after all, to say nothing rather than be ridiculed or resented.

So, I continued to fall. I stopped trying, my limbs weary from the effort of it. I stopped screaming and shouting, and my voice grew silent as my falling turned to floating that seemingly would never end.

The steady rhythm of school-homework-sleep continued in a ceaseless cycle. I found some comfort in drawing as a means of escape, my sole means of expression.

Eventually though, that too began to grow stale. I held the pencil in my hand, turning it slowly in the pencil sharpener, urging for a perfect shape. I gazed at the graphite meeting the minuscule blade, the rotation echoing the cogs in my mind. Thinking, thinking but what was I even thinking? I felt empty. My mind felt blank as the scraping sound filled my ears.

The lead of the pencil snapped and I stopped, frozen. The hint of unwanted tears began to brim in my eyes. *What are you crying for?* My gaze was still transfixed on the tiny blade with the piece of graphite stuck behind it. Its fragile plastic casing was cracked in places after years of wear and I wondered ...

It fell away all too easily as I pulled on the casing, removing the graphite and the blade itself. It lay solitary in my hand, the screw through its middle rendered useless. Conscious thought had entered my mind once again and I caught myself. *What are you doing? You've broken it now. That's completely stupid. Throw it out.*

18

I didn't throw out the broken pencil sharpener. Instead I felt compelled to hide it under a stack of books on my desk.

Most days I managed to talk myself out of it. Until the day I failed to do just that.

***

I was used to being alone. Before Rachel came along, and on the days she wasn't there, I would sit on my own at lunch every day, dive into my work and repel everyone away from me. No one ever spoke to me or approached me. I focused on keeping my mind and hands distracted to fight off the growing envy in my heart as I watched their happy faces amidst their group of friends.

I felt like I was living in some sort of movie but not a modern movie where there was action and romance at every corner, but instead like one of those old movies that had to be manually turned by hand in order to be played, in order to be seen, and showing nothing of great interest.

"Samantha, did you hear me?" I remembered that night all too well. It was years ago now and I could still recall it clearly. I had gotten lost in my own thoughts again, the voices of my family muffled in my ears. Mum's irritated voice broke through to me. My eyes refocused on the plate of food before me, untouched. It felt like the day had passed in a blur, with little participation on my part.

"What?" I said, attempting to drag my voice off the ground.

"*What?*" Dad jeered "Don't talk to your mother like that." He bore into me with his pale blue eyes. There was food caught in his moustache which made him difficult to take seriously. The army medal hanging from his striped shirt pocket clattered against the edge of the table as he leaned forward. I rarely saw him act so assertively.

I caught Mum shooting him a glance before she turned back to me. "I asked how your day was." She held my gaze for a moment, with a smile stretched across her face, urging some kind of interesting response.

Mum was someone who cared a lot about appearances. She was wearing a retro-style dress; blue on top, with a white skirt. It was her go-to style mostly every day. She always had impeccable, but subtle, make-up on and usually wore her hair pinned back into a bun, to keep it out of the way. I couldn't see much of myself in her, nor her in me. I often envied her positive attitude and her determination to see the best in things, no matter what.

"Same as always," I answered, monotonously, already knowing it wasn't the answer she wanted.

She sighed with her entire body and her smile

died. A tortuously long moment of silence fell. "Can you at least try to be happy?"

Because it's as simple as that. I looked across the table to my older brother, Gerard, who held a fork full of potato, frozen halfway to his lips. His dark, cropped hair was still wet from the shower and he really needed a shave. His red jumper was emblazoned with the name and logo of the local rowing club. He was watching us both, as if expecting some kind of explosion.

"I guess not," I mumbled. I hoped she hadn't heard me but of course she had. They all had.

"That won't do you any good, you know," Mum said.

"What?"

"Being so negative all the time. It's not going to make you feel any better. And after the day I've had, all I wanted was a nice, cheerful dinner with my family. You just need to try a little harder, sit up a bit straighter. How can you hope to make any friends acting like that?"

It wasn't worth the energy to argue. I didn't have it anyway.

I ignored her protestations as I feigned an upset stomach and excused myself from the table. My body felt ten times heavier as I dragged myself up the stairs. I was all too aware of my heart beating loudly in my chest.

I shut my bedroom door heavily. I made my way towards my bed and stopped halfway to look in the mirror. My stomach began to churn as I took in my reflection. *Why can't you just be happy? Don't you know how lucky you are? You're just bringing everyone else down. No one wants you around.*

Suddenly something began to stir within me. The numbness quickly subsided, replaced by a sudden urgency ignited by anger and frustration. I kicked at my wall and banged my head against it as emotions flooded through me. I reminded myself to remain quiet as I didn't want to draw attention; I didn't want them to come knocking as they surely would.

Before I knew it, before I had fully decided on what to do, I walked over to the desk and tossed the stacked books aside, the blade beneath shining up at me. My hands moved to pick it up and within moments it was done. I pulled the blade across my skin, more viciously than I had intended. The blade fell from my hand as the pain registered in my brain.

I gripped at my arm while I watched the line of red appear and deepen, the blood steadily seeping out over the edges. My tears had been halted in my eyes, my anger and frustration had been instantly subdued as the physical pain of the cut overwhelmed me. A part of me wondered if I should grab a tissue or bandage before it started dripping but I found myself transfixed by the blood, transfixed by the rush of pain.

As the blood began to clot and dry, I sneaked out to the bathroom to get tissue to clean the smeared blood from my skin.

My mind began to reel with the realisation of what I had just done. I had long contemplated it, but always told myself that it would be ludicrous to do such a thing. It would solve nothing, yet still I remained tempted, I remained curious. The feeling was something I had never had before. In that moment everything I had been feeling had been released, expunged through the smallest of wounds. I felt in control again.

I finally understood.

4.

I secretly gathered some flowers from the park nearby and placed them upon her grave. I came here at least once a week, preferably Sunday afternoons. I used to visit with my family, but I wanted to be alone here, alone to talk to her, like I used to.

Mine was not a tale of grief. I would not sully her memory by blaming her for my melancholy. She was my ray of hope and maybe I clung too tightly and snuffed her out too soon.

Grief is often fuelled by anger; anger at the deceased, anger at the universe, anger at the fates. However, I was not angry with her - I couldn't be. I remembered how I had had to watch her die for over a year and how I wished to be her ray of hope and peace too, although there was little a fourteen-year-old could do.

I loved my nan. I loved her like she was my oldest friend. When I was a young child, her home was like my second home, full of warmth and comfort as she picked me up and swung me around. She towered over me as I gazed up at her, a miraculous giant dressed in floral print. She'd always greet me with the biggest smile on her face as if I, too, was her greatest ray of sunshine.

Oh, and Gerard. I guess she liked him too.

But she was always mine, *my* nan. She didn't live too far away from our house so I could call over to visit whenever I wanted although I usually went with my parents in tow.

Whenever we visited, she had a freshly baked cake ready and waiting on the counter. The sweet smell would fill the house and make our noses twitch and our stomachs gurgle as soon as we crossed the threshold.

Then we'd sit in front of the TV together - me, Nan and my brother Gerard - and watch some old movies. Nan knew every one of those movies as if she had seen them a million times before. She would answer any and every question that I had about anything, never once seeming to grow impatient. She explained to me what a witch was and why her skin was so green. She warned me to never, ever get into a van with a creepy old man no matter how many sweets he had. She showed me how every book and every painting has an even greater story to tell; leap right into the pages of a book and you'll find yourself in another world, reach into a painted canvas and find yourself transported to another dimension.

Nan opened my eyes to the world. She imbued in me a true sense of childlike wonder. *Mary Poppins* quickly became my staple favourite and I'd ask to watch it again and again, much to Gerard's disgruntlement.

The scene where Mary Poppins, Jane and Michael jump into Bert's street art had always been my absolute favourite. I'd find myself scooting forwards on the chair, even sitting on the floor, as the scene unfolded. Gone was the dismal and grey world of old London; here in its place was a vibrant, magnificent and magical world.

Nan would later tell me stories of how as a child I'd come over every week, pull out some paper and crayons and start drawing the craziest, most bizarre things that my young mind could conjure up. She claims she even caught me energetically jumping up and down on them on a number of occasions, proclaiming that I wanted to get to the 'magic world'.

Sometimes I wonder if that's where my interest in art began; the desire to create new fantastical worlds full of wonder and colour. Nan was wonderfully unceasing in her encouragement. She always had paper ready for me and new crayons and pencils whenever I needed them. Even as I got older, she bought new materials for me and would quietly watch over me for hours as I scribbled and sketched. She told me about how she used to be an artist before her "hands got too bad."

"How did your hands get bad?" I once asked her, at the mere age of nine. "What did you do to them?"

She laughed. "Oh, I didn't do anything to them,

sweetie. They just got old, like me."

"You're not old, Nanny."

"You're too kind to me." She watched me patiently as I continued my drawing of a magnificent dragon, swirling around a castle. "I want you to promise me something."

I stopped for a moment, feeling that this was one of those serious conversations I would have with my parents sometimes. "Promise what?"

"Don't let anybody stop you. Don't let anyone tell you 'no' or tell you to stop dreaming, okay? You can do whatever you like, be whoever you want," she said with a gleaming smile and glistening eyes.

"What if ..." I paused, looking down at my dragon drawing, "I wanna be a dragon?"

She started gripping her sides as the laughter overtook her. "Then you be a dragon. You be the best and fiercest dragon of all."

***

By the time I was fourteen, they had found a nursing home for her on the outskirts of town. Nan had tried until the bitter end to refuse as she didn't want to go there; she didn't want to admit defeat. However, it seemed in the end that she was just too tired to argue anymore.

The building itself looked rather nice, perched up

27

at the edge of town. From the outside it looked almost like a mansion. The garden was overflowing with life and colour which truly made the home feel like a place to gain a new lease of life and not, "the place people to go to die", as I heard Dad describe it once.

The building was incredibly long and incredibly tall. I thought, for sure, that there must be hundreds of people living there.

As we exited the car and walked towards the front doors, I started to think, maybe it wouldn't be so bad. A place this beautiful could be a real haven to live in. Maybe it truly could be the bridge between here and the next world.

Then… there was the smell.

The inside of the building was almost entirely different to the outside. At first glance it looked like it belonged to a different era, as if nothing had been updated or redecorated in quite a long time. The walls were a murky yellow colour with a few stains in places.

A nurse passed us in the hallway, pushing a man asleep in his wheelchair in front of her. She offered a pleasant smile and greeting to us as we intercepted one another.

A chill went up my spine. The air stung my nose with the aroma of something putrid. I stumbled for a moment to breathe, clamping my nose shut with my hands to force the air through my mouth alone.

"It stinks!" I couldn't help but say, much to the

disgruntlement of the receptionist.

"Shhh," Mum warned me, raising a finger to touch her lips as a sign to be silent.

"It is pretty bad," Gerard agreed with me. Sometimes he'd be good like that and step in beside me but only sometimes. "Wanna know what that smell is, Sam?"

"Stop that, Ger. Be quiet." Mum tried to cut in, but he continued.

"Old people - old people and death."

I let out a startled gasp. The look on my face must have been hilarious, as Gerard let out a substantial laugh, causing Mum to scold us again.

"No, it's not. That's just the smell of bleach and cleaning stuff."

"Oh yes," Gerard said, "To clean up all the poop."

"Stop that!" Mum said.

I couldn't help but feel even more nervous as we walked through this building of old people, death and poop.

***

I lay awake every night back then feeling scared and undeserving, imagining her lying alone in the place people go to die. I wanted more than anything to be able to rewind the clock on life and return to how it once was. I knew that she was slowly, but surely, disappearing from my life, and I was powerless.

29

Whenever we visited, she would beam up at me as I entered the room. I'd run into her arms each time and breathe in her warmth and comfort. She still smelt the same, despite everything. She was still just as warm and full of happiness as ever before. Her as-yet-unnamed illness was showing through on her skin; it looked almost purple in its paleness with a web-like pattern of lines etched across her face. Her hair had become a lot thinner than before and was somewhat clinging to her scalp. She shook slightly as I held her, and I tried not to squeeze too tightly.

A few weeks after she moved into the home, during one of our weekly visits, we were delighted to see her sitting upright in her armchair for once, instead of sunken into her bed. My heart leapt pre-emptively in my chest with a sense of hope. "Nanny, you look so much better!" I said excitedly.

"Not as well as you. Look how tall you've gotten!" She'd say that every time, as if I somehow grew a whole foot every week.

"It's so great to see you sitting up, Mum," My mum chimed in. I glanced over to see her eyes shining. I supposed she felt it too, that glimmer of hope.

"Well, if I'm going to be here, I'm going to make the most of it," Nan responded as she tried to push herself up slightly. The effort seemed to be a great strain on her as she dug her hands into the arms of the chair, trying to support herself. Mum motioned forwards to help her but Nan held up her hand, stopping her. "I'm all right, I've got it." She was stubborn sometimes.

Silence fell between us with the only sound being the terrible gameshow on the small TV hanging on the wall. Small talk was made, as one hour, then two, went by.

"It's great to see you doing so well, really it is," Mum said.

"Well, I'm doing what I can," Nan smiled.

After a while, it was suddenly time to go. It wasn't exactly exciting to sit there for hours on end, at times in total silence, but it still felt wrong to leave. I felt like we were abandoning her.

My parents and Gerard gave her a quick hug and kiss goodbye; Mum lingering a little longer than the others. I waited to be last for that bit more time with her. She pulled me in close, tighter than she had done before, and with my parents hopefully out of earshot she whispered, "You know, my little dragon, I am always here for you, always."

I hated leaving her there, leaving her alone, but she promised me that she was happier now and safer. I hung onto that hope every day.

***

Grief is something everyone faces at some time in their life but honestly, watching it creep over the horizon

31

seems even worse than the grief itself. Knowing what to say to someone in pain can be difficult; so difficult, in fact, that saying nothing at all can sometimes be the best option.

"I can tell you're upset about something, so don't lie to me," Rachel urged me to begin. The words started flowing from my mouth before I had even fully decided to talk. I told her how desperately afraid I was feeling. Nan had been such a cornerstone of my life, I couldn't imagine the world without her. I told her about the torture of watching her fade away, more and more, as the weeks passed by. I told her how much I yearned to take the pain from her, I just wanted my old Nan back.

She held me for a moment and let me cry into her shoulder.

I had to get a hold of myself as I looked like an absolute fool. I shut my eyes tight to expel the remainder of my tears and tried to control my breathing.

Rachel must have taken this as a sign that I had calmed down a little and so released her embrace before attempting to console me. "This is just ... what happens."

"What ... what do you mean?" I asked her, feeling rather dumbfounded. Was that the best she could come up with?

"Well, I don't have any grandparents anymore. I lost my granddads before I was even born and then my grandmothers when I was young, so I don't even remember them much.

"So ... well ... this just happens, you know? People get old and die. It's life."

In my mind's eye I saw myself reaching out with my hand and slapping her across the face. Of course, the logical part of my mind knew she was right. I wasn't stupid, I knew that people died, all people die. I knew that Nan would die eventually too, but why right now when I needed her the most? I didn't want Rachel to remind me of that. I wanted to be told that it was going to be okay, even if that was a lie. I wanted to be told that *I* would be okay.

I couldn't find the words to respond to her. I felt my lip quiver as my emotions started to bubble up again, but I refused to give in and held myself back as I searched her face for further meaning. No, she meant it. Her eyes glared at me from behind her glasses, but I couldn't read them. I couldn't tell if she was genuinely concerned or genuinely bored.

I decided to simply excuse myself for need of the bathroom and splashed water on my face in an attempt to remedy its redness.

It's just what happens.

5.

It happened a few weeks after that. I had already started mourning her loss, which seemed like months ago, and so what happened came as no real surprise.

My mother had called up to me in my room, easing open the door in an attempt not to disturb me from my cocoon. I already knew before she had uttered a word, her face betraying her every thought. The pencil slid out of my hand and fell to the floor while I waited for her to confirm the cause of my fear gripping my heart.

A shaky smile flashed across her face for just a moment, but she couldn't hold it, not this time.

"Samantha ..." she said, kneeling down before me. She must've thought it would be easier, the blow would be softer if she came down to my level. She needn't have bothered; nothing could make those words any kinder.

"What?" I asked, even though I already knew, hoping against hope that it was something else, even *someone* else.

"I'm so sorry, Sweetie." Her words felt like they

were floating in the air as she spoke. I tried to latch onto them, to make sense of them, to make sure they were true. "Nan passed away this morning. In her sleep." She blinked as tears escaped and fell down her face.

I didn't know how to respond so I sat in silence for a while, trying to analyse my thoughts, but at the same time I felt like I didn't really have any. I felt a wave of emotion wash over me and at first I couldn't tell what it was. Was it a wave of sadness? Or a wave of relief? Images flashed before my eyes, recalling the last few times that I had seen her. Over the space of just a few weeks she had started to sink lower and lower into her chair with each visit.

She had remained determined to stay seated in the chair, although she surely would've been more comfortable in her bed. I watched as time went by, and the smile she usually greeted me with became a rarer occurrence.

During our last few visits together we didn't say much. We just sat together and watched the TV in her room, although I wondered if she was truly watching it at all as she would easily drift off to sleep.

I wondered what kind of life that must be, to just sit there, day after day, each one looking more identical to the next. I could see the pain etched into her face, the pain she tried so hard to hide, and I yearned more than anything to take it away for her.

It was cruelty defined. That was not the kind of

life deserving of such a wonderful woman. That was not a life at all. You could barely call it existing.

***

In the run-up to the funeral, I remained at home while my parents made the last preparations for her send-off.

A coffin had to be picked out for her. I wanted to be the one to do so, but Mum assured me that they already had it chosen; she was going to get one similar or identical to the one my granddad was buried in. I never met my granddad, but I knew she'd be happier now to finally be reunited with him in the afterlife after so many years apart.

Feeling helpless, there was nothing I could do but wait whilst my family got the funeral arrangements in order.

I didn't think I could handle seeing her. I didn't want to. It was almost as if, up until that moment, some part of me was still sceptical, some part of me had yet to fully grasp the idea that she was truly gone. I wanted to pretend that this was all some sort of farce and that she was still at the nursing home, waiting for me to visit but I wasn't allowed to anymore because she had finally become too sick for anything.

Mum grabbed my hand while we walked into the funeral home, to begin the removal ceremony where I'd get to see her one last time before she was gone forever. She must've sensed my hesitation. She tried to offer words of comfort to me, "At least she's not in pain anymore, love." Maybe so, but I couldn't say the same about myself.

I glanced over towards Gerard and searched his face for some sign of emotion, but there seemed to be nothing. He was never as close to her as I was, but still, I expected something, some form of response, some evidence of his grief. I felt somewhat betrayed by his placidity.

"How are you so calm?" I asked him as he casually glanced around the lobby of the funeral home, his eyes reading the few names lit up on the screens above each door; another name, another soul, another life ended.

He must have deciphered my true meaning. "What? I'm not being calm, I'm upset too you know."

"Are you? Upset?"

"Of course he is," Mum jumped in, as if Gerard couldn't speak for himself. "He just doesn't want to show it." Oh right, I had forgotten. Men aren't allowed to show it, while women can be blubbering idiots. *Oh well*, I thought, *I'm sure I'll cry enough for the both of us.*

Her name was written on the screen furthest back, the last in line; Eileen Sullivan. The words didn't seem real even as I read them, white font on a startling backdrop of blue. It felt cold and formal and I was reminded that this kind of thing truly is a common occurrence. It's just what happens.

I glanced around briefly at the other names in the hall, knowing that behind each door was another family's loss, another's heartbreak. I could hear a mass being held within one of the rooms, the murmur of the priest's voice just loud enough to decipher.

My feet began to pull me through the entranceway, towards her name. The sign passed over my head as the doors before me opened suddenly and I felt the breath catch in my lungs. My heart began to beat faster, and I wondered if I might just die here too. This time, it was Gerard who caught my hand, who whispered assurances in my ear. A glimmer shone in his eyes as he tried to maintain his composure. I wanted to tell him it was okay too, that he was allowed to be upset and to show it, but I couldn't say anything because if I had I would've lost my grip on myself.

The room was beautiful. That much was true. My eyes floated quickly over to the right, away from where I knew she'd be. Rows of chairs were lined up in the room, filling the space between me and her. A number of flower bouquets stood equidistant along the walls and the sun was glaring in from the back window. It was beautiful, almost heavenly.

Then I had no choice. I had to look. I had to look at her.

I started looking along the floor, following the pattern in the carpet. I found the array of flowers that were arranged around her and her coffin. I saw the wheels that were prepared to move her at any moment. I saw the decal in the coffin of Jesus sitting beside his twelve apostles. I saw the brim of the white satin around the coffin's edges.

Then I could avoid it no longer. She was there, right in front of me. Lifeless, yet brimming with beautiful peacefulness. The kiss of illness and death remained evident upon her skin. They had brushed and styled her hair a little so that it no longer clung to her scalp. They had even given her make-up which was strange to look at because she hadn't worn any in years. There was almost too much rouge on her cheeks and her lips were too pink. They were trying to mask the appearance of death, but I wished they had let her be as she was. Death could not be made softer.

Her skeletal hands were clasped across her chest with a rosary bead wound around her fingers. I wondered what the point in that was. It was a little late for praying now.

I stood back as I watched everyone go up to her, kiss her and say goodbye. My extended family had begun to arrive and quickly the room was getting almost too crowded. I watched, as person after person approached her, but I couldn't move. Mum continued to reassure me, saying that it was okay, that I should go up and say goodbye, but I couldn't move. A tear slid down my cheek.

I waited until Nan was finally alone again without someone leaning over her before I urged my feet forwards. My legs were shaking and I feared that I would fall over at any second and make a fool of myself. I touched the edge of the coffin, the velvet soft beneath my fingers, and laid my eyes upon her face as tears continued to blur my vision.

As I forced myself to lay a hand upon hers, I could contain my emotions no longer. The coldness of her skin confirmed it all for me, removing any last remnant of disbelief. My lip began to quiver uncontrollably as my eyebrows pulled together. I took a deep breath and wiped away the tears so I could kiss her face without splashing on her. I wanted to tell her I was sorry - sorry for all she had gone through, sorry for how much she had suffered. The words were stuck in my throat, I couldn't get them out no matter how hard I tried.

I felt the weight of an arm appear around my shoulder. "It's okay, it's okay," the voice whispered to me. Gerard took my hand that was clinging to hers steadily away and assisted me back to a seat. I let myself cry into his shoulder.

***

The funeral came and went in something of a blur. I felt like I was simply going through the motions as I dressed up in black and followed my family into the church. My feet were being pulled along by some unseen force and I was helpless to resist.

I wondered what she'd think of all this. Nan hated black. She'd always tell me about the wonder of colour and how colourful clothes brought out the sparkle in my eyes, yet still, everyone was donned in the traditional black of funeral garb, informing all others that grief and death had struck home. It was as if she had taken the colour out of life along with her.

I contemplated wearing something else because I knew she'd prefer it but that probably would've caused a scene. So I kept my mouth shut and rode the tide of events.

I walked behind her, gazing up at the coffin cradled atop the shoulders of six men as they walked through the cemetery towards her final resting place. My dad was at the helm, his arm stretched across my uncle Seamus' shoulders. Gerard followed behind Dad, just about tall enough to offer his shoulder for support. Other family friends followed him in turn to help carry her towards her final resting place.

Rachel walked alongside me in silence. I was so thankful that she had been there, as if grounding me in reality. I had forgiven her for what she said before, "it's just what happens," although she never really apologised; we just carried on like nothing had happened. I didn't care about that right now though. Her presence was the root I needed to stay standing.

We followed the coffin in silence. There was nothing either of us could've said, and I had no inclination to talk. She hooked her arm through mine, and I tried to focus solely on that support as I followed Nan to her grave.

We continued walking for what felt like an age, with each step more careful than the last. I glanced around at the other headstones surrounding us; some of them had become decrepit after years of neglect and little maintenance, while others remained cherished and attended to years after their initial erection. I noticed the smaller of the headstones standing out amongst the crowd and would strain my eyes to read the names of the young children taken too soon without even having the chance to truly experience life. Then I found myself wondering if they were missing much at all. In the end, we all end up in the same place.

As we neared the back of the graveyard, the crowd began to move even slower as we reached what would become her final resting place. I watched as the pallbearers slowly shifted the coffin towards the ground and into the mechanism that would welcome her to the earth. I gripped Rachel's arm tighter, using it as a support to help hold myself together. The words of the priest's sermon seemed to be coming from some far-off place as my eyes remained locked on the coffin. My mouth moved to offer the relevant responses, but I didn't hear a word.

42

Then, all too suddenly, she was lowered into the ground and my heart sank with her. Rachel pressed a rose into my hand that someone else had given her. She guided me forwards, towards the large hole in the ground. I watched as others approached and tossed their flowers into the grave, offering one final goodbye. The rose fell from my hand and landed with all the others within the earth. I thought I should say something as everyone else was, but I couldn't find the words.

Eventually, tortuously, the sermon drew to a close and that was it. She was gone. Murmurs echoed around me as we turned to leave the graveyard.

My heart continued to beat steadfastly in my chest as if to say, *I'm here, I'm here, I'm still here.* I felt like I was suffocating, surrounded by endless inevitable death. I had no control; this was just what happens.

"You'll be all right," Rachel said, "You'll get through this. We'll get through this together." Sometimes she could be really great. I tried to force a smile as she attempted to distract me with idle small talk. I did my best to participate, but she ended up doing most of the talking which she didn't seem to mind. I tried to listen to her as we started to leave but my head felt fuzzy and I just wanted to go home.

As I looked around the graveyard, something in the distance caught my eye. I squinted to try to make it out. As we got steadily closer, I could tell that it was a person sitting on the ground in front of a small headstone.

My curiosity refused to let me look away from the boy crouched down on the ground with his head leaning on his knees. As if sensing my gaze, he glanced up and looked straight at me. His stare bore into me and I took a second too long to break it. I knew who it was; even from a distance, I could see the bruise still evident on his cheek.

Michael stared at me for a moment, before his eyes shifted to skim over the crowd of people walking behind me. He looked back at me one last time with a hint of sympathy in his smile.

I forced myself to smile back at him. What was he doing in a graveyard and all alone too? This wasn't exactly where you'd expect to find a teenager on a Saturday. I didn't know it then, but this wouldn't be the only time we'd find ourselves here, together in the graveyard.

6.

So the globe kept turning and the lives of its citizens continued to steadily crawl forwards. Time waits for no man, after all. I wanted more than anything to just curl up into a ball and roll endlessly down a hill to escape everything; to escape the world and all I thought I knew.

But I couldn't. I couldn't just lie back and let the darkness take over, even though that would've been the easiest thing to do. I had to keep going. Somehow, I had to.

I left the graveyard and my Nan behind with yet another promise to do better, to *be* better. It had been two whole years since the day I said goodbye to her for the last time. I knew that she would want me to be happy. I felt like I was letting her down.

I knew I had to keep going. Every morning I'd pull my unwilling limbs out of bed and drag my feet along the road towards school. Some people misunderstand the importance or impact of monotony. I had heard so many tales of people going through severe trauma, abuse and bullying to find their darkness. "You should count yourself lucky," I'd hear them say. Indeed, I should've been glad that I had no traumas to haunt my dreams at night; or at least, not yet. I should've been glad that the worst that had happened to me was that, but still, the darkness would persist, linger and grow, as if their judgment was giving it life.

"Hey, I've been meaning to tell you something ..." Rachel began during the lunch break a few weeks later. I rubbed my eyes to wake myself up a little as I had begun to slump more in my chair. "I wasn't sure how to, but I guess I just gotta now."

"What's the matter?" I asked, trying to keep myself from yawning in her face.

"I'm going away," she said, plain and simple. I waited, wondering if that was going to be the extent of information I'd receive. Then I realised she was waiting for me to respond.

"What do you mean you're going away? On a holiday?" I urged.

She laughed in response, "Nothing as simple as that. It's Dad. He's got a new job up the country and, well ... we gotta go with him I guess." She shrugged her shoulders and continued eating her lunch, as if it what she'd just said was the most natural sequence of events imaginable.

"You're moving away?" The realisation began to fall upon me like a tonne of bricks.

"Yeah, to Galway," she said, taking a slurp of her

46

Coke through a straw.

"Galway? That's so far away."

"Hence why we have to move there," she said sarcastically.

"When're you going?"

"Next week."

"Next week?" The words practically exploded from my lips.

"Shhh. Don't make a scene," Rachel warned me. She looked around and laughed it off to those who had turned in response. "It's no big deal."

"N-next week?" I brought my voice down to a near-whisper, "That's so soon. Why didn't you tell me until now?"

"I dunno, I guess it just kept slipping my mind," she said simply.

"Slipping your mind? You just kept forgetting it was happening? Or you kept forgetting to tell me?"

"Don't be like that."

"Like what?"

"Like that! Making it all about you, again. There's a lot on my plate right now, and it just didn't come up until now, okay?"

Rachel returned to eating her lunch and seemed to have no inclination to say anything more. I didn't know if I was angry or upset and I didn't know if I had the right to be, but there was little point in arguing or complaining about what was happening.

"We'll ... we'll still be friends though, right? We'll still talk and see each other?" I asked after a lengthy silence.

"Of course!" she said, offering her familiar smile. She pulled me into a hug as if everything was perfectly normal. The conversation quickly died as others approached and interrupted us, talking about some show or other that was on the TV last night. I failed to bring her back to that conversation that day, and despite her reassurances whenever I did ask, I knew that I was losing my one and only friend.

***

Sometimes, I would feel like I was floating through life. Sometimes the sound of my own name didn't sound right; *that's not my name*, I thought. Sometimes my mind would go blank mid-conversation and I just wanted to sleep.

Rachel left last week, her absence leaving an instant void in my life. She had landed me with the bombshell of desertion, and I hadn't a clue what to do with myself. I needed to keep myself distracted; I didn't want to think. All that mattered right now was the pencil and the lines it drew. Every spare moment was taken up with my sketching. I'd sketch out the most mundane of things, from the clock on the wall to the book laid out before me. It didn't matter the subject once it took up my thoughts.

As I sat in the school entrance hall with my sketchbook in hand, I sneakily worked on a life sketch of a group of girls sitting nearby, being careful not to be seen by them. However, no one ever seemed to notice me sketching. Maybe I was just really good at hiding my work as my pencil flew across the page, making the paper grow darker and darker by the second.

I studied their forms; how they sat together in circular fashion so that everyone could see everyone else clearly with no one being excluded. They were sitting on top of the table, disregarding the purpose of the chairs beneath their feet. One girl in particular with flowing blonde hair seemed to be leading the conversation while the others soaked in her every word. It must've been a very funny story as they'd often burst into uncontrollable fits of laughter.

I wanted to capture that look, that atmosphere. As I sketched, I loosely drew in the lines of their features, trying to capture that moment of glee and laughter. A few of them were in fact some of the girls who had often hung around with Rachel, and, by extension, me. We had talked, we had laughed and they had admired my sketches. That seemed like another world now. Not one of them seemed to notice me, no matter how long I stared. Without Rachel, it appeared as though they couldn't see me anymore.

Oh no - I felt my hand suddenly begin to quake. I

could feel it starting again, emotions bubbling up beneath the surface, threatening to overwhelm me and explode. I closed the sketchbook quickly and packed away my supplies. I sat still, gripping my arms.

And waited for the bell to ring.

7.

It's one of those things that people won't really be able to understand unless they've experienced it, unless they've felt those feelings and thought those thoughts. People would see it purely as a choice, and offer no sympathy in the face of my stupidity.

As days turned into weeks and weeks turned into months, I knew it was useless. I knew it wasn't helping anything, not really. But still, I continued. Still I yearned for that rush of pain, for that instant sense of relief and that instant distraction. It offered me control as I failed to keep my heart at a steady pace, failed to keep my eyes from spilling over.

The marks quickly began to litter my arms and I never let them fade. They became an expression, as if they could somehow release the brewing darkness within me. With each bead of red, I would feel myself falling further as numbness overtook my senses. Anger and frustration would fuel my motions as the collection continued to grow.

I could never let them be seen, not for a second,

not by anyone. I didn't want their stares, their laughter; I didn't want to face their confusion and lack of comprehension.

So I'd remain silent and oh so careful to never be seen. I'd tug at the end of my sleeves as if they could never be long enough, and laid things against my bedroom door to stop anyone from catching me.

In school, I felt the heavy weight of each and every pair of eyes glaring at me, as if they could see right through me. I felt their judgment pouring out, even if they didn't know. I felt watched.

The material of the scratchy uniform I was obliged to wear itched at my skin and I could feel every scab brushing against it. I yearned to rip it off, to let them breathe, but of course that would surely make me look insane.

On the rare occasion of a hot day, I felt them staring at me as I refused to roll up my sleeves or wear t-shirts without hoodies on top, and declined to wear a dress which was never an option for me.

I kept the blade hidden in its stained state and soon took to carrying it around with me, lest it be discovered by probing eyes. The dull blade that had become my partner seemed to weaken after a while so I soon found another. I thought about other methods that would surely heighten the pain I yearned for. I had seen it in countless movies and TV shows; it was always a razorblade, for some reason. There were none in the house and I hadn't any money so I stuck with feeble sharpener blades.

Until the day *that* fell into my hand.

For a moment, I thought Mrs Cohen, my art teacher, was mocking me, chastising me as she handed me the blade, coyly curled up in a plastic case. I reminded myself to not be an idiot - she doesn't know - as I watched her hand a similar tool to another student. We were to use it to cut into pieces of foam board to begin one of our projects. My hand shook as I held it; as if this thing, this piece of metal and plastic combined, held some sort of power over me.

I glanced around the room certain that they must all be looking at me, waiting for me to snap, waiting for me to betray myself. But I was invisible to them all as they focused on the task at hand, carving their boards into something from their minds.

I pushed the blade up out of its casing, slowly and carefully. I could sense someone watching me.

"It won't bite!" Mrs. Cohen said, as she passed by me again. I must've been staring at it for longer than I thought for her to notice my hesitation. I forced a tiny smile at her and pushed the blade out of its casing. I glanced up just in time to see one of the other students happily slicing the blade through their piece of foamboard. The sound of the board splitting sent a tingle down my spine. She pulled the pieces of foamboard apart with a final crunching sound.

Something panged.

I forced my eyes back down to my own board and tried to focus before anyone else noticed and questioned my hesitation.

Of course, our teacher demanded the blades be returned at the end of class.

But she never locked the door.

***

My seventeenth birthday came and went without much of an event. My parents urged me to do something, anything, with the bounty of friends they somehow assumed I had. The topic of Rachel came up who had, at that point, been in Galway for about three weeks. Little did they know I hadn't spoken to her since before then, or at least not properly anyway. They offered to take me to see her - a "proper day out", Mum called it - but my stomach churned at the thought.

I realised all too late that Rachel had never been a good friend to me, not really. She'd keep me company in class and during lunch breaks and maybe we'd hang out outside school sometimes, but she never truly fulfilled the definition of a friend.

She was the friend that would talk to you simply because you happened to be there but never made much effort to seek out your company otherwise. She was the friend who would make no hesitation in asking you for things but would seldom offer anything in return. She was the friend who made excuses for not hanging out or contacting you when the truth was she simply couldn't be bothered. She was the friend who had too many friends to remember you existed.

But she was the *only* friend I had.

A while later, I decided to let my anger go. I wanted to see her, I wanted her to give me an excuse to get out of home, at least for a little while. For weeks, I asked again and again if I could come up and visit, but she'd always come up with some excuse; she was too busy with homework as the school in Galway was a lot stricter about it than my school was and she couldn't be late with anything; or her family were busy getting everything in order with their new life, and she had to help organise the house and put the new furniture together. She had naturally made a lot of new friends and had already made plans with them. Sometime soon, she promised.

I decided to call her one night when I was particularly suffering. I had seen countless posters and messages online, even on the street, urging people to talk. They promised me that I was loved, I wasn't alone and that there was always someone there to listen. They failed to tell me that not everyone would listen.

I'd wonder later, why she was the one I chose to go to that night. In the past, she had always said that she'd be there, but I should've known. I should've seen the signs by now.

I dialled her number and waited for her to pick up whilst playing with the stolen craft knife in my hand, revealing and unrevealing it steadily. The blade was crusty and red after weeks of meeting my skin, but it remained as sharp as the day I crept into the classroom to take it. I waited as the tone dialled and wondered if she'd even answer. Oftentimes she didn't, and I'd receive a half-hearted apology a few hours later.

She picked up this time. I heard her familiar tone and for a moment, felt my heart rise slightly with it. My worries suddenly slunk in my mind and I found myself making small talk. I glanced down at the red marks littering the skin on my forearm just as she said, "Hey, look, I love talking to you, but I have a lot of family over so I'm gonna have to go." There it was, the excuse, barely five minutes into our conversation. A lump caught in my throat as I quickly decided what to do. I hesitated for just a moment because that's all I had; she'd hang up on me if I didn't respond quickly.

I tried to form my words. "Wait, I wanted to talk to you about something ... important."

"Oh, two seconds." I waited and listened to the shuffling sounds in the background. I guess she really did have a lot of visitors over. She was moving to a quieter location to hear me better. "What is it?" I tried to discern her tone but couldn't. I decided to continue, to just blurt it out and see what happened.

"Well, um ... I haven't really been doing so well lately ..."

"Aw, you miss me?" she asked.

"Of course I do! But that's not what I'm talking about, not exactly ..." I didn't know how to say it. The words were right there, printed in front of my mind's eye like a teleprompter. I knew what to say but I didn't know how to say it. A silence started to hang between us on the phone and I wondered if she was growing impatient.

"What is it?" Rachel asked, urging me to get it out.

"I really mean, I'm not doing well. I want out of here."

"C'mon. Tíreen's not that bad. You'll be graduating soon and then you can go to college someplace else." She said this with a hearty voice as if she had finally stumbled upon the heart of the problem, as if that was absolutely what I meant to talk about.

"I don't mean Tíreen, I don't even mean Cork. I mean here, life, I'm tired of it." A longer pause ensued. I felt it was still my turn to talk. "I've been ... doing things ... to myself. I've been ... harming." I could barely get the last words out. My ears were greeted by static. "I just want out of this, Rach." I could feel the emotions bubbling again and tried to keep them down, but allowed a few betraying tears to slide down my face while I awaited her response.

I started to wonder if I would ever get it. I called

out to her to make sure she was still there, and she assured me that she was, she just didn't know what to say. Maybe she should've stopped there. Maybe she should've known that sometimes admitting that you don't know what to say is better than saying the first thing that comes into your head, but that wasn't like her.

"I think ... maybe you need to get some help. Professionally, I mean. If you don't, well then ... I think you're just being an attention seeker."

I froze in place, the phone glued to my ear, my senses numbed. It's safe to say that wasn't what I expected to hear; it wasn't what I wanted to hear. I wanted to be told that it would be okay, no matter how much of a lie that was. I wanted to be told that I wasn't alone, like those posters promised me.

Professional help, was that it? Had I truly fallen so far that I had become too much for anyone else to handle, too much for anyone else to want to try to help? Was I not worth it?

Those other words hurt me the most, resounding in my brain every day since – attention seeker.

Don't be so dramatic. You're always so dramatic.

Those words played back to me as if on some recording in my mind. She didn't take me seriously. She didn't care, this was just another one of my ploys to garner attention, to be dramatic. That's all it meant to her.

I thought about saying all this back to her. I

thought about telling her how I had debated spilling my heart out to her for weeks on end, had debated ending my own life for even longer. I never expected that my decision to talk to *her*, my most trusted friend, instead of a trained health care professional whom I had never met, would label me as nothing more than an, 'Attention Seeker', someone not to be taken seriously, someone who doesn't matter.

Instead, I said nothing. I let the silence hang between us and wondered, maybe, just maybe, she'd realise her mistake and quickly take her words back and apologise. I was even ready and willing to forgive her, as I always did, yet still, it lingered, and the tension grew.

"Listen. You need to get help, okay? Call me back when you do. I need to go."

And she was gone. She didn't bother to wait for my response, to wait for a goodbye. The beep of the end tone rang in my ear. I tossed the phone aside, the anger boiling up inside of me as I let my emotions loose.

I left the ball in her court and waited, but it never bounced back.

8.

Rachel was no longer a part of my life, not then anyway. Her words floated through my mind for days on end afterwards, taunting me. Funnily enough, her ultimatum for me to seek help was little encouragement.

As weeks and months passed, I became increasingly aware of my state of mind and steadily became terrified of losing it completely. I had hoped I was wrong. There wasn't anything wrong with me, not really, surely? The marks on my arms said otherwise.

I couldn't be crazy. I couldn't be so insane at the age of seventeen to require professional help to find my way back to normality, back to whatever constituted sanity. So, I hid. I hid and pretended that nothing was wrong, not really ... or at least, not wrong enough.

I began to question myself each and every day, suddenly unable to trust my own thoughts. Nothing seemed real anymore. I wondered about the thoughts in my head, presented as absolute truth; what if they were all lies? What if I wasn't as lost as I thought? What if I wasn't as detested and despised as I thought? What if something in my brain had broken and was constantly tricking me into thinking these things?

I found myself spending hours online, researching symptoms of numerous mental disorders, quickly falling down a spiral of possibilities. My head began to swim as I found myself identifying with thousands of bleak statements.

Clinical depression, bipolar, borderline personality disorder, anxiety - the list went on. I became consumed by it, finding myself agreeing with each and every statement, determined to put a name to how I was feeling, determined to take the blame off of myself. That made it easier somehow; knowing it wasn't entirely my fault, but still I feared being told that I was entirely unhinged.

The fear continued to grow within me until it reached boiling point and I thought for sure that I was losing my mind.

I'd look at my family's faces as we ate dinner together, the three of them happily chatting between mouthfuls, whilst I had little to contribute. I'd look at them one by one and wonder what they'd say if the revelation of my deteriorating sanity became known to them. I imagined they'd react just as Rachel had; they'd tell me I was being silly for worrying about stupid little things like my inadequacy. They'd tell me to stop being so dramatic and stupid. They'd tell me to stop being so negative, that it wouldn't get me anywhere. Or maybe they'd tell me I surely must be mad.

Then they'd haul me off to the nearest hospital and demand I be kept in some psychiatric ward for months on end until I snapped back into my old self. I'd become the talk of the town, an instant disgrace to both myself and my school.

Then again, maybe they'd say it's just part of being a teenager and they wouldn't do anything at all.

Truth be told, I never once fully considered talking to them - the people most likely to care enough to do something, the people who would help me see through the cloud of darkness over my head. I had kept it from them for fear that they, too, would reject me and cast me out. I didn't want to become a burden or an embarrassment to them. Mum was a primary school teacher in the local boys' school; the last thing she needed was her reputation being tarnished. They'd whisper in the streets, "Did you hear Mrs. Ward's girl is a lunatic who cuts herself?", "Can we really have someone like her teaching our kids when that happens to her own?" They'd question whether my brother - who studies chemistry in college - was searching for some sort of cure for the family lunatic. They'd wonder what my veteran father thought about a young girl complaining about her life after all the war he's seen.

My bedroom had quickly become something separate to the world I lived in outside. In there, I was myself and I held nothing back as I didn't have to pretend to be happy. Outside of that door, I'd spend every minute in pretence, focusing on making sure my face didn't look too sullen, that my eyebrows weren't burrowing into my face. I forced the corners of my mouth upwards each time I entered an occupied room. I didn't want to raise questions; that was sure to break the fragile wall surrounding my façade.

For years, I remained vigilant to keep myself covered, to keep myself hidden. My arms were littered in scabs and scars. My legs were quickly catching up.

Then some days I'd slip up and they'd almost see. Mum would come into my bedroom to wake me and I'd hastily dive under the covers, my pyjama sleeves having rolled up too far, praying she hadn't noticed. Or I'd stretch myself out in the kitchen, unaware of their eyes and have to explain why I was writing on my skin. Or I'd become ill, the fever making me sweat, but refuse to remove my dressing gown or jumper to keep myself covered.

I thought they'd surely figure it out, someday they'd realise. Sometimes, they'd ask me twice how I was, not believing my automatic answer of "fine."

"Just stressed out from school," I'd say, to stop them from enquiring further. It was a valid excuse. The Leaving Certificate had been all anyone talked about through fifth year as the teachers rushed to prepare us for the incoming storm of exams. With it, came talk of our futures and what we were going to do once school ended. I didn't care about the exams. I seemed to always do well enough with moderate effort, so I wasn't worried. I didn't feel the need to stay up all night to cram excessive knowledge into my brain; knowledge I'd likely never use again.

The future seemed shrouded in darkness. My teachers would urge me to follow my "artistic passions," as I was surely destined for great things, but I had begun to lose hope even in that. Over the years, my art had grown steadily darker. Gone was the vibrant landscape with a towering castle in the distance, beckoning the prince to save the trapped princess; in its place, the unending expanse of a lonesome graveyard covered in grey.

I figured I would worry about the future later. At times I wondered if I even had one.

***

I had come to hate summer. Each year, it passed tortuously as I waited for the three months to pass, each day dragging out into oblivion. As monotonous as my life had already become, summer seemed to heighten the feeling that I no longer had any reason to get out of bed, get dressed or leave the house at all. So I didn't.

"C'mon, it's time to get you out of the house for a change," Mum declared, pushing my door open once again, without knocking. She quickly sped back down the landing without waiting for my reply.

"What?" I was a bit annoyed to be disturbed whenever I was busy drawing. It was like being pulled back to reality.

"No arguments, we're going out, all of us," she shouted from her room.

I groaned as loudly as I possibly could. I glanced out my window and saw that it was a pretty nice day for once. Ireland's weather was often very unpredictable. Despite being the middle of July, it would rain more often than not, and 'summer' in terms of hot weather, would only last a week even during a good year.

"Where are we going?" I shouted back.

"Wear something light, it's roasting out there!"

"Where?" I shouted louder.

I tried to resist, to find some way to back out of it. The last thing I wanted to do right now was to go outside, but she wouldn't hear my claims of sickness or tiredness.

"Don't be such a spoil sport," she said when we were setting off in the car, "You need to get out. I don't like you spending so much time in that room of yours."

"I don't have anything else to do."

"Well we need to find you something, but never mind that for now. I want us to have a nice day out while the weather's good."

"Which probably won't be long," Dad attempted to joke from the passenger seat.

About thirty minutes later, we pulled up to the beach. It seemed that most people had the same idea to try and take advantage of the good weather. We were lucky to find a spot just big enough for the four of us to spread out comfortably.

I wish I could be one of those people who enjoyed the beach. Mum was dressed in all sorts of summer attire – swimsuit, sarong, sunhat and sunglasses. She was even bringing along a lounge chair. She was the essence of blissful relaxation as she was laid out beneath the sun.

"I thought I told you to wear something light?" She scrutinised me, her eyes peering out over the top of her glasses.

"This is light," I said, tugging at my thin hoodie, the lightest thing I had.

"Jeans?" She pointed at my legs.

"I don't have any other pants."

"I've bought you skirts and shorts before, surely I have."

"Yeah but ..." There was no way I was wearing any of those. "I prefer jeans."

She sighed heavily and returned her glasses to the bridge of her nose. "Well, make sure you stay hydrated. I've put more water bottles in the car."

I expected her to fight with me, to force me to remove my jumper, but thankfully she didn't. I guess she had vowed to herself that she was just going to relax today rather than fight with her angsty teenager.

I glanced over to where Dad was, spread out on a towel on the ground. I could see the sheen of sunscreen spread across his chest and he looked to be asleep. He was wearing long pants too, but of a lighter material than jeans. I suppose he didn't want anyone to see his legs either.

"Hey, you coming for a swim?" Gerard called from behind me, looking like he had already been.

"Um ..." I said, glancing down at myself. "Obviously not."

"Didn't bring any togs?"

"No, I didn't even want to come."

"Ah, don't be like that. Come up to the water with me, at least. Roll up your pants."

He seemed unrelenting so I gave in and did what he said. I hated the feeling of the sand in my toes. I hated knowing I would have to spend ages later trying to remove the grains from my feet. The sand was almost too hot to bear but as the water of the sea washed over my toes, it was incredibly soothing.

"Feels good, right?" Gerard asked.

"I suppose."

"You're allowed to be happy, you know."

"What? What do you mean?"

"You don't have to play the part of the grumpy teenager all the time. Smile, enjoy yourself."

I wanted to. He had no idea how much I wanted

to just let down my guard, soak in the comforting rays of the sun and just embrace the miracle of life. God, it was so hot, I wanted desperately to fling my jumper away, but I couldn't. The anxiety was gripping me tightly, holding me back. I couldn't be seen, I couldn't let them be seen. How was I supposed to relax and enjoy myself when I was so busy worrying about hiding?

"I am enjoying myself," I replied after a moment of silence. He looked at me with a confused expression, his head slightly tilted to the side. "No, seriously, I am. Mum was right, it's nice to get outside."

"See," he said, punching me playfully in the arm. "That wasn't so hard now, was it?" He seemed pleased with that. "Well, I sure need a swim. Just relax, okay? Build a sandcastle or something." He patted me lightly on the shoulder and ran out into the ocean. As soon as he was far out enough, he dove down and disappeared into the waves.

I wasn't much of a swimmer. Gerard was the one with the talent. I felt the waves steadily brushing against my ankles. I wanted to step out further and keep going as far as I could. I took a couple of steps forwards until the water was level with the end of my rolled-up jeans.

Gerard was so far out I couldn't see him anymore. I had never felt fully comfortable in the water. As I struggled to find him, my mind's eye began to fill with intrusive visions of never finding him again as the waves swallowed him whole. I glanced out across the horizon and saw in the near distance a group of people happily jumping off a cliff. I felt my stomach plummet along with them as I watched them fall, their screams echoing in the wind. What if they never came up again?

My heart began to pound louder and faster, as the water around my calves rose. I stared back at the people on the cliff. They were all gone now, having taken their leap of faith. I couldn't see or hear anyone. They were surely dashed to pieces on the ocean floor. Where was Gerard? I cast my eyes over the waves before me which were growing bigger by the wind. The colour of the sky was beginning to change with the bright blue steadily receding. A loud noise reverberated through the air as a rumble of thunder sounded.

"Hey!" Someone grabbed my arm. "Are you all right?" It was Gerard, thank God. There was water on my face.

"Yeah, I'm ... I'm fine. I ... I couldn't see you." I mumbled the last few words. I felt so stupid now. I knew he was a great swimmer, I knew I had nothing to worry about. It was stupid to worry.

He laughed. "It's all right, but hey, looks like summer's over now." There was more than just tears on my face. Rain was beginning to fall.

Mum and Dad had already gotten everything packed away by the time we reached them.

"Should we wait it out?" Mum asked. Clearly she hadn't had enough time to relax yet.

"Hey, at least we got a few hours," Dad said, "Who knows how long it'll take to blow over and with that thunder too I think we'd best call it a day."

Mum was rather sour-faced as she relented, returning to the car to go home. I couldn't have been happier to leave.

9.

Two weeks - I had made it through another two weeks, constantly resisting the urge to cut into my skin. My final year in school had finally begun, and I wanted to start over. Still, with each passing day, the urges grew stronger and the thoughts got darker until I was too tired to fight against them anymore.

I'd hold the blade against my skin and wonder how easy it would be to go too far, to cut just a little too deeply; how it could all end in a moment if I released my controlled grip just a little more. Then fear would catch at my heart at the last second and pull me back from the edge.

A dismal sky looked in upon me from my bedroom window, as if reflecting my own mind. The clouds were sure to open at any second, letting their pent-up precipitation loose. It was six o'clock in the evening, in the middle of September, but already little light remained in the air and the streetlights had come to life.

I felt myself growing restless. I couldn't stand

these four suffocating walls anymore. I needed to get out. The spatter of a drizzle on the window warned me that it would be unpleasant, but I thought for sure that the walls were soon to collapse in upon me if I didn't escape right then and there.

I walked carefully down the stairs, one step at a time, as quietly as I could. The creak of a step threatened to betray me and I paused for a moment, mid-step. I didn't want to be seen, didn't want to be heard, didn't want to be questioned.

I could hear the TV blaring from the living room as usual, some program or other with an instilled laugh track. Dad guffawed along with it, oblivious to anything else. I noticed Mum's coat was missing from the rack; she must be out shopping. Good, this would be easy then.

I picked up my own coat from the coat rack and eased the door open slowly before stepping outside.

A walk in the rain. Who decides to go for a walk in the rain? The fresh, moistened air hit against me instantly, promising comfort and distraction. I pulled up my hood and tightened my coat around me as the cold began to set in.

With no real destination in mind, I allowed my feet to guide me forwards without question. The escape from my cocoon felt like a weight lifted from my mind.

The cold wind brushed against my face and I felt a shiver run down my spine. Perhaps I should've worn a few extra layers for warmth but the cold felt like a new sensation and I actually found myself welcoming it.

The clouds in the sky above were dark grey, and I knew that at any given moment they would break completely and let their weight loose. I should've turned around. *You'll catch a cold in this weather*, I told myself, but I didn't seem to mind all that much.

There was not another soul around. I spotted a few birds flying above me that quickly took refuge in some nearby trees. I could hear nothing but the sound of the steadily growing rain, as it collided with the pavements and the innumerable cars lined up against the kerbs. Tíreen was a small town but still rather well populated, with almost every house occupied by a buzzing family.

I didn't mean to end up there. I had never even considered it, or at least not consciously. I surprised myself as the gates to the graveyard seemed to suddenly appear ahead of me as if there was nowhere else I could've possibly gone to.

The graveyard itself, attached to a small, infrequently-used church, was situated on the outskirts of the town but it still only took me under half an hour to reach.

Ancient and huge, the gates towered above me, rusted over with age and neglect, slightly bent at the top. They looked in need of replacing but still, this lent the graveyard a more rustic, embellished feel, promising innumerable stories within.

The gates squeaked loudly as I pulled them open. The noise seemed to echo in the air, as the rain fell down upon me. My clothes were almost soaked through, clinging to me from the weight of the moisture but still, I continued on.

I looked out over the graveyard as I stepped through the gate. It seemed to inhabit every past resident of Tíreen within its massive grounds. To the left, graves of souls from the early Eighteenth Century could be found whilst the right featured more recent passing's.

I always felt some sort of morbid curiosity being here. During other visits I had ventured into the older portion of the graveyard and peered at the names, trying to decipher them through the erosion and decay of the stones. I wondered who these people were, who they had once been, how they had all ended up here, eternally together. So many of them had died so young, it seemed a waste.

The older graves were a lot more modest than the newer ones. No one really cared before for giant crucifixes or life-size angels, like they do nowadays. A modest stone, sized similarly to the rest, seemed the popular choice in the older days. Everyone was equal in death, but every grave over the last one hundred years or so was perfectly unique. No two graves looked the same, every one of them spoke of a different person, a different soul. I suppose it also made it a lot easier to find the one you wanted to visit. It must've taken people ages before, having to visit everyone else before they found their loved one.

It didn't take me long to find her; I knew exactly where she was after all. I stood before the white marble stone and read their names: Gerard Sullivan and his wife, Eileen.

She had been buried with the granddad I'd never met. I touched the stone gently, my fingers easing along the embedded text of their names. I stuck my hands back in my pockets and stared at the stone, suddenly unsure. Mum would tell me to pray, but I wasn't one for that. I thought maybe I should talk to her as if she was still here, tell her whatever was on my mind like I used to, but what would be the point in that? She couldn't help me now. She couldn't do anything for me now.

I felt a pang in my heart for how I missed her so dearly, nearly three years after I had lost her. I readied myself to cry, to let my tears mix with the falling rain, but nothing came. Serenity seemed to overcome me as I stood in silence, remembering her.

Then came a sound, something in the distance mixed in with the rain, barely noticeable, tickling my ears. The rain had begun to ease just a little bit, but was still falling at a steady pace. I turned around and peered across the expanse of the graveyard only to find it empty.

I turned back to the grave, reassuring myself that I had simply imagined the sound, but then I heard it again, much clearer this time. It was someone shouting. I looked around with more vigour as my ears pricked up. I felt my hair standing up as a tingle fell down my spine. I couldn't see anyone.

I stood still, waiting and listening, looking all around to find the source of the sound. My heart began to beat loudly in my chest, telling me to leave. I began to walk back towards the gate, the sound growing louder as I did so.

I stopped, realising that the voice sounded distressed, not threatening. I still couldn't make it out fully, but could sense its anger and frustration. I questioned myself as my feet moved away from the safety of the gates and towards the sound of the voice as it reverberated through the air.

I began to walk further through the graveyard as the forestry in the back came into view. The voice grew louder still, clearer with each exclamation. Slowly, a blurred shape became visible amongst the trees. I could tell now that the voice was definitely male, and the person's silhouette seemed to match that conclusion.

My pace slowed as I questioned whether this person was safe to approach, but then a feeling of familiarity began to spread through me. I still couldn't see his face, still couldn't recognise him, but felt I knew him all the same.

When I was close enough I came to a stop, intuitively knowing that I shouldn't get too close. His back was turned to me and he seemed to be blocking something from my view as I could see from the movement of his shoulders that he was working at something with his hands.

I tried to discern what he was doing as his shoulders lifted up, down, up, down with the pace of his heavy breathing. Of course, it was obvious. What else could it have been?

I watched as he let the rope go, stepping back and leaving it to swing for a moment in the wind. I stared dumbfounded at the noose tied at its end.

With effort, I tore my eyes away from it to look back at him and instantly knew who he was. I could never mistake his side profile with the bruise around his eye, seemingly renewed with greater invigoration.

"Michael?" I called out.

77

10.

The sound of my voice clearly startled him. He turned around to face me, the remnants of his screaming evident on his blotchy face.

We stared at each other in silence, the noose hanging nearby, swinging in the breeze and demanding attention. I supposed that I had startled him. He had likely come all the way out here, on an evening like this, with the express intention of being undiscovered and uninterrupted.

"You're-" he started. I wondered if he even knew who I was. We had never spoken a word to each other; I only knew his name from roll call and the occasions of overhearing him being scolded by teachers for being late for the umpteenth time. I recalled the day our eyes met right here in the graveyard, after my nan's funeral. I had forgotten about that, I wondered if he was remembering that now, too.

The pause continued as if he was searching for my name in the depths of his memory, so I helped him out. "Samantha." I shook my head, disliking the full version of my name. Only Mum calls me that. "Sam. From school." Just to make sure.

"Y-yeah ... of course. Sam." He started to glance around nervously, looking for a way out of this incredibly awkward situation.

"I'm sorry if I scared you. I heard shouting," I said, feeling as if I needed to explain myself.

A look of realisation seemed to dawn on him then. "Oh, I didn't realise I was ... shouting," he admitted, looking down at his feet with his arms crossed over his chest in a protective stance. He looked up at me after another while with a look of puzzlement. "What are you even doing here? In this weather?" he asked, as the rain gathered speed and ferocity once again. He had the right to question me, no one in their right mind would choose to go outside in such weather, much less visit a graveyard.

"I was just going on a walk and it started raining," I began. My eyes wandered over again to the rope hanging from a tree's branch and suddenly I caught myself. I wasn't the one who needed to explain their actions here. I struggled to take my eyes off it.

Noticing my gaze, he moved to stand in front of the hanging noose, attempting to hide it from me, as if that would halt my curiosity.

"And what exactly are *you* doing here?" I asked. He turned away from me again and I could physically feel the nervous energy expelling from him. I knew it was a stupid question as his intentions were obvious, but I didn't want to judge him or scare him further.

"It's nothing, please, just leave me," he said. The rope extending above his head had stopped swaying as he held onto it.

A chuckle escaped my lips. His ears pricked up, surprised to hear a laugh at such a moment. "You think I'm just gonna turn around and leave you like this, with a noose in your hand?" I said as his shoulders slumped downwards.

"You don't even know me," he said, finally turning around to face me again. He was gripping the noose in his right hand and I tried to mentally urge him to just pull it down, visualising the tree's branch snapping as he did so.

"I know you enough to care," I responded. Now it was his turn to chuckle, but I knew it wasn't time to smile yet. My mind started to race. I didn't know what to do. I tried to puzzle out what it was he'd need to hear at a time like this. I needed to get him to step away, to leave this graveyard with me. I knew that much, but I wasn't sure how to go about it.

"I know that may sound funny," I said, responding to his chuckle, "But it's true. I mightn't know you all that well but that doesn't mean I don't care whether you live or die." I tried to search his face to gauge a reaction, but he was shielding himself. He looked back rather longingly at the rope in his hand. I detected a slight quiver in his lips and eyebrows. "Don't do this, please. This isn't the answer. Whatever it is, you deserve to live. Don't let the demons win."

Suddenly he dropped to the ground and landed on his knees, not caring about the muck gathering beneath us as the rain melded with the grass. He had been holding his composure fairly well since I found him, but now he lay crumpled in front of me, shaking with muffled sobs.

His t-shirt and jeans were clinging to his skin as the relentless rain continued to beat down upon us. I had to get him out of here. Somehow, I had to.

I lowered myself down to him, the grass slumping under my weight. I didn't care about the muck seeping into my clothes either. "Michael." I tried to call to him, to get him to look up at me but he kept his eyes trained on the ground as his body rocked with sorrow and misery. I thought about reaching out to him, to touch him or hug him, but I worried that he would react badly to that, so I kept a respectful distance between us. "You need to get out of here. Your family... I'm sure they're worried sick about you at home." He glanced up at me for just a moment with piercing brown eyes.

He shook his head vigorously, the rain collecting in his hair shaking off in every direction. "I can't go home."

I wanted to ask why, but something told me to stop as it wasn't my business. "Do you ... want to talk about

81

it?" I asked. I waited a while for his response, but didn't seem to be getting one. His shaking had subsided, and I hoped that the frustration within him was calming. "I couldn't make out what you were actually shouting earlier but I figured you were fairly pissed about something."

He let out a noise which sounded like laughter mixed with tears, and I wondered if I had messed up again. "That's one way to put it," he said, "I figured I owed it to the tree. I wanted to tell it everything before I used it." I glanced up at the old tree, standing forebodingly above us. I wondered if he was the first to choose it.

"I used to think about it a lot," I started. I felt his gaze turn towards me as I kept my own trained on the tree before me. "Sometimes I still do, but never long enough to actually do anything about it. I'd wonder what it'd feel like, to just slip away." A voice in my mind began to caution me. Why was I saying all of this? He was practically a complete stranger, and these were my innermost thoughts. Why was I sharing them with him? "It sounds so easy, right?" I glanced over at him. He looked away, as if in shame.

"You don't have to tell me anything if you don't want to. I get it, but this can't be it. This can't be the only answer." I turned away, my eyes falling on the noose swinging above us. His eyes fell heavy upon me again. The words seemed to flow out of me. "I want to

82

live. I want to live so badly but I don't ... want to live like this. So I have to believe that things will change. I have to tell myself every day, every moment of every day, that things will change; that where I am now is just a temporary stage in life. Sometimes, that works, but sometimes, it doesn't." I wondered if he believed a single word I said. I could barely believe them myself. "I will get out of here someday, and so will you. Whatever it is that brought you here, you're not bound by it. You have a choice. You are in control."

I couldn't look away. The noose had me caught in its presence as it swung dramatically in the wind. I felt the rain fall down upon me as silence filled the air. He wasn't looking at me anymore, his hands distracted by plucking out clumps of grass by his feet.

"Do you honestly believe that?" he finally asked, after a lengthy silence.

"Believe what?"

"That things can just ... change," he said, continuously plucking out the grass. His fingers were covered in soil now.

I kept my doubt to myself. Whether I believed that or not didn't matter, I just needed him to believe me long enough to leave this place; to leave this place and keep on living.

"I have hope ..." I said, quietening the voice of hypocrisy in my mind, "that someday we will have the power to demand it."

83

"It's already been ... so long. Ages in fact." He sighed heavily, taking another look at the noose hanging above us, "So much has happened, I-" He looked me right in the eye for the first time that night. "I can't ... I can't talk about it. I just ... I've had enough." Another few tears fell down his face and he bowed his head as if to hide them from me.

I waited as the pain wracked through his body, feeling helpless, wishing I could do something.

He wiped his face on his already sodden t-shirt and looked back up at me. "Things are bad. Things are really fucking bad, but you're right ... this won't help anything. I'll only make it worse. It was stupid to even come here." He suddenly jumped up from the ground.

"Don't say it like that. This isn't your fault."

"Isn't it? I'm the one that let this all happen. I let it get this bad. I got this rope, I came here. That seems like it's all on me, so far."

I decided to stay quiet, not sure what to say. It was probably best to just let him say what he wanted to say, even if I disagreed with him.

Silence grew between us again for a long moment. "I'm sorry," he said as he turned to the noose and untied the knot that allowed it to fall limp from the tree branch. "You were just trying to help, I shouldn't be getting upset at you. I ... thank you." He offered me a weak smile through instances of sniffling. "I should get going." I watched him turn to go, remembering his earlier claim that he wasn't able to go home. He was a fast walker and I had to skip to catch up with him in his urgency to get away.

We walked through the expanse of headstones, leaving the woodland behind us. The sky had become a lot darker since I left the house. How long had it even been?

"Are you going home?" I had to ask.

He shrugged his shoulders. "I guess I have nowhere else to go."

We neared the old gates of the graveyard and stepped outside. I felt like a weight had been lifted from my shoulders. I felt like we were safe now, he was safe now. I had saved him.

Still, I worried about leaving him. "Will you be all right? What if you ..." The question was in my mind, but I suddenly wasn't sure if I should ask it. I didn't want to bring about an option that didn't yet exist in his mind.

"Go somewhere else and do it?" he asked, chuckling again at me, as if I was silly to worry about such a thing. "Don't worry. That was my only rope." The expression on my face must've been enough of a reaction for him. "Kidding! Kidding ... but also not kidding."

I couldn't believe how quickly he had started joking after something so serious, after what he had almost done that night. "Sorry," he said, somehow sensing my train of thought, "Bad taste, I know. I

85

shouldn't be joking about it now after all you did. I'll be fine. Straight home, I promise." He smiled at me, but I could tell it was less than half-hearted. "Thank you for everything again, Sam, but, um ... I have to ask you - will you please keep this a secret?"

The request flew through my mind, offering up a series of potential scenarios. I could tell a teacher, the principal even, and they would tell his parents and maybe offer counselling or some other means of support to ensure it wouldn't happen again. I thought about telling the guards. Is this even a matter for the police? Would they investigate what may have led to this? I would be betraying his trust, the trust of this near-stranger if I did that. His eyes were pleading with me, urging me to agree as if the revelation of tonight's events would be far too harmful for him. I was hesitating too long.

"I know it's a lot to ask," he said, interjecting my hesitation, "It'd only make things a lot more difficult for me, so please... promise me you won't tell anyone."

I couldn't really say anything other than yes. "Okay, I promise. I won't say a word."

"Thank you. Thank you so much." He seemed truly glad about my promise. "I'll see you in school."

We said our brief goodbyes and turned away from each other. He took the path leading right from the graveyard, walking at a fairly hurried pace. My home was actually the same way, but I had the feeling he wished to be alone so didn't pester him to walk with me. I waited a while until he was out of sight before turning around myself and making my way back home.

11.

He wasn't there the next day. He didn't turn up for any classes. I tried not to worry too much, reminding myself that we only shared a couple of classes so I could've simply missed him.

The lunch hour dawned, and I spent the majority of it looking around eagerly to try to spot him in order to ease the anxious voice in my mind. I couldn't find his face amongst the crowd of faces in the entrance hall. I thought that maybe he was eating outside instead but his usual group of friends were seated at their usual table. He was nowhere to be seen. I reminded myself that I had barely paid him any mind before. He could be anywhere. Just because he wasn't where I could see him was no cause for alarm.

And so, I waited.

I didn't see him the next day either nor the next. Suddenly it was a week later, and he still hadn't shown up in school. I couldn't be that ignorant and he couldn't be that evasive. I grew increasingly worried and wondered if I should say something to someone about what had happened, despite promising to keep it a secret.

What if the anxiety buried in my gut was right? What if I stopped him that night, only for him to succeed the next night instead? I didn't know what to do. I thought about going up to his friends, just to ask where he was, but again, the possibilities of embarrassment and ridicule played out in my mind instantaneously, halting me in my tracks. I tried to pose the question as vaguely as possible in my mind. *Where was he?* I'd ask. *What?* They'd ask back, wondering who the hell I was and why I was interested in their friend's whereabouts. They'd gang up protectively in front of me. My anxiety would surely get the better of me then and I'd stammer *n-never mind* and scurry away, their laughter reverberating in my ears. Then, they'd question him about it when they saw him later that night, doing whatever they do. They'd ask, *what was with that weird girl earlier?* Then he'd know I'd broken my promise, or at least as good as broken it. He'd hate me and never speak to me again and that'd be that.

So, I bundled up my worries and waited. It was another week later until I finally saw him.

I had almost forgotten to even look for him, automatically assuming that he wouldn't be there today either. I sat down in my usual spot in school for lunch and by complete chance, glanced up at the exact place where he sat. Despite being partially turned away from me, I knew it was him, and the knot in my stomach which had been building for weeks, suddenly seemed to release with confirmation that he was at least still alive. In my mind's eye, I saw myself running up to him and asking where he'd been, but that would've been crazy; I had no right to ask or to worry, just because we talked that one night. That didn't make us friends, not in the slightest.

He turned as if feeling the weight of my gaze and we locked eyes for a moment. He looked away almost instantly and turned further with his back fully facing me. He was ignoring me.

I told myself it wasn't any of my business. I told myself that that small feeling I felt, that feeling of some sort of connection was but some kind of far flung fantasy. I helped him out that night by saying some words he needed to hear and that was it.

***

He seemed to put extra effort into avoiding me after that. We had never properly met or talked before that night in the graveyard but he had never so purposefully avoided my gaze as he was doing now. Again and again our eyes would meet by chance as we passed each other in the hallway, but each time he'd turn his head without a word.

I'd try to catch his gaze from across the entrance

hall during lunch but for mere seconds only as he'd instantaneously find something more interesting to look at. In every class we shared, he'd sit further away from me than before, and then he'd leave the classroom before I could even contemplate approaching him. Not that I ever would have done anyway.

I told myself it didn't matter. I had met him at what was a severely awkward time for him and maybe he just didn't want to face it. I knew this, but it didn't matter. I felt slighted, cast out, unimportant and as unwanted as a stain on the floor.

The walls I had built to protect myself from the ignorant outside world were growing steadily higher, brick by brick, snapping into place until they towered over me, impenetrable and comforting in their suffocation.

I glanced over to him once again as the wall solidified in front of me. I tried to convince myself that I couldn't see him anymore and so, as always, I was alone. That was the safest way to be.

*****

I had heard all the stories before. The stories of horrendous bullying and vicious torture. The broken childhoods and broken homes. All those lives smothered in darkness. Of course they couldn't take it, of course they just wanted to end it all. Wouldn't you

91

have?

If I did what all those posters told me to do and talked to someone, what would I even say? I could already hear the most inevitable question on everyone's lips - *Why?* I wouldn't be able to tell them. I hardly knew myself. I had no trauma to speak of, no abuse nor torment. I should be happy. I had no right to complain.

No one ever mentioned the isolation, the exclusion; that feeling that you simply didn't belong anywhere. No one ever mentioned the suffocating loneliness either.

I could go days without saying barely a word to anyone – weeks or even months. I'd mutter one-word responses to my parents and anyone else who dared to pose a question as if it required the greatest bout of effort. Some might try, at first, to break down my wall, but soon realise it was futile. I was locked in here, within myself, and who could know where the key was?

I thought maybe he had one too. As I watched the noose swinging above us, it seemed as if the bricks from his wall had fallen down around him. He had let himself become exposed. He tried to pick up the pieces as I approached, but it remained shattered. I thought maybe he'd understand what it was like for me. Maybe he could be the first person to listen, and really hear me. Maybe he could see past my wall too, maybe even see through it.

Or maybe, just maybe, he would see *me*.

92

12.

The lines started flooding across the page, turning it darker and darker with each stroke. I didn't fully know yet what the lines were trying to say or what image they were trying to create. I just let them run wild and coalesce until they began to stretch out and slowly merge together.

The pencil grew light in my hand and scurried across the page to add elements of tone and shadow. Then the pencil buried down, taking the weight of my hand with it to add greater depth which enhanced the darkness of the lead.

An indiscernible image began to form on the page. I drew slowly at first, but then all at once my hand grew more erratic as if this was an image that needed to be destroyed. Loops, circles and jagged lines flew out of the pencil until, surely, whatever image wanted to exist, had been lost. What lay before me now was nothing more than a mess of confused lines with no real purpose.

I tore the paper up into the smallest pieces possible and let them fall to the floor of my bedroom. I hadn't been able to draw anything for days. All I could manage was one mess after another. I tried to conjure up interesting images in my mind, but all I could see was a mass of lines, rendered colourless and lifeless.

I gazed down at the other mess of lines on my forearms; their startling red contrasting brightly against the whiteness of my skin.

An idea floated through my mind in an instant, but strong enough to be instantly understood and recognised. A voice of reason somewhere in the distance told me it was crazy and to not even think about it, but I couldn't stop myself.

I pulled the blade out from my drawer and noted the building rust from the stains of blood upon it. I had tried to keep it clean in an attempt to hide its true use but ultimately had grown tired of such a task and so let the stains gather. Despite being so well used, it worked just the same; as sharp as the day I stole it.

I pulled it across my skin and felt the familiar rush of pain. It flooded through my body, offering not just physical pain, but relief and proof of my being alive.

My arm began to sting as I watched the blood peter out slowly, the beads merging across my skin into a steadier flow.

I brought a blank piece of paper closer to me and focused on the image in my mind. I took a small paintbrush that I had nearby, stiff enough to draw the image well. The coarse bristles poked into my skin and the pain flared in reaction to the sudden intrusion. The bristles quickly developed a reddish hue as the blood seeped into the brush. Knowing it would dry quickly, I hastened to bring the brush down on the page and drew out the image that longed to be free.

I pulled the paintbrush around the page a number of times, stopping to re-dab the brush every once in a while. Slowly, the image of an eye formed before me; an oval accompanied by a series of circles. The redness of the eye glared up at me as further redness seeped down from it. It began to grow mournful; its expression speaking of desperation and hopelessness.

As the blood dried, the image became ever fainter but still, it continued to stand out against the stark white of the paper. The pain in my arm had begun to ease into a barely noticeable stinging sensation. I stared down at what I had done, at what had been created, and I felt content.

I hid the paper away in a box beneath my bed where I was sure no one would ever find it.

***

It swung before me, the wind pulling it this way and that. The frayed edges of the rope stood out clearly as it pulled against the branch above with an almost expert knot tied midway down that allowed a loop to form at its end. I wondered what it would be like, to feel that rope tied around my neck, to feel it tightening as the ground gave way beneath me. I thought about how painful it must be.

I knew from history lessons in school that hanging was often used as a means of execution. A sort of trapdoor was set beneath the prisoner's feet, and as the executioner pulled on a lever beside it, the door opened and the victim fell helplessly, their neck broken by the force of the rope pulling against gravity.

Truly, that must be one of the worst ways to die. Why would you choose to go like that? I had heard stories of people who would be left hanging for ten minutes or more until they finally died. It seemed too cruel and torturous. I would want to go much quicker. I wanted to be able to just slip away and to say my goodbyes to this world as the light faded from my eyes. I thought I would likely overdose on something or lay with my sharpened friend as the blood poured endlessly from my veins.

I had seen it done many times in films and TV shows. Even the Internet was desperate to tell me that I'd been doing it wrong all along. *Remember kids, it's down the road, not across the street.* Someone had even made a meme out of it, passing it around like some sort of macabre public service announcement. It made me sick to my stomach, but still it managed to stick in my mind.

It seemed that was the way you were supposed to

do it in order to really threaten the body, challenging its ability to clot blood and save the heart from bleeding out. The vein leading to the heart was right there, right beneath the skin, so that a single well-positioned cut would do the job.

In every film and TV show that I'd seen featuring such incidents, they had all chosen to do it in a bathtub with the water overflowing, allowing the reddened water to seep out into the hallway. I always wondered why they'd choose to do it like that as it seemed so impractical. I thought of my mother coming up the stairs, seeing the beige carpet suddenly growing dark. Her eyes would follow the stain towards the bathroom door and she'd know that someone had left the bath running. She'd run around, shouting and knocking on doors to seek out the culprit. The others would claim innocence. She'd finally come to my room and see I wasn't there. Then maybe, just maybe, she would grow concerned and would finally open the bathroom door to find me lying there amidst the sea of red with my body limp and lifeless.

I could never do that; it seemed too horrible. I'd prefer to slip away unnoticed. Maybe I'd even leave and go somewhere they would never think to find me so I could simply disappear from their lives and they would go on living happily.

I thought about it constantly. I thought that maybe I should just try it to see how it felt to be on the brink of death, to feel the greatest sense of relief of all, but I'd hesitate at the last moment as I drew the blade across my skin horizontally - non-fatally.

I made the choice to keep living.

13.

I wanted to ask him about that night. I wanted to talk to him, to know how he felt. What was it that truly put him there, that made him sure it was the right thing to do? What was he shouting about? Still, I couldn't bring myself to approach him. He wouldn't even look me in the eye.

I kept to myself as always and buried my head in a book, preparing for an upcoming test in history class. I had always enjoyed history. I loved learning about things that had happened in the past, why they had happened and how they had affected the world for years to come. The topic of choice was World War II. I tried to drill the names and dates into my brain. I loved history but I always mixed up the dates and couldn't remember every name, so I thought I'd best have them stored in my short-term memory before going in.

Suddenly I felt the table sag with the sudden weight of another person's arms. This was usually no cause for alarm, but I could feel the hairs on the back of my neck stand to attention. Slowly, I looked up from my book and froze.

The names and dates I had been cramming into my mind instantly disappeared as I looked at him, suddenly mere inches from me. He sat with his head bowed and his hands clasped on the table in front of him. I looked around and noticed that his friends weren't with him. It seemed he had sat here on purpose. I looked at him, waiting for him to look at me, wondering if he ever would. I felt unsure as to what to do, so I looked back down at my textbook and waited for him to do something or say something – anything at all.

Minutes of silence began to achingly stretch out as he remained sitting there. I could feel his eyes boring into me, but I pretended not to notice and tried to focus on learning the important dates of World War II's events.

"Hey ..." His voice was barely more than a whisper as he finally spoke. I gave myself permission to look over at him then. His head had risen so I could see his face. It looked the same as always, with the slight yellowish tinge of a healing bruise surrounding his left eye and his dark hair almost long enough to cover it, but not quite.

"Hey," I said simply. Words began to catch in my throat. I wanted to say so much more and ask so much more but held myself back. He had finally decided to speak to me and I didn't want to say anything that would change his mind.

"I, um, wanted to talk to you," he said. I noticed that his eyes were restless, shifting around, checking if anyone was listening. "Not here though. Can I see you later?" His eyes returned to look right into mine.

I obviously couldn't refuse. "Um ... sure."

"Sorry, I just ..." he started glancing around again, "I don't want anyone overhearing."

"Yeah, I get it. Where?"

"Will you wait outside for me later? Give me maybe half an hour after school." I found it a bit odd, but I agreed to his request that I'd meet him at the entrance after school. He offered me a quick smile of thanks and left me again. I watched as he exited the area, my thoughts swirling.

***

I stood against the wall outside the school gates, feeling increasingly awkward as more and more people passed me. I had left the last class fairly quickly, eagerly gathering my things to get outside in case he managed to arrive early and didn't want to wait around for me.

It was a nice day for once. The usual grey, rainy weather had eased and the sun was peeking out behind some clouds. I glanced around, praying I wouldn't have to wait too long. Several other students appeared annoyed as they had to careen around me while I waited on the other side of the wall. I thought about moving somewhere less intrusive, but I was worried he would bypass me, thinking I had decided not to meet him. I wanted to make sure we spotted each other.

Slowly, the crowds dispersed and I found myself standing entirely alone. I checked the worn watch on my wrist and found that it was now forty minutes since class had officially ended but I kept waiting.

Another ten minutes ticked by and my heart began to sink. I picked my bag off the floor and decided to leave. I wasn't going to be a fool waiting around for some boy. I started walking down the street towards home. I became faintly aware of the sound of someone running behind me. I was about to turn to see who it was just as he bounded ahead to stop me in my tracks.

"Sorry, sorry ..." he said, somewhat out of breath. "Took longer than I expected."

I gave Michael a few minutes to catch his breath but couldn't help laughing a bit at the sight of him bent over with his hands on his knees. He echoed back my laughter.

Eventually he managed to gather himself. "Had a bit of a run first, did you?" I said, in an attempt to break the ice.

"Well, you know, I already asked you to wait half an hour for me ... and then I ask you to wait even more. That's not on. I thought for sure you'd be gone."

"I thought about it ..."

"But ...?" he said, sensing I had more to say.

"But you said you had something to talk to me about. Well, I wanted to talk to you too." If this moment had become somewhat carefree, that feeling quickly began to change, as the matter reared its ugly head again. I could see that he, too, was recounting that night in his mind. Perhaps he had re-lived it every day since, just like I had. I didn't want to avoid it anymore; it would surely swallow me whole if I did.

"Um ... yeah," he began, his feet shuffling nervously. "Can we go to the park nearby? I feel like it might be a long talk." He offered me that smile again, and I couldn't say no.

***

I hadn't spent much time in the park or at least not in recent years. The park was pretty large, situated about a ten minutes' walk from the school. We talked casually as we walked; about our classes and our worries over the impending exams.

A moment of silence would fall at times but, for once, I didn't feel the overwhelming need to fill it. I assumed that he needed to get his words in order, to decide exactly what he was going to say, and how he was going to say it. Words began to fly around my mind too, desperately trying to find some way to fit together, to make coherent sense. I didn't want to upset him. Nor did I want to cause him to lock up again and avoid me.

I knew I would have to let him take the lead on whatever this was. I would have to be careful.

The park in Tíreen had always been well cared for. Of course, if you ventured far enough and investigated well enough, you were sure to find deposits of beer cans and syringes, but apart from that, the park was overflowing with colour; so much so that it looked like a vibrant painting created by one of the masters. Tall trees stood in the foreground, their seemingly never-ending branches reaching up to the sky. Their leaves were an array of colours as they began to decay and fall, littering the ground beneath. The grass was a mass of green, each blade cut to the same length. A path extended throughout the park from front to back, careening off to each side. Along this path, a number of benches had been planted to allow people to relax on a rare day of good weather. In the background, a small playground had been set up with swings and slides. A number of children who had just finished school for the day were running around.

I followed Michael as he walked towards one of the benches near the centre of the park. The park itself wasn't that busy so there would surely be no one within earshot of our conversation.

I sat down beside him, the old wood feeling slightly unstable. He was staring forwards, and I could almost hear his mind whirring as he decided what to say. I waited until he was ready to begin.

"I feel like ... I need to apologise," he said.

"Apologise?" I said.

"I thought you'd be pissed with me."

"About ...?"

"After what happened ... I couldn't-" He still hadn't found the right words as he broke off to re-assemble his thoughts. "I ignored you. For weeks."

I had hardly forgotten it. I had been yearning to ask him why, but I never expected him to apologise for it. I almost didn't know how to respond.

"Do you have a reason for that?" I asked. I had grown up thinking that if you were sorry for something, truly sorry, you'd have some reason as to why you had done what you did. Or, at least, people would always come up with some excuse to aid their apology, even if it was a fabricated one.

"I ... it sounds so stupid. It took me so long to realise how stupid it was. How stupid *I* was." He laughed at himself. I didn't feel the need to interject and allowed him to continue. "Needless to say, that wasn't a good night for me, Sam. It wasn't a good night at all. I still owe you so much for it - I do. Every night and every day since, I've thought about it. I've practically re-lived it and I'd repeat the words you said over and over but then ..." he broke off for just a moment. "I'd see you. I'd see you in school, in class, at lunch and I just couldn't ... I couldn't bear to look at you, I couldn't bear to be near you because it was just a constant reminder of that night and I'd end up re-living it yet again.

"But then ... I dunno ... Maybe you'd call it an epiphany or something but suddenly, the other night, I realised that was so stupid. You had saved my life, literally saved me, and this was how I thanked you? By completely ignoring you? By not being able to even say hello? I hated myself for it. I owed you."

His words floated through me like a breeze. I had never thought about it like that. I never realised that he could possibly be feeling that way. He seemed almost ... embarrassed by it all.

His leg had begun to shake beneath him, which caused the bench to shake too as he awaited my response. I didn't realise that I had left a silence to grow.

"Do you ... is that okay?" he asked. I could see the nervousness in his eyes.

"You don't owe me anything," I finally managed to answer.

He laughed, as if I had said something ludicrous. "Oh, only my life."

"No, I'm serious. You don't. I mean, yeah, I was somewhat hurt that you were ignoring me. I guess I just didn't understand why but ... I never thought about it like that."

"I am so sorry, really. You didn't deserve that. It's such a bullshit excuse but I just needed time to wrap my head around it ... and I'm still working on that bit."

A moment of silence grew between us as I considered his words. It made sense, he was embarrassed and afraid to confront what had happened, what had drawn us together. I couldn't say that I would've acted any differently.

I was ready to move past it, but then I remembered. "You were out," I said.

He looked up at me, straight in the eyes, his expression puzzled.

"You were out, for at least two weeks afterwards. I mean, ignoring me is one thing but ..."

"Oh God, you thought ..." he interrupted me, daring to laugh.

"Yeah, I thought! I thought you had gone and done it for real. I mean, it mightn't've been my right, but I was worried sick. I was gonna report it if you didn't come back the day you did."

He almost started to laugh, thinking I was joking, but then a spark of fear took over him. "You didn't, did you? You haven't told anybody?"

"No, but like I said, I was going to, if you didn't show up. I mean, can you imagine what that would've done to me if I knew you were feeling like that but didn't report it and then you turn up weeks later, dead? I would've died too." The words spilled out of me before I could stop them.

It seemed like I had made him speechless as he glanced around the park. He was breathing rather

107

heavily, and his leg had suddenly stopped moving. "I didn't even think about that," he said, staring off into the distance, "I am so stupid." He bent over and placed his head in his hands. "You're so right," he said after taking a few deep breaths. He looked back up at me, straight in the eye. "If the situation was reversed, I would've been worried sick. Hell, I would've gone to the guards the next day if you hadn't shown up, but you kept it for two weeks?"

"Guess I'm good at keeping promises. Too good," I said. I could feel a knot building in my stomach.

"I am really so, so sorry. There's so much going on right now, I wish I could tell you. Just please let me make it up to you," he said. His eyes were looking at me, pleadingly, as if he truly believed that he had committed a great wrong.

"Michael, it's fine. You don't owe me anything. Just a hello once in a while would be nice, I guess."

He laughed that adorable laugh and I thought I caught the glimmer of a tear in his eye.

"Let me buy you lunch. It's the least I can do." He stood up from the bench and offered his hand to help me up, even though I didn't need it.

"Lunch sounds good."

14.

I slept better that night than I had in a long time. The day raced before me and I urged it to slow down, but all too soon, the sun had begun to set, and I returned to the familiar confines of my room.

Lunch with Michael had been effervescent, magical. We talked about the most mundane of things, choosing not to linger on the event that had drawn us together. We talked again of school and its endless torture. We shared our dreams for the future and our common desire for escape, for more. I wanted to know him. I felt there was more than a coincidental event tying us together. Michael even jokingly said it "must've been fate" or some great intervention from beyond that brought me to him that night. I told him he was crazy and that there's no such thing as fate or destiny. Things just happen and we just have to go with it. He didn't much like that way of thinking.

I went home feeling elated. It had been ages since I had spent such a long time in someone else's company. Even at home, I'd hasten to make excuses to leave the kitchen table, preferring the isolation in my room over the mundane questions that sufficed as conversation with my family. But with him, it was different. Even though he was a complete stranger, I didn't buckle under the weight of his gaze nor want to run away in fear or anxiety. I didn't feel suffocated by the presence of momentary silence between us.

Instead, I wanted him to open up to me. I wanted to see what he was thinking; what was going on inside his head. I knew there was something behind those eyes. I could see the hurt as plain as day written on his face, but I knew he daren't talk of it. Besides, I was hardly in a position to judge, being ever so careful to keep my skin covered, even if the café was too warm and I yearned for the sweet release of air on my skin.

Dreams began to overtake me. It seemed I had suddenly reached the limit of exhaustion. I'd usually spend each night battling with my thoughts, trying ceaselessly to quieten them. Often, I'd lay awake into the early hours of the morning, tossing and turning as I chased sleep. But the more I chased it, the further away it seemed.

This night, for once, my mind felt eerily calm. I felt no anger, no frustration and no overbearing numbness. It was contentment - the strangest form of contentment I had ever felt.

Or perhaps my subconscious had simply stored my worries for later. Maybe it chose to give me just one good day.

***

I was in a town I didn't recognise, and the world was devoid of colour. I wondered if I had managed to step into an old film and soon, a random tornado would come by and whisk me away. I was standing amidst a large group of people, many of whom I knew. They were gathered in a circle, glaring downward as if something had captured their attention.

I made my way through the crowd, icicles trickling up my spine. I pushed my way through the last few people at the front to witness what they were all staring at. My heart leapt in my chest. A noose lay on the ground, bloody and broken at my feet.

A scream escaped from my throat. I glanced around at the faces of the other people but not one of them seemed to care. They remained emotionless and uncaring. Slowly, their eyes began to shift up to focus on me instead of the noose.

I felt more screams rising up within me and tried to keep them down, but it seemed I no longer had control over myself. Their eyes bore into me, their stillness almost suffocating. I met the gaze of my mother who gave me a look of complete and utter disappointment. Or was it disgust?

I found myself fleeing from the scene with all my

might, failing to understand what had happened. The weight of their gazes tore into me as I ran; scream after scream escaping from my chest. Tears had begun to blur my vision and I had no idea where I was going.

Suddenly I saw them in front of me which was impossible, as they had been way behind when I had left them. I ran into my father, his eyes forlorn as he silently entreated calmness in me, but there was no calming the storm raging within. I pushed past him and continued to run forwards, until I was halted in my tracks by the sight of my brother. He was the first to laugh.

I thought for sure that I was going mad. I ran and ran and screamed and screamed but there seemed to be no escape. Everywhere, people were looking, laughing and judging. I didn't understand what I had done and I didn't understand what had happened. I wanted to disappear more than anything, ever.

The world began to spin, and I tried to keep running, but the laughter only grew louder until, eventually, everything had faded away into complete blackness.

That dream would visit me many times thereafter. No matter how many times I dreamt it or lived through it, it remained the greatest terror; of losing my mind, of losing myself.

My throat felt sore and dry and I wondered if I had been screaming in my sleep but surely then someone would've heard and woken me? The dream had infiltrated my mind so deeply that I continued to feel those feelings of desperation and despair throughout the day after. I could barely face my parents afterwards, as all I could see was the memory of their dream-like laughter, etched upon their faces, directed straight at me.

***

We'd visit Nan's grave occasionally as a family. In the beginning, we visited a lot more often, but as time went on, the visits became even more infrequent. I tried to visit when I could, but even *I* found myself forgetting after a while. I had no excuses, Nan. I could say life got in the way, but what life? I could say that exams were occupying my mind, but I still found plenty of time to draw.

I tried to hold on to the blissful memories I had of her, and tried to forget how she looked as she lay dying. The headstone was all that remained of her now and was all that I would ever see again.

I wasn't sure if I believed in an afterlife. It all seemed so impossible. Mum would tell me to, "just believe" whenever the topic came up. "You can't believe in nothing," she'd say. I couldn't help but question it all, none of it ever made any sense to me. How could anyone say for certain that there was another life after this - a plane of paradise for the lost souls - with nothing to show for it? We all came from nothing, that much was true, and so it seemed sure that we would return to nothing. I tried to stop that thought from keeping me up at night.

During our most recent visit as a family, we stood in silence together for a few moments, 'praying' or talking silently to Nan. I felt too weird talking to her in front of the others. If there truly was any hope of an afterlife, I hoped she could hear me.

The sound of a ringtone broke through the tranquillity of the scene.

"Samuel!" Mum gasped, using Dad's full name to scold him.

"Whoops," he said, pulling the phone out of his pocket. I watched his expression change from embarrassment to confusion as he read on the screen the name of the person calling him. He walked a few steps away and answered the phone. I couldn't hear what he was saying from where I stood so didn't pay him much attention.

A few minutes later he returned, looking rather glum. "Who was it?" Mum asked.

Dad was about to answer, but then caught me looking at him and changed his mind. "Nothing. I'll tell you later."

As we said our goodbyes to Nan, I found myself glancing towards where I had first seen Michael sitting in front of a grave. I was still curious about that - whose grave was it? I wondered if I would ever find out, but it wasn't something I could just ask him out of the blue.

The forest at the back of the graveyard seemed to be calling out to me. My heart began to beat faster, and a shiver went up my spine as the sound of his shouting echoed in my mind once again. What if I hadn't listened or ignored it, instead reasoning it was some drunkard deciding to argue with God? I silently thanked whatever it was that brought me here that night and gave me enough courage to walk towards him.

***

"Samantha love, come down," Mum bellowed from downstairs, a few days after the grave visit. The tone of her voice meant I couldn't refuse. I pulled myself away from my desk and went down. "Your dad and I have to go out for a bit." She and Dad were dressed all in black. She looked as impeccable as ever as she helped Dad with his tie. He was leaning on his walking stick which I thought was strange as he hadn't used it much recently.

"Where are you going?" I asked. I looked over towards Dad. As Mum finished fixing his tie, he hung his head low, breathed deeply and turned away from us.

"One of your dad's friends, from the army, he ... passed away a few days ago. We're going to the removal," Mum explained. That must've been what the phone call was the other day.

"Is he all right?" I said, watching as Dad sat back

at the table to finish his coffee.

"He will be. Just a bit of a shock right now." She glanced back at him and I could see she was worried. "Anyway, Gerard's still out training but he'll be back soon. Could you help clean up a bit? Do some hoovering?" Again, I could hardly say no.

As I watched them go out the front door, I wished I could do something more. I didn't know who the man was or how close he and Dad were, but I could see the grief written into his features like the scratches on a cutting board.

116

15.

The page grew darker as I pulled my finger across it, smudging the graphite continually until I achieved the right tone. Shapes began to further form with each stroke of the pencil. The crumbling tower began to come to life in elements of black and white; the various tones showcasing negative and positive spaces. Rubble gathered at its feet as it stood defiantly against the amassing army of attackers on the opposite side.

Suddenly the page was overcome with a widespread dark tone. A large shadow loomed from behind me, blocking my source of light.

"Well, that's incredible," he said matter-of-factly, "I always thought you just doodled but that's one hell of a doodle." Michael sat down beside me as he commented on my work.

"It gives me something to do," I said. That, and I have to get so much better too.

"That's some serious talent you've got there," he said. His eyes were scanning the image and my heart began to hammer in my chest as I awaited his criticism.

I closed the book suddenly. "Hey!" he protested, like I had switched the channel on the TV during his favourite show. "You don't need to be shy about it," he laughed. I wanted him to go away and leave me alone so I could continue in peace by myself, just to *be* myself.

"Sorry, I'm bothering you," he said.

"No, no, I just …" I began, but I had no idea how I meant to finish that sentence.

He eventually broke the silence for me. "Look, um, it's none of my business, if you want me to leave you be, I will. I just thought, you know, you might like to have lunch with us ... instead of-" The unspoken words, "being alone," hung on his lips, as if acknowledging my isolated existence was sure to offend me. I looked into his eyes and saw that look I had seen on so many other faces, that look of pity. I didn't want to be pitied; by them or him.

"Who's us?" I asked.

"Oh, well, my friends back there. Just two guys, not too crazy," he said, as if sensing my trepidation. "Sorry, I know it's weird, but they'd kill me if I ditched them for a girl so ..." he explained. I both hated and loved the smile he offered me. It was a smile that promised comfort and safety but at the same time, I worried about what could be hiding behind it.

I felt I had no choice as declining would've just been rude.

I was already hatching a plan of escape as I neared

their table; a table of people that had always been in my class but to whom I had never spoken. I pushed myself forwards, not wanting to look pathetic by running away with my tail between my legs.

My mind began to race as I worried about small talk, or indeed talking in general. I worried that my words would get stuck in my throat as I waited politely for others to stop speaking first, which often rendered me altogether silent. I wouldn't be winning any awards for conversational skills.

"Don't look so worried," Michael said just as we approached the table, "They won't bite." He hadn't a clue.

His friends looked up as we approached, and I could feel the weight of their judgment as my stomach plummeted. My heart began to race again, and I wanted more than anything to turn around and run, but something pulled me forwards. I waited for their rejection, for their outbursts of mockery, but it never came. Instead, they smiled and nodded, and I realised that, of course, he had already warned them, so they could get their impressions of me under control. They introduced themselves as Mark and Cian although I already knew that from our classes.

Despite my fears, it was fine. My heart consistently hammered in my chest, and I was surely visibly sweating the entire time, but it was fine. They did most of the talking amongst themselves and I was left to simply smile and laugh in the right places. Then suddenly, every now and again, they'd turn to me and ask me a question directly. This would catch me off guard as I was so used to being the outsider, even just the observer, in a conversation. Rarely would people actively invite me in. I felt Michael's gaze on me and wondered if this had been some kind of test.

"Tell me something," I asked Michael afterwards, as we left school, "If you don't mind. I was just wondering if they ... know." I let the sentence hang between us.

"If they know what?" he said, seemingly unsure of what I was hinting at.

"You know ..." I started, taking a moment to make sure no one was within earshot of us. "About what happened ... that night." I saw him stumble as he realised what I meant and I quickly added, "Not that it matters, I was just wondering."

"No they ... they don't. So, please-"

"I won't tell," I interrupted, already well attuned to his concern for secrecy. "Who you tell is your business, after all."

"It doesn't matter anymore anyway. That was just one stupid night and a stupid decision. It won't happen again."

"I sure hope not." I wanted to quiz him more about it. I was burning with questions, but it was clear he wanted to just leave it in the past, forget about it and

120

pretend it had never happened in the first place. I let the subject drop. His reasons were his own and I had no right to judge, just as I hoped he would never judge me were I to ever dare confide in him.

***

There were a lot of days when Michael wouldn't come to school. I tried not to worry whilst the image of a noose floated before my eyes. I'd take out my phone to ask him how he was and try to ignore the hammering of my heart and the voices in my head as I texted the number he had given me. All he'd say in reply was that he, "wasn't well" or "wasn't feeling up to it" that day, which I couldn't help but doubt.

It still wasn't my place to pry. I kept myself quiet, not wanting to bother him or come across as clingy. Was it strange that I missed him when he wasn't there?

Weeks later, I was surprised to find Mark and Cian, sit beside me at lunch. They must've noticed my hesitation and claimed that we were all friends now, which I found hard to believe, but nonetheless I enjoyed their company, even if I did feel quite awkward about it at first.

Mark was captain of the basketball team and had, in fact, just lead them to victory against a neighbouring town, a fact he had no shame in boasting about. His dark hair was much longer than Michael's and hung below his shoulders. He kept it tied up neatly out of the way in a ponytail most of the time though. He was well built from the years of practice.

Cian, on the other hand, hadn't much interest in sport but attended every one of Mark's games for support. He seemed the type to truly value friendship and loyalty and I felt truly envious of their bond. Cian kept his blonde hair short, but just barely long enough to keep him from being labelled a skinhead. His hands were mottled with tiny cuts and contusions. I questioned him about them once and he talked at length about his love for woodwork and making things with his bare hands. He said it was like watching things come to life. He showed me the chair he was working on for his Leaving Certificate project and it was truly something immaculate that I'd expect to find in any furniture shop – or even a museum; too unique to be sat upon.

I told them about my interest in art, of my hopes to attend Crawford someday and to see my works framed on a stranger's wall. After some pestering, I handed over my sketchbook and they flicked through it, uttering gasps of awe as they did so. I blocked out the worried voices in my head and allowed myself a moment of pride as I took in their startled eyes.

I decided to ask them about Michael. Surely, they'd know what was going on? I posed the question a number of weeks after we had first met, and it seemed I wasn't the only one who was wondering. "Why is he out so much? It's almost every week now."

"Dunno," Mark said in between bites of a sandwich, "We ask him but-"

"Apparently he keeps getting sick," Cian finished for him. I was so glad that I wasn't the only one that doubted Michael's excuses.

"You don't believe him either, then," I concluded.

"Ha!" Mark said, whilst devouring his sandwich.

"He's not a very good liar," Cian whispered, as if it was some sort of secret. "I've known him almost all my life. I've never seen him sick. Well ... apart from that time," he trailed off.

"I figure," Mark butted in, gulping down the final bit of bread, "He just can't be bothered. Ever."

"Yeah, maybe ..." Cian said, but I could see he wasn't convinced by that suggestion.

"You don't really think that, though," I said.

"Nah, not really," Cian admitted, "Like I said, I've known him forever, longer than Mark has. Michael was never the type to just ditch school. He was almost snotty in primary. I had to convince him to stop working most of the time as he'd always say he could never do enough – that project could always be better – stuff like that."

"Yeah, but people change," Mark said.

"Maybe, but I don't think it's like him, and this is our last and most important year. You'd think he'd just push through and give it one last shot. And that's coming from me," Cian joked.

Michael would never admit that he was ditching

school or avoiding it for some reason. "There's no point anyway, it's not like I'm missing anything," he said when I asked him about it one day, "Everything we do in class is straight out of the textbook so I can just learn on my own at home." I'd try to argue that point, but it didn't seem worth it. After a while, he'd become increasingly annoyed about the questions, so I let it go.

16.

It had become almost commonplace, but somehow still remained taboo as something to discuss in hushed tones at late hours when no one could hear. Then, every once in a while, the news stations would light up with word of another celebrity who'd died by their own hand.

The headline would glare up at me, "Rock Star Found Hanging at 50" with a simple description of them found hanging in their hotel room in the middle of a tour. The dismissive way they reported such a story said it all to me: "Oh well, there goes another one who just couldn't be bothered." The comments I'd read online beneath the numerous identical articles were a mixture of grief and anger. Sometimes, even laughter.

Amongst them all, it was the words of disbelief and shock which stood out the most; devoted fans who just couldn't believe their hero was no more. A shining ray of hope had suddenly been wiped from the world and nothing seemed sacred anymore. I had never been one to stake my faith in something so vulnerable, but I understood. I understood the feeling of depending on something so thoroughly, on focusing on someone or something so fiercely that should they leave or be taken from you, it was like having the ground beneath your feet suddenly cave in on itself.

All too soon, the familiar question of "Why?" would raise its head as people struggled to comprehend the fact that the bubbling, happy-go-lucky comedian just couldn't take it anymore. Sometimes they left a note to offer some sort of explanation for their actions, their decisions or for their suffering, but more often than not their death was made all the worse by the silence surrounding it.

I'd hear the comments in reaction to yet another death and felt the world grow stale from caring. The word 'selfish' crept into conversation as people offered their condolences to the actor's wife and children. I wanted to shout at them, I wanted to tell them that they didn't know. How dare they act like they knew? I didn't know either, but I knew it was not out of selfishness, but in fact the complete opposite.

Sometimes, I'd find myself fantasising about it. I'd imagine the blood pouring out of me, I'd imagine the last breath escaping my lungs, I'd imagine the feeling of my throat collapsing as the rope drew tighter and tighter. I'd imagine the feeling of my heart beating faster as it struggled to keep me alive and then steadily failing as my vision blurred into nothingness.

I'd imagine my family finding me and wonder

how they'd react. Would they be surprised? Devastated? Relieved? Or would they say the same as everyone else? Would they grow angry and claim that I was nothing but a selfish cow whose only concern was her own feelings and suffering? Would they call me weak for not being able to deal with it or would they curse themselves from not noticing the obvious signs?

Would I survive? Would they find me just at the last second, resuscitating me at the vital moment before I could slip away? I could see their angry faces flashing before my eyes, screaming, "Selfish, selfish, selfish! How selfish can you be?"

The fantasy and the questions would re-play in my mind over and over again, even as I sat at the table with them, silently eating my dinner, and I'd wonder if they'd care.

***

I went downstairs to fetch a glass of water late one night near the end of November. The house was quiet, and for a while I didn't even notice he was there. Dad was sitting alone in the living room, the TV on, but muted. Mum was in the bath upstairs.

I tried to sneak back out unnoticed, but he caught me. "Sammy?," he called.

I turned back on my heel and went into the living room. "Yeah?"

"Come in and sit with me for a minute." I felt

cautious, but went in anyway and placed my water on the table. I sat down on the couch opposite his armchair. He had a photo album open on his lap. "How've you been?"

"Uh, fine."

"Really?"

"Y-yeah."

He looked like he didn't believe me. He sighed, giving up quickly and went back to looking at his photos.

"Are you ... all right?" I mumbled.

He chuckled, but didn't answer me. "D'you know what these photos are?" I tried to get a closer look, but I didn't recognise them. "These are from my army days, way back when. It's been so long now." He looked wistful. "Ten years of my life, that was, and it would've been a lot more if it wasn't for my damn leg." He stomped it on the ground. He turned the page of the album and sighed even heavier than before. "Here it is," he said, "This is the one I wanted." He passed the photograph album over towards me.

I took it hesitantly. The photograph showed two men dressed in army uniform with a large tank behind them. They were both very young, but Dad's trademark moustache was already blossoming. The man beside him was a few inches taller and much thinner. I had no idea who he was.

"That's me and my closest friend, Sean. We

128

joined at the same time and served in the Lebanon several times. He was my main man, always looking out for me and I looked out for him." He grew silent for a moment before continuing, "He died. Last week. And Jim died, Matt died, Eddie died - all within a month of each other. One by one, they're all going." I didn't know what to say. "But Sean ... he stayed in the army a lot longer than me. When he finally went home on leave, I don't think the same man returned. He was different ... his view of the world changed forever. I tried to help, I really did. I always let him know that I was here for a chat, for a drink, anytime, but that didn't matter. He went and did it anyway." His voice grew increasingly quieter as he talked and I didn't know what to do or say. I could see he was trying desperately to hold himself together.

After a few minutes, I silently handed him back the photo album. "I'm so sorry, Dad." It was all I could say.

"So am I," he said, sighing, "It's not always easy, I get that, everyone gets that. But just ... giving up like that ... I don't get it. Those poor kids."

I was starting to sense some anger in his voice. His hands clenched and unclenched as he took a couple of deep breaths to steady himself. "Sorry, Sammy." Another deep breath. I waited, unsure and unable to move.

"Thanks for staying with me, Sammy, but just

promise me something, okay? When I ask how you are, I want to actually know. You ever need someone to chat to, you come to me. You kids and your mum are all I have. I wouldn't be here without you." He leaned over towards me and placed his hand on mine. "You mean the world to me. Don't you ever forget that." His eyes were glistening with tears. I didn't know what to do.

"I know, Dad." It was awkward to get up and leave him after that, but as he closed the album and put the volume of the TV back up, I hoped he would be okay.

***

The school hallways would be almost completely empty within minutes of the bell's final toll. However, I was in no particular hurry and walked casually to my locker to collect my things. I saw Mark and Cian ahead of me and for a moment considered calling out to them, but they had rounded the corner before I had time to weigh that option.

I took my time as I dropped some books into my bag, returned others to the locker, and shut the creaky door, securing it.

I adjusted the straps of my now over-burdened backpack as I walked through the hallway towards the exit, peeking into each classroom as I passed. My eyes were focused on the tiles at my feet, made dirty from the day's traversing. A mystical, soft sound in the distance caught my attention and I stopped in my tracks, mere feet from the entrance hall and the exit.

I found myself turning on the spot, following the sound. It sounded so lonely and out of place in this almost deserted building. I followed it and soon realised it was coming from the music hall. I edged ever closer, my original destination now forgotten. It was the sound of a guitar being played, and I wondered why anyone would still be here; a music student? I thought to back away as they probably wanted to practice in private which was surely why they were here after hours. But still, the music pulled me closer, and within moments I was standing at the closed door to the music hall.

I stood and listened, allowing each plucked note to flow over me like a river. I took a careful step towards the door and looked through the small window etched into it. It was difficult to see into the room, as if it held great secrets that needed to be protected, but then I noticed the unmistakable ponytail hanging from the nape of his neck. Mark had never mentioned an interest in music to me before and as he turned and walked to the other side of the room, I confirmed that he wasn't the one playing. Then I noticed Cian was there too, sitting on a desk, but he didn't have the guitar either. That left but one possibility, although he remained out of view.

My hand shook as I moved it onto the door handle. I took a breath and forced myself to open it just as the guitar played its final chord.

"Ah-ha! It works!" Cian shouted triumphantly, raising his hands up into the air as I entered. Mark turned around at the front of the room and stepped aside so I could finally see him. Michael was sitting on the foot of the stage with a guitar in his hand.

"W-what works?" I asked.

"Nothing," Mark said, shooting a warning glance at Cian.

"Was that you playing?" I asked Michael, turning my attention towards him.

"Duh. Le guitar," he said, motioning to the instrument in his hands.

"It sounded really nice," I said.

"I appreciate the critic's kind words." He stood up and mockingly took a bow. We laughed in unison.

"I didn't know you played. Or that you even studied music. How come you didn't tell me?" I said.

"No reason. Guess it just didn't come up." I found that hard to swallow. We had been friends for months now. I was sure I had asked about his interests many times; when there had been many opportunities for him to mention his love of music. "I'm just practicing for the practical exam."

"And wanted our sagely advice," Cian said.

"Shut up, you imposed."

I watched in silence as he played a few more songs. I could've happily stayed there all day, listening to him. I watched his hands as they danced up and down the fretboard dexterously, the guitar emitting subtle tones as they did so. He hummed along softly with the music which made it sound all the more magical and ethereal.

I had almost forgotten that the others were there as I watched him play, allowing the music to wash over me completely. I wanted to put him in a music box so I could play it over and over. I felt completely at ease, every worry of my mind suddenly silenced.

There was nothing but the sound of music.

***

Afterwards, we headed to the park, Mark and Cian making some excuse not to join us. I was still stunned he had managed to keep this talent hidden from me in the few months that I had known him. He told me that he wasn't one to gloat or even call it a talent, it was just something he liked to do to pass the time.

I asked if that's what he wanted to do with his life, to play music, to awe crowds of people and inspire their senses.

He laughed at me. "I'm not that good - yet. I made so many mistakes in that last one just now."

To my untrained ear, I hadn't noticed any errors at all.

He claimed it was just a hobby, but I knew that

wasn't entirely true by the way his eyes lit up as he talked about it.

"Music is probably the most important thing in my life," he said. "Honestly, it saved my life so many times. I can't understand people that live without it."

It wasn't that I didn't care for music, but I didn't have the same connection to it that he had. Still, I understood what he meant; art and drawing were much the same for me.

From then on, he started walking me home each day after school. When I asked him where he lived, he told me it was a half hour walk through the town. I'd try to talk him out of walking me all the way to my front door as I was all too aware of the questions that it would likely invoke from my family if he did, but he'd keep insisting.

We'd share a quick hug goodbye before he'd turn to leave, and that would be it. Then one day, he turned to kiss me on the cheek. I instinctively stiffened at his touch, unsure how to react. I stood still and silent, almost afraid to respond.

I felt him tense underneath my embrace. "Sorry, was that weird?" he said, pulling away from me and breaking the hug. He looked uncertain, embarrassed. "That was weird. Don't know why I did that. Sorry."

He seemed to wipe his hands as if ridding himself of the evidence of a great crime he had just committed. "No, it's fine," I said, allowing a moment of awkward laughter to ensue between us.

We said goodbye and he turned to leave. I waited at the door until he was out of sight.

17.

I had thought this was it - the change I had been waiting
for - when the boredom and loneliness would finally end
and I would be able to embrace happiness.

I waited. I waited for it to happen, for the darkness
to finally seep away, but it remained all the same. The
anger bubbled up within me. I couldn't understand it.
What was I looking for? Why wouldn't it end? I should
be grateful that things were *finally* changing. I should be
happy that I had someone in my life again. But still, the
blade would meet my skin on an almost daily basis; still,
I'd put great effort into hiding my shame, and still, I'd
contemplate the release of death … and remain silent.

My parents often caught me in a sombre mood and
encouraged me to just look happier, smile, as if that's
all there was to it. I'd question whether they thought a
plaster could heal a broken bone to which they'd reply,
"Don't be so negative"; a favourite phrase of theirs
repeated like a stuttered lyric on a broken record player.

I thought that I didn't need to tell them as I already
knew their response. They'd call me dramatic, negative,

a disgrace, an attention seeker. There would be no point.

Michael had become like a break in the fog, a glimmer of light that promised hope. I focused on it, focused on him, as I dragged myself out of bed each morning, knowing that I needed to just be with him again, to talk to him, to feel the warmth of his light, however brief.

But that light would sometimes appear disjointed as it flickered, much dimmer than before.

I hadn't heard from him all weekend. We weren't exactly on a daily-talking basis but still, something felt wrong as Monday night drew to a close. I told myself not to text - I didn't want to seem clingy - but the knot in my stomach was telling me otherwise. I kept my words casual:

Hey, how're you?

He didn't respond for quite some time and while I waited, I tried to put my mind at rest, telling myself that I'd see him tomorrow and everything would be fine. It was stupid to worry just because I hadn't heard from him in a couple of days. Eventually, he wrote:

Hey, I'm okay. You?

It was a normal response but the knot in my stomach groaned further.

                                    I'm okay. Hadn't
                                    heard from you in
                                    a while.

Awww, miss me?

                                    Shut up.

You   did,   you
missed me. ;)

I could feel his humour creeping back in, but wondered
if it was forced. Before I had even responded, he quickly
wrote another:

Haha it's okay.
Missed you too.

                                    You did not.

I did! Would've
text but ...

                                    But?

Crazy weekend.

                                    Oh? What happened?

Secret crazy
weekend!

                        Boo, no fun

I felt I had reached the point where he'd stop talking if
I pushed too much, so instead tried to change the topic:

                        What are you up to
                        now?

Oh, just the same
old, same old

                        Haha and what
                        would that be?

Blaring music
until I can hear
nothing else.

                        At this hour?

Haha what, am I
disturbing the
neighbours with
my melodramatic
tunes?

                        Perhaps

Oh well!

                    You're a nut.

Nonsense. I'll
have to show you
some sometime,
then you'll see
what you've been
missing

                    I should get
                    going, up early
                    after all

Hmm? Why? Got
somewhere to be?
:P

                    Uh, school?

Duh, I know that,
you little nerd

                    Oh right, yeah, I'm
                    the nerd, Mr.
                    Mathematician

Hush now, that's a
secret

                    I gtg, night

```
Don't go


                            What?

Don't go yet

                            Why not? I'm afraid
                            I need my sleep to
                            tackle the day
                            ahead!

Yeah, I know.
Sorry. I'll see
you in the
morning, Sam.

                            You sure you're
                            okay?

I'm fine! Don't
worry about me.
Just like talking
to you is all.

                            I like talking to
                            you too

Now go get that
beauty sleep.
```

I went to sleep soon after and felt lighter for knowing he was okay, or for at least having his word that he was okay, whatever that was worth.

***

On Monday, he sat at one of the tables in the entrance hall, resting his head on his arms. I sat myself down alongside him, announcing myself as I did so. Slowly, he turned his head to peer up at me and there it was - the dimmest light of all.

Dark circles hung under his eyes and he looked a lot paler than usual. His hair was greasy, as if he hadn't washed for a few days which was unlike him. He sat up slowly, grunting in apparent pain.

"What's wrong?" I asked, suddenly worried.

"Nothing, nothing. Just woke up wrong." Suffice it to say, I didn't believe his explanation, but Mark and Cian bounded into view before I could challenge his honesty.

"Whoa, what happened to you?" Cian said, blunt as always.

Michael smiled meekly, telling them to shut up, he just had a rough night sleeping. They, too, seemed hesitant to believe him as they nodded sarcastic assurances.

I probably should've known as surely the signs were all there. Yet I could never put the pieces together to discover what was really hurting him.

***

Late on Friday night I lay on my bed, my sketchbook open before me, and focused on the image in my mind. I sketched out the foundation tonal ground to begin with. As I began to overlay darker areas, the image of a figure started to appear. The figure appeared distressed and clutched its head as if in agony.

I continued drawing the image, erasing away areas to form the mouth and eyes; endless voids in the skull of the figure. His scream echoed through the drawing as I worked on solidifying his arms and torso at the edge of the frame. I drew in other elements that made it look like his skull was dissipating, breaking off into the distance as he tried desperately to cling to the remainder of it.

The image seemed to bore into me as I drew the last lines and finished the shading. If I allowed myself a moment to feel pride about my skill, I thought the image was highly expressive and evocative. Despite acknowledging my talent, I felt it was just another drawing I would never show anyone for fear of their judgment and questioning eyes. They would surely see right into my mind through the lens that this image provided.

I pulled out the large box beneath my bed that housed all the other images that I knew would never see the light of day. I placed the new drawing on top of the stack of others and put it back under the bed, releasing it from my mind.

I lay back down on my bed, and stared up at the ceiling, not sure what to do next. I was just contemplating doing some exam revision when my phone buzzed:

```
Are you awake?
```

It was Michael. I checked the time in the upper right-hand corner of the screen: half past ten at night.

```
                    Yeah,   of   course.
                    Bit   early   yet.
                    What's up?
Um, I'm here.
```

I puzzled over what he meant.

```
                    What do you mean
                    you're here?
Outside, right
now.
```

The sound of heavy rain hitting my bedroom window drew my attention. He must be joking as no sensible person would step outside in this weather, let alone walk as far as my house. He was playing a trick, surely:

```
                    Haha, nice try.
```

```
                          Not falling for it.
I'm    serious,    I'm
here. I'd ring the
door       but      ...
Awkward
```

He was right. If he really was here, I wouldn't want my
parents to be the ones to greet him. I decided to give him
the benefit of the doubt. As my room was at the back of
the house, I had no choice but to open the front door to
see if he was telling the truth. I started to mentally
prepare my reaction if this turned out to be a trick, but I
hoped he wasn't the kind to play that kind of ruse.

First, I checked the hallway outside of my room
to make sure no one was around. I could hear Gerard in
his room playing video games, shouting and laughing
with his friends online. He was distracted and wouldn't
notice me moving downstairs. I could hear the sound
coming from the TV in the living room where both my
parents sat watching it. The door to the room was also
closed, making it easier to slip by unheard.

I took gentle steps towards the front door, being
careful not to be betrayed by the squeaky wooden floor.
I began to wonder why it even mattered to remain
unheard - I could just explain it after all - but something
told me to remain as silent as possible. I peeked through
the peephole in the front door and could discern a
moving shape in the darkness beyond. I gingerly placed

my hand on the doorknob and released the latch, pausing to make sure no one had heard. Satisfied that no one had, I quickly opened the door and stepped out onto the porch, carefully closing it behind me.

He stood before me, dripping wet from the rain. He was shaking from the cold as his wet clothes clung to his body.

"What are you doing here?" I asked. "I honestly thought you were joking."

The dim light in the porch made it difficult to see properly as I tried to make out his face, but he seemed to be almost hiding it from me.

"What, I can't just come see you sometimes?" he said to the floor. He peeked up at me briefly so I could see his eyes beneath the mass of hair that clung to his forehead. They were red and startling, betraying his attempt at humour.

I motioned to the rain that was falling even heavier now. "Well, it would certainly be a first ... and I highly doubt you'd choose to come out in this weather just to see me," I said. I felt like I was almost scolding him as I watched him shuffle back and forth.

He laughed. "It's not that mad an idea."

It still felt too weird to me. I considered inviting him inside where it was warmer - I was already beginning to shake with the cold so couldn't imagine how he felt with his jacket and pants soaked through. However, I didn't think I would be able to sneak him in unnoticed; his footfall was much heavier than mine and he was likely to leave a trail of dirt and rain behind him.

As if he had been reading my thoughts, he asked, "Can I come in?"

I was startled and stuttered out my hesitation, "Everyone's still up ..." His shoulders sagged and his head hung even lower, the rain on his hair falling to hit the floor. I felt awful.

"Maybe this was a mistake. Sorry. I'll go."

"No," I said as he began to leave, "You came here for a reason. I want to hear it." Michael stood still, facing away from me and I could see from the rise and fall of his shoulders that he was taking some very deep, purposeful breaths. Something was clearly very wrong. I waited as the familiar air of desperation flooded through me.

My mind flashed back to that fateful night which I hadn't thought about in quite a while; to that event which seemed to have happened in another lifetime. I heard the echo of his screaming and shouting once again and saw the noose hanging from the tree branch. That same feeling of misery and frustration was emanating from him now, only instead of venturing to the graveyard to find some ill-fated tree, he had come to me instead. To think I had almost turned him away…

I suddenly didn't care about my parents seeing us talking on the porch in the pouring rain, nor if they noticed their teenage daughter sneakily bringing a boy upstairs late at night. There were worse things I could do, after all.

"I'm just worried about my parents ... they'll ask questions if they see you here so late," I confessed. He nodded as if he understood. "You have to try to be as quiet as you can." He nodded silently and turned back to face me. Now my eyes had had time to adjust to the darkness, I could better see his face; the face which wore the same look of hopelessness as before.

I carefully opened the front door again and ushered him inside. My parents were still happily distracted in the living room. Luckily, they seemed to be watching an action movie at a louder-than-necessary volume that would hopefully cover the sound of our joint footfall.

We stealthily made our way upstairs, Michael purposefully walking on his toes in an effort to make less noise, although it still sounded like thunderclaps to me.

By some miracle, we made it to my room undiscovered.

"This is not how I wanted this to go." Michael said as he entered my room.

"What do you mean?" I said, trying to keep my voice low.

"Not how I planned to gain entrance to your chambre." He laughed, slightly hunching over. I told him to remove his wet shoes and coat, placing them on

148

the warm radiator to dry in time for his return trip home. In the meantime, I offered to get some fresh clothes of Gerald's which I could steal from the hot press, but Michael assured me he was fine and would soon dry out. I told him he'd catch a cold.

"There are worse things," he said, taking a seat on the edge of my bed.

I finally got a proper look at him as the room's light illuminated his features clearly. His slim arms were a myriad of colours, littered with bruises. His hands were etched with tiny cuts across the surface and there was a reddish hue staining his skin. He swept his wet hair away from his face and only then did I see it.

The familiar bruising had returned; the bruising he almost always seemed to have. I had questioned him about it before, but he always claimed he had banged his head against something in his clumsiness, a clumsiness that I had never seen demonstrated.

In the midst of those bruises was a contrasting smudge of dark red on his temple.

"Michael, you're bleeding!" I said, jumping towards him to inspect the wound.

As if suddenly remembering the cut, he attempted to cover it again with his hair and brushed me off. "It's nothing, don't worry about it. It's not bleeding."

"How did it happen?" I asked. I watched him as he tried to think of an excuse, a lie to cover what had actually happened. "The truth, this time." I knew now that he had been lying to me all along and had kept something hidden. "You turn up here with blood on your face, so tell me what happened."

My words seemed to have some effect. He looked at me sorrowfully. "You're right, but it's not that simple. I can't just—"

"What?" My mind was reeling for answers. I tried to find some possible reason for the laceration on his face. I had never seen him play sports, never even heard of any slight interest in the likes of rugby or football or anything else that could've caused such an injury. I had serious doubts about his supposed clumsiness as I didn't know how someone could be constantly walking into things.

I wondered if, maybe, he was being bullied all this time and I had somehow missed it. I didn't think that was possible however as we spent almost every day together in school. Besides, I'm sure Mark or Cian would've said something about it if they noticed anything like that. Michael wasn't the type to get into fights either, unless he somehow had a hidden persona I didn't know about.

I knew he didn't have any siblings, so ruled out those kinds of fights too. I was struggling to puzzle it out as I watched him, waiting for him to speak, not wanting to push too hard and frighten him into silence.

"I have no idea what's going on, Michael, but I want to know. I want to help you." I sat down beside him. I could see he was struggling to find the right words as he moved to start talking, but then stopped himself at the last second. "Whatever it is, you can tell me. I'm here." I attempted to embrace him, but when I did so, he whined, flinching away violently in response as if I had stabbed him.

"What is it? What's wrong?" I asked, jumping back from him. Slowly, he pulled up the hem of his shirt to reveal the greatest bruise to date. It almost completely covered his left side and was a deep, dark red. I let out a stifled gasp, my hand over my mouth. I had no idea what to say. Michael's eyes were tearing up and he was biting into his bottom lip in an effort to stop them from spilling over.

He quickly pushed the shirt back down to cover the bruise. "Michael ..." I didn't say anything else as he reluctantly let his tears fall.

151

18.

In that moment, it felt like the world was imploding in on me. The possibility of something I had never before considered, started to become clear in my mind. I didn't want to say it out loud or ask the question, for fear the idea would become real.

I wanted to hold him, but didn't want to hurt him again. I waited as he tried to regain his composure. I didn't know what to say or do, or even if there was anything that would have made this better.

After a good while, Michael began to steadily calm down as his shoulders ceased in their wracking. He started taking longer, deeper breaths and I could hear the pain rattling through him. I silently left the room to fetch some pain killers from the medicine cabinet in the bathroom. He took them gladly with a quiet, "Thank you."

After a while, he was finally able to talk. "Thank you," he said again. His face wore an expression of immense embarrassment and he seemed hesitant to meet my eyes.

"Michael." I had to find some way to get the truth out of him. I knew all the excuses he had given before were complete lies. I felt hurt that he didn't think he could trust me enough, but I knew that didn't matter right now. "I don't think you can come up with any excuse to explain this one."

He nodded solemnly, understanding my meaning and confirming his dishonesty. "I had to come here ... to you ..." he began, "because ... I didn't know where else to go ... I don't have anywhere else to go."

"Well, I'm glad you did," I said. I wondered why he chose to come here instead of to either Mark or Cian but again, that didn't matter. At least he was here and not standing beneath some ill-fated tree.

"I want ... to tell you ... so badly, I want to tell someone ... but I can't."

"There is nothing you can't tell me. You can tell me anything. I have literally seen you at your worst, you know," I said. He laughed slightly but it hurt him to do so.

"I guess you have." He took a moment to breathe. He seemed to be feeling slightly better. "This is much more than that, though."

Silence began to grow between us again and I knew I had to urge him to continue. "Who's doing this to you?" A look of surprise flickered across his face at the sound of my accusation. "Don't tell me you're just clumsy again." I expected him to laugh but instead his

153

face began to drop further, and he hung his head, looking down at the ground. "Whatever it is, whoever it is, you can tell me. I want to help you. I can't just sit back and do nothing anymore." My stomach was in knots.

"Sam." He looked at me earnestly. "I appreciate you so much, you have no idea. I love that you care, I really do, but you have to understand that this is complicated. It's not something with an easy solution, it's not something you can just *fix*. If I tell you ..."

He didn't need to finish the sentence as I already knew its ending. "Are you serious? How can you ask that of me? If I know someone's hurting you, I mean seriously hurting you, how can I keep it a secret?"

"Then no one's hurting me." He looked me sternly in the eye and I knew he was serious. I didn't want to make that promise, not again, but I knew he wouldn't say a word if I didn't promise secrecy. I felt powerless. I cared about him, I wanted to help him. I could feel his pain within myself and it hurt even more not being able to do anything about it.

I needed to at least get him to tell me the truth.

I felt the presence of the scabs on my forearms, reminding me of my own secret that I daren't confide in him or anyone else. The secret whose discovery was impossible to contemplate. It would be the end of me if anyone ever found out what I had been doing to myself and thus, discovered to what depth my sanity had fallen.

Maybe he felt the same.

I sighed deeply, still not wanting to be sworn to secrecy. I thought for a moment of giving a false promise, but I would never want to betray his trust and risk losing his friendship. "Okay," I said, "But I'm not happy about it."

"Thank you. It would just be far too awkward, too complicated. I'm ... working on it," he said, flinching as he adjusted himself to turn more towards me. He grabbed my hands which I had been keeping in my lap. Perhaps he found it easier to speak to them rather than my face. He kept his head bowed slightly, only looking up at me every once in a while. I kept quiet, allowing him to find the right moment to begin.

"It started about five years ago when ... my dad died."

An image flickered in my mind's eye. I saw him again, in the graveyard, sitting in front of a headstone. "I saw you that day, after Nan's funeral."

"Yeah. That was Dad's grave. I like to go there sometimes, visit him when I need somewhere to think. I dunno, it helps me. I know that might sound weird." I assured him that it wasn't, as I would sometimes do the same. And somehow, that had brought us together.

"Anyway, he died when I was twelve, nearly thirteen." I tried to offer belated condolences, but he shushed me. "It's alright, it doesn't really matter anymore... One day, he and I went out on our own.

155

I can't remember where Mum was, just at home, I think. He liked to take me out on long car rides sometimes and we'd go to the city, see a movie, get some McDonald's. It was the best." He grew wistful in his nostalgia as a smile played across his lips. "Whatever happened, I ... I can only remember flashes. I've tried so hard ever since to remember more, thinking I missed something somehow, thinking I should've been able to stop it from happening ... somehow.

"It happened on our way home. I was so happy that day, that much I remember. We were driving along a fairly empty road, singing with the radio, playing games during the long journey back. Then out of nowhere ... he came speeding right at us.

"I didn't know at the time, but I found reports later on, that said the other driver was well over the drink limit and supposedly on his phone as well, not paying the slightest bit of attention."

"Wait a minute," I said, "You were in the car crash that killed your dad?" I could hardly believe that he had failed to tell me about any of this before.

"Yeah. Lucky for the other guy, he died too," he said with not a hint of remorse in his voice, "It was a head-on collision, there was no hope for either of them. They said it was a miracle that I had survived. Thank God for seatbelts, they said." He tried to joke but the laughter quickly died on his lips.

"I remember being in the hospital for a while,

completely confused. Mum ... Mum was a wreck, she just couldn't understand it, she couldn't understand what had happened. Nothing I said seemed to make her feel better. She lost him and that was too much."

"She still had you, though, right?"

"Little solace, it seemed." He was finally getting to the heart of the matter now and I kept my impatience in check as he continued, "She completely changed after that. I mean, I had always been closer to Dad than I was to her, but not for any particular reason, that's just how it was.

"So, when Dad died, she couldn't handle it. It was as if the entire world had transformed. She got worse and worse, and day after day I'd come home to the sound of her crying or I'd find her passed out on the couch, bottles everywhere.

"That was truly the start of it. She was constantly drinking from then on. I asked her about it a few times at the beginning and all she'd say was that it made her feel better, it numbed the pain in her heart.

"But some days, the drink wasn't enough. She started lashing out, demanding explanations, demanding reasons for her unhappiness. I'd try to keep her calm, try to keep her from hurting herself. I once walked in on her crumpled on the floor, surrounded by the remains of a broken wine bottle.

"I'd try to talk sense into her, but it only seemed to make her even angrier and well ... then she turned her anger against me." He sighed exasperatedly, having finally gotten to the pivotal moment, the revelation, the answer I had been waiting for. Somehow, I felt that I already knew. The shock quickly subsided within me as I listened to his story.

"Long story short, she only got worse and with every attempt I'd make to try to help her, it'd all suddenly be my fault."

"Your fault?" I said, unable to resist interjecting, "How could it have possibly been your fault?"

He laughed meekly. "She never tires of reminding me ... that if it wasn't for me, he would never have been in that car in the first place. He wouldn't have been driving that day if it wasn't for me. He wouldn't have been on that road, wouldn't have met that driver ... if it wasn't for me."

As his eyes bore into mine, I could see that he wasn't just reciting her words - he believed them.

"That's ridiculous. It was an accident."

"Yeah ..." he trailed off and looked away from me.

"So, you're telling me ... she hits you because she thinks the accident is your fault?"

"I know it sounds ridiculous but ... she has said it many times now, and I guess, other times I just end up in the wrong place at the wrong time and run into her angry side. The next day, when she's sober, she'll remember what she did and become incredibly apologetic. I'd wake up sometimes to find her crying outside my bedroom door and then she'd hug me for ages, begging for forgiveness."

"You should've told me. Why didn't you tell me?" I asked him softly, carefully placing my hand on his shoulder.

"Why would I? There's nothing you could've done."

"Michael, you need to report this. You need to tell somebody."

"No, no," he said, suddenly pushing away from me, "I can't tell anybody, I can't report it."

"Why not? She's abusing you!"

"Why not?" He let out a half-hearted laugh as if it was the stupidest thing to consider. "Because if I did report her, she'd be taken away and locked up God knows where. I can't do that to her. She needs me. I need to look after her."

"Look after her?" I couldn't understand how you could want to protect someone who was needlessly hurting you. "It's not your job to look after her, she's supposed to be looking after *you*."

"You don't understand," he said. He stood up abruptly and started pacing agitatedly, his hands on his head.

"I'm trying to," I said, rising to join him. "Just tell me something - that night in the graveyard - did she push you to it?"

He stopped suddenly, coming to meet me. His

eyes were glistening with more reluctant tears. "I'm just tired. I am so tired, Sam."

I decided it would be best to hold back my anger for now as I drew him to me and wrapped my arms around him. I let him cry into my shoulder and offered to let him stay the night.

19.

I woke up a lot earlier than usual so I could sneak us out of the house unnoticed, but perhaps it was unnecessary. After all, what's the worst that would've happened if we were spotted? There would be questions of course, far too many questions; not just about having someone secretly in my room, but a boy no less and a clearly injured one, at that. The cut on his face had begun to scab over in a vibrant, dark red and I did my best to help him clean it. He tried to pull his hair over it like he always did, but not even that could hide it this time. I suggested he should see a doctor in case he needed stitches, but he just shushed me away and promised he'd be fine.

A new bruise was beginning to develop on his cheekbone, again. I wondered if it ever got much time to be healed. I worried that his ribs were bruised too given the sight of his chest, but still he refused to get it looked at. "It'll get better soon enough," he said, as if from great experience.

I didn't want to let him go home. He stayed with

me all through Saturday, but eventually he had to return to his mum. She had been calling his phone all day and I encouraged him to ignore it until he eventually turned it off as the gap between each call narrowed. "I bet she's all sobered up now, ready to apologise," he said.

He had nowhere else to go. He said it wasn't really her fault. She was sick after all and needed help. He couldn't just abandon her, even if for his own safety. He thought that would be selfish of him to do that. He had to look after her in order to protect her from herself.

I wanted to hate her, I really did, but I knew he was serious about everything he'd said. He never blamed her, not even once.

He promised me he'd do something this time, that he wouldn't just accept her apology and her half-hearted promises to stop and get better. He swore that he'd sit down with her properly in her sober state and that he'd get her help. If he truly meant to keep the abuse secret, he needed to encourage her to seek professional support, otherwise it would never stop.

I asked him about it over the next few days in school. I felt like there was no time to waste; he had to confront this problem now before it got even worse. At first, he'd just say that it wasn't that easy to broach the subject, that he couldn't just jump into a conversation like that; he needed to find the right time to talk to her in such a way that she'd listen and take him seriously. Then he told me he had talked to her. She'd agreed she

162

needed help and that she'd look into AA meetings, and maybe even see a doctor for therapy. His mother's positive reaction seemed too easy and I grew suspicious as he appeared to be as battered as before.

He quickly grew angry at me and my persistence. I tried to tell him that I simply cared about him and wanted him to be safe and happy, but he saw my urgency, my 'nagging' even, as a misunderstanding of the situation and he asked me to just leave it alone as I was only stressing him out even more.

I didn't know what to do. I had truly come to care for him deeply and it hurt me to see someone abusing him like that. It hurt me even more to feel as though there was nothing I could do about it.

I wanted to talk to Mark and Cian about it, but Michael had sworn me to secrecy, even from them. I wondered why he had never confided in his closest friends or how they had never guessed what had been going on all these years. I kept my mouth shut when he lied to them about the cut on his face, and how the bruise on his chest made it difficult to breathe. "Just need to work out more," he joked.

***

Sometimes, I'd have great moments of clarity and know exactly what I needed to do to fix things, to change things, to finally make my way out of the darkness and towards happiness. I knew I needed to at least spend less time in my room, even if that just meant spending the day downstairs instead. That alone would be a step forwards. I wanted to quell my compulsion to hurt myself as I knew perfectly well that it was only making things worse. However, these moments of clarity were sparse and quick to fade.

About a week after the night of Michael's confession, I felt the overwhelming desire to be anywhere but in my room. I packed away what little homework I had been inclined to do and went downstairs to make myself a sandwich.

I could hear the sound of gunfire and explosions coming from the living room and ... screaming? I peaked in and saw that Gerard had decided to move downstairs too for the evening, since Mum and Dad were out.

He turned around to look at me from the couch. "Hey Sam," he said, before turning back to his game just in time to stop a zombie in a Nazi uniform from killing his character. His attention was completely taken.

I joined him silently and finished eating my sandwich. My presence didn't seem to deter him in the slightest. Then eventually, he lost.

"Fffffuuuuu-" he started to shout, but somehow managed to stop himself.

"Oh, tough luck," I said.

"You want a game?"

"What? No, I'd be useless at it."

"No you wouldn't. It's easy."

"It didn't look very easy."

"All you gotta do is point and shoot, and just do what I say. Easy!"

I wasn't much of a gamer and he knew that, but he seemed persistent enough as he pressed the controller into my hands. He said it was an easy game but honestly, I think I just made it a whole lot harder for him as he had to spend so much time looking after my character and constantly reviving them instead of solely focusing on the enemies. Surprisingly, I found it really enjoyable. It felt just like old times when we were kids, and nothing else mattered but having fun and enjoying ourselves.

"All right, I think that's enough," he said after a few hours. I hadn't realised we'd spent so long playing as I hadn't felt the time pass by. "We haven't done that in a long while. I barely see you anymore."

"Well, whose fault is that? You're so busy all the time, between college and the rowing club and everything."

"That doesn't mean I don't have time for my baby sister," he said, ruffling my hair. I fixed it back into place, making my annoyance known. "Anyway, what's new with you?"

"Uh, nothing really. Same old, same old," I answered automatically.

"Ha! Lies."

"What?"

"Who's the guy?"

"What? What guy?" How could he ...?

"Ooooh someone's blushing! Last week, on the porch, the guy you were talking to. I just got up to close my curtains and saw ye."

"Oh, he's ... a guy from school." I got the impression that Gerard didn't know I had invited him in, and I wasn't about to tell him.

"That's it? Comes over late at night, in the pouring rain, but he's just a guy from school?"

"I mean, yeah ... we're friends. That's all. We're not going out or anything."

"Sure, sure, whatever you say," he said snidely, "Just hope you're being careful."

I laughed. "Seriously? Are you going to have the 'talk' with me?"

"No!" He guffawed. "I'm sure I don't need to, but I mean, emotionally, as well as physically." I punched him playfully on the arm and we laughed the moment off.

I found myself asking for advice before I even knew I wanted it. "What would you do if ... a friend ... was in a bad situation, and you wanted to help them, but they've sworn you to secrecy?"

He paused before answering. "Like a ... criminal situation?"

"What do you mean?"

"Like, do you wonder if you should call the guards?"

"I guess so, yeah, but the friend keeps promising that they're sorting it out, they're handling it, but you know they're not. What do you do? Before it gets ... worse."

He looked at me for a long moment and I feared that I had said too much. I knew I could trust Gerard, but I couldn't tell him exactly what was going on.

"This wouldn't happen to be ... about a certain someone?"

"No ... it's purely hypothetical."

"Sure, sure," he said, completely disbelieving me, "I've had those situations too and they can be tough, but I guess it depends on the exact circumstances. I mean, if they're in danger, literally, or they're harming others, then, fuck it. What does loyalty matter if they're dead, you know?" I had thought that myself before. Michael could be mad with me all he wants, he could hate me and refuse to see me, but if I knew he was alive and safe, that'd be all that mattered.

"Is everything okay?" Gerard asked, after a moment of silence, "Is this guy up to something?"

"No, no, everything's okay, really. Thanks, Ger. I'm gonna head to bed." I got up to leave.

"Hey, you can tell me anything, you know. I'm always right here, whatever it is."

"I know." I said goodnight and left.

167

***

Weeks passed but nothing seemed to change, not for either of us. I felt completely hopeless. I was lying on my bed for what felt like hours, staring endlessly up at the ceiling as if expecting it to cave in at any moment. That feeling began to overcome me again; that feeling of absolute nothingness.

My phone lay several feet away from me, tossed onto the floor, occasionally buzzing. I tried to move, to pick it up and answer it, but my brain wouldn't send the appropriate signal to my legs, so I just lay there for even longer.

The light beaming in from my window slowly began to fade as day turned into night. The buzzing continued just as unwarranted tears began to blur my vision. I cursed myself. What was wrong with me? I had no reason to be crying right now.

I wanted to turn it off. I wanted to throw it against the wall and stop the incessant buzzing coming from that stupid phone. Eventually it stopped, the silence continuing to ring in my ears in its absence.

As if on autopilot, I found myself sitting up and dragging my legs over the edge of the bed. I moved slowly, one foot dragging behind the other until I reached the phone on the floor. I couldn't even remember why I had tossed it there. The number of missed calls and text messages assured me that it had indeed been a few hours since I got home and lay down on my bed.

I thought back on the school day and on the week I had just dragged myself through. It had been nothing different or spectacular but it also felt like the worst week ever.

I picked at the scabs on my arms, causing them to slightly bleed again. I looked over the scars that had taken permanent residence on my skin. Some of them had become so faded they were barely visible. I pulled out the blade I kept hidden in my drawer and brought it over my skin again, re-drawing the faint lines. I barely reacted to the pain anymore, but its affect was everlasting. It broke through the numbness of my mind and reminded me that I was still a living, breathing, feeling human being - even if I didn't want to be.

The phone buzzed again with a new text message. I didn't want to read them. I just wanted to be left alone right now. I didn't want to explain or talk through the nothingness I was feeling. I wiped away the blood seeping on my arm with some tissue that I had nearby. Finally, I convinced myself to pick up the phone and scroll through the messages. They were mostly, "hello's" and "how are you's?" - nothing in particular - but then as time passed, they had become more persistent and questioning, "Hello?!?!" He had also attempted to call me three times.

The phone began to vibrate in my hand again and his name lit up. A voice told me I was being stupid. He wasn't calling out of concern for me. Something must have happened to him; I must have missed something which was stupid of me.

I pressed the pick-up icon and raised the phone to my ear. I forced a smile across my numb face and pushed out a, "Hello."

"Well, hi stranger," he said. I could hear the sound of wind intercepting the microphone's signals. For a moment, I started to panic, thinking he had decided to show up on my doorstep unannounced again.

"What's wrong?" I said, suddenly agitated.

"I was about to ask the same thing," he responded.

"What?"

"I've been trying to call you for a while now, started getting worried."

"Why? I just ... didn't feel like picking up the phone," I said simply. Hopefully that would be enough to bypass that question.

"Yeah, I get that too sometimes but, I dunno, I just had this feeling ..."

He let his statement hang for a little while, urging me to ask, "W-What feeling?"

"Do you ever get like, this knot in your stomach? Like you know something's wrong but you've no idea what? That feeling. It might sound crazy but when you didn't pick up the first couple of times, I started to get

170

that knot in my stomach. I got worried. Sorry if I bugged you, though."

He was right, it did sound crazy but then again, was he wrong? I had felt it too, at times, on those days when he would offer silly excuses or claim he was fine. That knot in my stomach told me otherwise.

"I'm fine, really," I lied. Or was it a lie? I didn't feel particularly bad but I knew I wasn't good either. I felt nothing.

"Hmmmmm," he said, evidently not believing me, "You're an awful liar, you know. I know that sigh. The sigh I've sighed so many times. Come out."

"What? Come out?" My mind felt shocked as if I had just woken up from a long sleep.

"Yeah, I'm just out walking around. Come out with me. I'm almost at your house."

"You gotta stop doing that."

He laughed. "You can thank me later."

Luckily, it wasn't too late, so I could leave without raising suspicion, but Mum questioned me anyway and made that face again when I said it was Michael. It was like she was bursting with pride to discover I had finally made another friend whose friendship was enough to make me leave the house.

As I walked down the driveway, I knew he was there but he kept himself hidden behind the wall at the end. He almost startled me as I rounded the corner.

I was surprised to see him looking happier than

171

usual, his face substantially healed.

He greeted me with his usual charming smile, and I felt my spirits lifting a little. He brought me in for a hug and I wondered if he could possibly see right into my mind. If so, maybe I would never need to say a word to him. The pressure of his arms around me seemed to spark something within me and I felt my eyes brimming with tears. I was being ridiculous. Why on earth was I crying? I hugged him back tightly, feeling his warmth seeping through to give me instant comfort.

He let go after a moment and only then did I notice it standing behind him; a slick black motorcycle perched up on the kerb. I had never noticed it before and wondered who it belonged to. He saw me looking and turned to follow the direction of my gaze.

"Oh, you like it?" he said.

I wasn't so sure if I liked it, per se, but I felt drawn to it nonetheless. It felt like it was urging me to come closer, to hop on and speed away into oblivion.

"Well, yeah, it's nice," I found myself saying, "But why is it here?" It was perched right outside our house, but Gerard certainly hadn't bought a motorbike as he was still saving up for a car. He always said it was much safer than a bike.

"Oh, I haven't a clue," he said, but his tone implied that he very much did have a clue. I watched him curiously as he approached the motorbike and picked up the helmet that had been strapped on to its

172

handles.

Without saying another word, he pulled open the luggage box that was attached to the back of the bike and pulled out another, albeit smaller, helmet.

He stretched out his hand and offered it to me. "Ready to feel alive?"

173

20.

I stared at the black metal of the bike, unsure what to do. He had never mentioned this to me before or even that he had an interest in bikes. Yet here he was, acting like it was no big deal and then asking me to take off with him, just like that.

"I'm sorry, what?" I said.

"It'll be great, trust me."

"Where did you even get this?" I couldn't imagine how he'd got the money to buy it. What else had he been hiding from me?

"I'll tell you later," he said, landing the helmet in my hands, "Just come with me."

I could hardly say no, no matter how much I might have wanted to. I glanced back at the house and wondered what my mother would say if she knew. I knew nothing about bikes except what I had seen on TV shows and in movies, when, more often than not, motorcycles in high-speed car chases ended up crushed beneath an enormous truck, the rider thrown aside. I had also seen them slam headfirst into a tree or another unexpected vehicle and I had seen the adverts warning drivers to be more wary of those travelling on bikes. I guess I didn't need my mother to warn me; I was doing it myself.

I must have been silent for a while as he asked me enquiringly, "Are you coming?" He placed his hand gingerly on my arm in concern. "Don't worry, it's perfectly safe. I'm well trained, passed all my tests. I'll protect you." He took the helmet back from me and placed it on my head. I was surprised to feel it easily slip over my skull, perfectly cradling it as if it had been made just for me. He clicked the strap into place. "Do you trust me?"

I nodded affirmatively, unable to speak. He chuckled and turned to put his own helmet on before elegantly swinging himself onto the bike. He offered me his hand to help me get on behind him. The seat was softer than I expected. I pulled the visor of the helmet down over my face and placed my hands gingerly on his waist. He quickly pulled my arms forwards and wrapped them around him, telling me to hold on. The fear brewed within me again and I wanted to tell him to stop, that I couldn't do it, but instead I held on silently.

All too soon, he gripped the handles of the bike and it roared into life, vibrating beneath us. I almost squealed as my fear rose drastically and I gripped him even tighter. I felt his body vibrate too as he laughed at me. *Ready to be alive?* Those were his words, his

175

invitation. I found it funny that hopping onto such a deadly machine could make someone feel more alive.

He kicked the bikes small stand back underneath and I gripped him even tighter as it began to sway. He pulled away from the kerb slowly and then steadily began to speed up. He swerved effortlessly down the narrow road and onto a much wider one. I was sure we would collide into one of the numerous parked cars on the way and tried to make myself smaller, certain that one of my protruding knees would bring about the end of us both.

Eventually the streets began to clear, and the buildings slid by, out of view. We passed the school and dozens of homes, the local shops and the church. We passed the graveyard that had brought us together and soon there was nothing either side of us but rolling fields of green.

I released my grip on Michael a little as my fear subsided. The bike was a lot steadier and more stable than I had anticipated. I knew Michael had complete control of it and I trusted him as he expertly balanced it this way and that along the stretch of road. I felt the wind push against us, trying to keep us back but failing to do so, as we were too strong, too fierce, too unstoppable and formidable. My fear was quickly replaced by adrenalin. I could feel my heart beating in my chest - *thump, thump, thump* – the blood coursing through my veins.

I felt I could fly away right here, right now. The world surrounding us was passing in a blur, creating a myriad of colour in my vision. I wanted to go faster and faster - faster than the speed of light - until we ended up in another dimension, another world and another time.

I felt the truest smile stretch out across my face as we rode on. I felt alive.

***

We followed a long road out of the town, until there was nothing but endless green on either side of us. Michael started to slow down and steadily pulled the bike over to the left side of the road. We disembarked, removed our helmets and started to walk up the hill, Michael leading the way. "I like to come here sometimes," he said, "One of my other haunts ... when I need to get away from everything."

"I guess that's exactly what this place is," I said, "Away from everything." The air was full of the sounds of nature; crashing waves from the beach nearby and seagulls flying overhead.

"Come up here with me," he said, suddenly picking up his pace and jumping ahead of me. I followed steadily behind, not seeing the need to suddenly rush. The sound of the waves grew stronger and I realised that we were nearing the edge of a cliff. A trickle of fear shivered up my spine; we were so close - too close - to the edge as it overlooked the endless abyss of water below, but he was fearless.

He walked with purpose ahead of me, stopping mere feet from the edge, looking out over the water. He urged me to come closer and extended his hand. I dragged my reluctant feet forwards, one step at a time.

"Don't worry, it's safe," he assured me, but unfortunately his words were little comfort as the ocean came into view, the ground running out beneath my feet as it did so. My heart continued to hammer against my chest, telling me that once again, I was tempting fate. Somehow, the person who often contemplates death, even yearns for it at times, was also afraid of it.

He took my hand as we stood mere inches from certain death. The wind brushed against our faces and the view of the endless sea was truly magnificent. I tried to find some solace in his grip and told myself that I was safe, but as I glanced down to see the water practically at my feet, I felt uneasy, almost quaking. I could see a small strip of beach below, almost hidden by the incoming tide, but still there. I looked around and noticed a small dip to my right in the hill we were on. I later found a path there, leading down to the water, its waves unrelenting.

"W-Why here?" I asked him. I was trying my best to resist the temptation to walk steadily backwards to safety.

"I dunno," he started, taking some time to

consider his answer. "I ended up here one day by complete chance. Then, time and time again, I'd end up staying here for hours just looking out, taking it all in. I find it quite relaxing just ... listening to the waves below. It's beautiful here, isn't it?"

It was beyond beautiful. The sun was just beginning to set, turning the blue sky into a mystical orange. The waves below were crashing steadily yet purposefully.

Suddenly, he let go of my hand and sat down, his feet dangling over the precipice. My heart leapt in my chest. "It's a bit dangerous here, though," I said, "We're too close to the edge."

"That's the best thing about it," he replied, "Don't you ever feel like that? Like you're constantly on the edge, constantly almost defeated, but there's still just a little bit of you left, still a little bit of hope and that's what keeps you safe, that's what keeps you alive."

I carefully sat down beside him, ignoring the worries in my mind. I was safe here. We sat in silence for a while, watching the sun set. It was truly one of the most beautiful sights I had ever seen. I could have stayed there forever.

I glanced over at Michael and wished I could capture the image of the orange sky framing him angelically. Desperately wishing I could sketch him at that moment, I tried to commit the image to memory.

"What is it?" he said, catching me staring at him.

"Nothing." I shrugged. I felt like I was seeing him for the first time. He had become so much more than the boy I found in the graveyard; the boy I saved. Something was stirring within me.

I inched myself towards him without thinking and lay my head on his shoulder. Before I could pull back, he quickly lay his head on top of mine and wrapped his arm around me.

We stayed there for a while in silence as the sun continued its descent into the horizon. Slowly, Michael began to move beside me. He kissed me gently on the forehead and I froze in place, unsure how to respond, or even if I should. I pulled back slightly and saw the same feeling of uncertainty in his eyes, as if his own action had surprised him, too.

Then, slowly and ever so steadily, the gap between us continued to close. Our foreheads met and the air between us seemed frozen. With hesitation, trepidation and anticipation, we inched ever closer to one another until finally our lips met.

The kiss was so soft and gentle at first and then he pulled me closer to kiss me more fiercely. I could feel myself almost melting into him, every worry in my mind silenced. My heart began to beat ever faster.

All too soon, the kiss was broken and we started laughing.

21.

The feeling of that kiss lingered on my lips for hours afterwards, and I never wanted to leave that moment behind. It became a memory that I would hang onto forever, bringing a smile to my face at each recollection.

We tried to keep it a secret at school, especially around Mark and Cian, as we didn't want it to create an awkward tension in our little friendship group. The secrecy was almost intoxicating. We started to sit together in every class we shared, and after a few days his hands searched for mine beneath the table where we'd remain entwined for the entirety of the lesson.

He started asking to see me increasingly more often after school. My days steadily changed from ceaseless monotony, into monotony with a twist at the end. Most of my classes dragged on as they always had, except for the few Michael and I shared. I told myself to be wary for he could leave just as quickly as he came, and if he did, I would be back to square one.

I tried my best to silence that voice of negativity and just live in the moment.

Of course, despite our attempts to remain nonchalant in front of Mark and Cian, the signs were there, and they surely knew. I found them after school some weeks later and asked them where Michael was. They sniggered knowingly, poking each other in their ribs.

"Oooh, where's lover boy, you mean?" Cian mocked.

I rolled my eyes and remained silent; this wasn't the first time I had been offered this response.

"Sorry, he left before us so, probably outside."

I separated from them for a while to collect my things from my locker. I assumed he was waiting outside for me again, as he had done for weeks now. I grabbed my things and stuffed them haphazardly into my bag before finally making my way out of the school. I couldn't see him at first and spent a few minutes standing on my own outside school, checking my phone repeatedly for messages from him, but there was nothing.

Then something flickered in my peripheral vision and I finally saw him in the distance to the right of me, except, he wasn't alone. I couldn't quite see who he was with at first, but he was clearly arguing with them. The other person was substantially shorter and as her wild hair flew out behind her, I knew who it was.

This was the first time I had seen her, and I felt a prickle of anxiety shiver up my spine.

I could just about discern the pair of car keys dangling from her hand which I assumed belonged to the red car, parked between her and her son like a barrier. They seemed to be having a rather heated argument and I started to think I should go over to defend him, whatever the problem was, but it was best I stayed away. I knew he wouldn't want me getting caught in the middle of it. I grew more anxious as I watched, my eyes tracking her hands with every move she made. In her agitation, she attempted to get closer to Michael but he'd quickly sidestep her, putting the car between them again.

Suddenly, his mother's hand shot out in my direction, pointing directly at me. I could feel the weight of her glare, even from this distance. I could feel her anger and resentment as if she was shooting it right at me through her extended index finger. Michael turned to follow it and looked right at me, his expression unreadable.

He quickly moved over to her and pulled her arm down. I thought, for sure, that would be it, the moment that she'd lose it and expose her true self, right now in front of me. Instead, she re-directed her finger of anger into his face and shouted something at him before jumping into her car and speeding off.

She drove in the direction I was standing and made the greatest effort to avoid making eye contact with me. She had the greatest expression of frustration and stress upon her face that I had ever seen. She was still a fairly young woman, younger than my parents at least, but the years of alcohol abuse had been wholly unkind to her.

He ran up to me as I watched the car disappear over the horizon. "I'm so sorry about that," he said, "You didn't need to see that. Sorry for keeping you waiting."

"What was that about?" I asked, although I doubted he would tell me.

"Oh, nothing, nothing," he said, disregarding my concerns.

"That didn't look like nothing." I tried to sound stern.

"Don't worry about it," he said simply.

"Uh-hmm," I replied.

"Listen, I, um," he said, shuffling his feet nervously, "I can't hang around today. I have to go home."

"What d'you mean?" It wasn't like him to cancel plans quite literally at the last minute.

"There's just stuff I have to take care of."

We had reached that point in our relationship, in our friendship, that I no longer needed to wonder if he was telling the truth or not. I just knew. I felt the hairs on the back of my neck stand up as my eyebrows began to furrow. I knew the truth even though he wouldn't say it outright. I knew it would only upset him if I said anything, if I dared to confront it, but I was upset too.

"Don't lie to me," I said.

He looked back at me and took a long, deep breath. "There's just some stuff I have to do," he said again, silently telling me that he didn't want to talk about it.

"Like what?" I asked, although I already knew what he'd say.

"It doesn't matter, just stuff, okay? I'll see you tomorrow." He began to walk away without another word.

"That's it?" I said, "Really?" He stopped dead in his tracks and turned to me with a sorrowful expression. "Do you really not trust me yet? Do we still have to keep secrets?" The words were out of my mouth before I could stop them.

"I'm not the only one keeping secrets," he said, nonchalantly. He smiled slightly, kissed me gently on the lips and left me there, speechless in the dust.

His words swum around my head continuously for days. What did he even mean by it? Could he somehow ... know? Or was it just one of those things that people say in the heat of the moment without really meaning anything by it? As time went on, I grew more and more anxious. My phone would light up at night with messages from him asking how I was, and my stomach would start doing somersaults in reaction. I felt as if I had suddenly been exposed, but there was no way of telling exactly by how much.

He had the power to make me feel completely transparent. I could hide from everyone else, remain invisible without effort, yet with him, I was laid bare. He could see right through the wall I had built around myself. The thought of him knowing truly terrified me, so much so that I couldn't think about it or bare to contemplate it. *Stop being so dramatic. You're just an attention seeker.* The words of Rachel's rejection remained imprinted on my mind. I couldn't stomach the possibility of those words being repeated by him.

It would surely only be a matter of time before he demanded to know everything - if he hadn't already figured it out – but I tried to ignore it as best I could, convincing myself they were just empty words that meant nothing. I wouldn't bring it up, I couldn't.

It seemed that, just as things were beginning to get better, they quickly got a whole lot worse.

Time and time again, we made plans to meet up but each date was cut short or cancelled. When we did meet, most times his phone would ring incessantly, his mother demanding he return home at once.

I'd try to keep him with me for as long as possible. It broke my heart to watch him walk away, to imagine what I was letting him go home to.

I tried to find sympathy for his mum; a woman consumed by her grief. I tried to see things from Michael's perspective; it wasn't her fault, never her fault, she was unwell and needed help.

Then I'd see the bruises renewed upon his face and my sympathy would vanish.

She was his mother. She was supposed to look after him.

22.

I was tired, so very tired of hiding every day, exhausted from being constantly too self-conscious, to the point of paranoia. A glance from someone across the room would cause the hairs on the back of my neck to stand up and I'd have to fight the urge to run and hide. I felt like I was constantly on show, and any minute now they would all catch a glimpse of who I truly was, and would realise how far I had fallen.

I'm not the only one keeping secrets. Those words reminded me every hour of every day that I was betraying the only person that I felt I could truly trust, but the thought of telling him everything, confessing my assured insanity, was too horrible. He would recoil in horror, and condemn me for finding my own life so miserable when what he had to suffer was so much worse. He would abandon me; he had enough to deal with without the extra burden of my problems.

In hindsight, it seems, I had worried for nothing.

We returned to the cliff about a week after he had said those words. It was starting to become a regular spot for us; somewhere to go where we wouldn't be disturbed or overheard by anyone. The grass was a beautiful green beneath our feet, despite the waning sunlight. The sky was threatening rain with an ominous dark cloud overhead.

"Sam, do you trust me?" he asked out of the blue. The question caught me off guard. Of course I trusted him. I trusted him more than anyone else even though he sometimes chose to keep things from me.

"Of course," I said.

"But ...?" he replied, easily reading my tone.

"But I wish you'd be more honest with me." I said it almost under my breath, unsure if I should say it at all.

I wanted him to open up to me, truly and fully, even though I knew that with each insistence, I was proving myself to be a massive hypocrite. I tried to tell myself that I couldn't demand such trust and honesty from him if I refused to talk about something that took up much of my mind for the majority of every day. I felt like I was betraying him.

"I am honest with you," he said calmly. I looked over at him with an expression that I hoped showed my lack of belief. He knew what I meant. "Maybe not about everything ..."

"I'm glad you agree," I said. I allowed a moment of silence to sit between us and again felt that tension grow. I decided to return the question. "Do you trust me?"

"Of course I do." He seemed incredibly genuine. "Even though I know you're not being honest with me, either." Silence fell between us again and I waited, trying to figure out where this conversation was going. "I think our problem is ... it's not that we're lying to each other but ... leaving things out. Omission."

I sensed he had more to say and so I kept quiet. "When it comes to me and my situation, there's not much you don't know. I just ... don't want to get you mixed up in it. It sounds clichéd, I know, but it's for your sake. There's not much you can do about it, I'm dealing with it. The things that've happened recently, you just don't need to know, it'd only hurt you, upset you.

"On the other hand ... I know something's going on ... with you." I started to pluck nervously at the grass by my feet as I listened to him. "I can't make you talk about it, I know that. I've been trying to give you the space you need until you trust me enough to talk about it."

My heart plummeted into my stomach. Could he really know?

"I think about that night a lot. The night I'm sure neither of us will ever forget." He was looking straight ahead with a look of pure focus on his face as if that memory was re-playing in front of him right now. "And I started to wonder ... how did you do it? How did you get through to me so easily? How did you know the exact words that I needed to hear right then and there? I thought to myself, well, it's obvious … you knew what to say because you had already said it, so many times, to yourself."

"That's stupid," I muttered.

"Is it? I don't think so. I mean, we had barely even met before and yet I felt like you understood me more than anyone else, ever. Like you were right there with me.

"Do you get where I'm going with this?" I thought I knew all too well what he meant. Perhaps I did have that conversation many times with myself, before then and since. Perhaps I had often talked myself out of that decision. I was hardly going to admit it, though.

"What are you doing, Michael?" I asked, growing more and more anxious by the second. "What is this?"

"I'm sorry, I just can't help thinking ... I could wait and wait for you to come to me, to be truly honest with me ... but what if you never do? What if it becomes too late? I just want you to know that I'm here for you and you can tell me anything. I want to help. I want to help you just as you've helped me."

He knew. I was certain then as he looked deep into my eyes and held my hands in his, that he knew. My stomach was in knots and my mind had gone completely blank. I didn't know what to do.

He waited for a moment before wrapping his arm around me. I felt like the words were there, floating right in front of me. All I had to do was say them.

I wanted to tell him. I wanted to be free of the burden of hiding, but I also didn't want to tell him, even if he already knew. I didn't want to admit it, to make it real.

For so long, I had feared that he would abandon me, that the exposure of my secret would prove my insanity and he would surely want nothing more to do with me.

The hand gripping my shoulder said otherwise. It told me I was supported, that I was loved and that I was not alone.

My heart began to beat faster and faster as the words turned over in my mind. I felt a ball growing in my throat, attempting to suffocate me at any moment as I tried to convince myself to just do it, to just let it out - to hell with the consequences. I was tired of lying.

He planted a kiss on my forehead again, just as he had done so many times before to remind me that he was still there and that he wouldn't rush me. He would always just be there.

"Don't be mad at me." The words came out as little more than a whisper.

"Why would I be mad at you?" He pulled back slightly to look at me. Suddenly, unexpected tears began to flood my face. I pulled further away and tried to hide them. "Hey." He pulled me back to face him and wiped the fallen tears away. "I could never be mad at you."

"I-I didn't mean to lie ... to you." The tears were making it hard to speak at all. I tried to wipe them away and focus on something to steady myself ... something other than digging into my skin. "I've just been ... too scared."

"You don't need to be, I promise you. You can tell me."

"You'll think I'm crazy." My voice was still barely audible.

"Aren't we all?"

"This is different. I know I shouldn't be doing it, I know that, but I can't help it. It's like a ... habit or maybe even ... an addiction and it's just been ... eating me up from the inside. I know it sounds so stupid ... and ridiculous and I've tried so many times to stop it ... but I can barely go a week without falling back into it."

"I get it," he said, reaching for my hands again.

I felt the marks on my arm burning as if they had a life of their own and knew I was talking about them. They wanted to be free, they wanted to be seen. I imagined the way he'd react if he saw them, the instant look of shock and disgust.

"I get it, Sam," he said again. I looked into his eyes, unsure how to say anything else, and yet I felt like I didn't need to.

"What do you mean?" I whispered.

"I wanted to let you come to me, but I won't make you say it, I can tell it's too hard," I tried to hold myself together as he spoke, but felt I would break at any moment, "I saw ... before. In school, a while ago now, a few weeks at least, you were busy scribbling away as always and I guess your sleeve rolled up just a little too far and I saw."

The tears were welling up in my eyes again, but I managed to fight them back. He'd seen them. I didn't know whether to feel relieved or terrified. I wanted to run and hide, pretend this wasn't happening.

I forced myself to stay where I was. "If you've known for so long, why didn't you say anything sooner?" I asked.

"I guess I didn't know what to say, or what to do," he admitted, "I won't lie, I don't really understand it and I thought it best not to say anything until maybe I did understand it, or until you found you trusted me enough to tell me about it."

I couldn't believe he was giving me such a calm response. "I can't believe that," I admitted.

"What do you mean?"

"You realise I've been cutting myself and only worried about misunderstanding it?"

Something passed over his face. I knew that wasn't his initial true reaction. Those were just words he had thought up in the meantime. It felt like a glossed-over lie.

"You think I'm lying?" he said.

"It's a little hard to believe," I found myself

talking rather quickly, "I kept it from you all this time because I was terrified of how you'd react. I thought for sure that you'd cast me out, call me a freak and want nothing more to do with me. I thought you'd claim that you already had too much to deal with and didn't need more drama in your life. I thought-" He cut off my words with a kiss firmly placed on my lips.

"You think far too much." He laughed. I didn't think it was such an amusing situation and remained stoic. "You really thought that? You thought I'd just dump you there and then?" The tears were rising up again. "You have been there for me literally through everything. It breaks my heart to think you've been going through so much on your own and not letting me help you like you've helped me.

"I told you I'm here for you, always. I'll admit I was startled at first when I realised what you were doing but truly, I thought I'd just stay out of it and let you come to me. I just didn't know how to bring it up."

I couldn't hold back the tears anymore as he pulled me into him and held me tightly. "I'm just so tired," I said into his chest, "I'm tired of all of it."

"It'll be okay. We'll get through this, together, I promise you."

***

For so long, I had anticipated his reaction. I thought that would be the end of it, the end of the light that had suddenly entered my life, but instead, he met me with overwhelming support and comfort. I was finally beginning to let myself believe that this was it, this was real and things would finally begin to change.

About a week or so after that day on the cliff, we were having lunch in the school's entrance hall as usual with Mark and Cian in tow. I lay my head on Michael's shoulder, unable to keep my eyes open for much longer. It was nearing the end of January now and our pre-Leaving Certificate exams were in full swing. I was spending nearly every night cramming information into my head for the exam the next day. Apparently, it wasn't good enough to put us through torturous exams once this year, we had to do a practice round too - a practice round that was deliberately harder than the real thing, just to assure us that we can never try hard enough.

I always wanted to do well. I hated getting bad grades, but it seemed that no matter how much I studied, I could never achieve anything higher than a B. Every day the teachers reminded us just how vital the exams were, as if our entire lives depended on the results. Whatever it was you wanted to do, you'd better be able to recount all this useless information that you'll never need again.

Michael liked to scold me about it, for staying up so late for an exam that didn't even matter. I never caught him with his nose in a book and yet he never seemed to fail either.

Later that day, I watched Michael as he practiced his music in the hall after school. His practical exam was tomorrow, as was my art exam, but I didn't want to think about that.

As we were getting ready to leave, he pulled me back and said, "I want to give you something." He put a small, brown bag into my hands.

"What is it?" I asked.

"Just something I thought you might like. Open it."

I opened the bag and a plastic square fell out onto my hand. A plain piece of paper was covering the front of it. I realised it was a CD case and I pulled it open to see the glittering CD within. The back of the piece of paper had a series of phrases written upon it; song titles and their respective artists.

"A mixtape?" I laughed.

"Mix *CD*. Get it right," he joked. Truth be told, I didn't own many CDs.

"Why though?" I asked, skimming through the track list again. I barely recognised any of the artists. I really needed to expand my musical horizons.

"Well, I was thinking ... music has always helped me on the bad days. Just throw something on, turn it up loud and suddenly that's all that matters. I might even scream a little with them."

I took his word for it until I truly realised what he meant. This mix of music was unlike anything I had ever

197

heard. All I really knew were the songs that played on the radio every day, each song sounding just like the other. The robotic sound of the vocalists would jar my ears and I was sure I would never enjoy listening to music if critics deemed these songs to be 'good'.

The songs on the CD were different however and when I researched them online later on, I discovered they were modern songs mixed in with 90s hits.

I was lying on my bed, late in the evening, listening to the music playing from my barely used CD radio player in the corner. I listened carefully, eager to hear every single word of every single song, trying to decipher their meaning although most were obvious.

He was right - even just focusing completely on those words left me little room to think about anything else. It was just me and the music.

Then the vocalist said something that caused me to sit bolt upright. I rushed over and replayed it to make sure I'd heard the lyrics correctly. I played the song again and again. My eyes began to fill with tears. Somehow, he had single-handedly put everything I had ever felt into words. In less than five minutes, I suddenly felt completely understood for the first time.

It was called *Iris*; a song by a band I had never heard of, The Goo Goo Dolls. The lyrics resonated with me, the sound of the singer's voice - his raw emotion - echoing my own pain. I was dumbfounded.

The people behind these words in my ears had felt

what I felt, had been where I was and had come out the other side. They used their darkness, their hopelessness to create art, to inspire and help people; to tell people, to *show* them, that they truly weren't alone in this. It was the first time I thought I could believe it.

23.

Michael told me to play it every time I needed proof that I wasn't alone in all of this, that he was there with me. I thought I would wear it out from playing it so much.

I really thought that things were beginning to change. I thought I finally had everything I needed to find this elusive thing called 'happiness', and some days, I did feel genuinely happy. I'd curse myself for having ever thought about ending my life, yet still the darkness would roll in over me, time and time again, like a passing wave. I could only hope that the boat on which I perched was strong enough to brace against the impact.

That week, the wave became constant, uniform. It continued to flow tumultuously against me and over me. I waited for it to cease but felt certain that it never would.

I promised I would stop. I swore to Michael that whenever I had the overbearing urge to harm myself again, I would listen to his CD, sit on my hands and sing my heart out until it passed. I promised I would call him, even in the dead of night, and we would talk about nothing until it passed.

I couldn't handle it though. I hadn't hurt myself in weeks, but the urges were getting too strong for me to hold back. I thought about calling him, like I had promised, but I never did.

> Can I see you today?

I really wish I
could but I can't
today

> Why not? You busy?

Sort of

> What are you up to?

Just stuff

Just stuff. Like I couldn't guess what that meant. I never expected him to just drop everything for me, but I didn't know why he had to lie when I already knew the truth. I guess he already had enough going on and didn't have room for me on top of it.

I had asked him several times how things were going, with his mum, with his home life. I'd always get the same response,

"It's fine, I'm dealing with it, don't worry about it," he'd say. It had been a couple of months now since he had shown up at my door, battered and bruised from her hand. His skin was still littered with bruises, some of them yellow and new.

"I don't think you are." I couldn't help but feel a bit frustrated.

"Don't be like that." He was getting frustrated too, with *me*.

"You know it's only because I care," I said.

"Well, please, if you really care, just leave me deal with it." He would never talk about it. Even when she dragged him away after school, or away from me on the days we'd arranged to meet, he'd act as if it was normal parental strictness. I was getting tired of the situation.

During the week, I had stayed downstairs and worked on my homework at the kitchen table, to get a break from my room. Dad entered the kitchen, limping, wearing a black suit – the one he only wore for specific occasions.

I could see how tired he was. "Hey," I said.

"Hey, Sammy." He came over and kissed the top of my head.

"Where're you off to?" I asked, although the answer was obvious.

He sighed heavily. "Removal. One of the guys from the army."

"I'm sorry." I didn't know what else to say. I remembered how upset he was that night in the living room as he looked over his old photographs.

"It's all right." He smiled meekly. I got the impression he didn't really want to talk about it, so I let it be.

We sat down to dinner the next day as usual, but Dad wasn't there.

"Where's Dad?" Gerard asked, as Mum seated herself down at the table after serving me and Gerard. The smile plastered on her face looked ready to crumble.

"Oh, he's upstairs, resting." For once, she wasn't very talkative.

"Is he all right?" Gerard said.

"Of course! Why wouldn't he be?" The smile began to stretch her face abnormally.

Gerard chewed silently for a moment. "Well, he's been through a lot lately, I wouldn't be surprised if he's struggling."

"No, no, don't worry, he's fine. He just needs to rest," Mum said. Gerard shrugged, giving up for now.

"Are you not gonna eat your food, honey?" she said, turning to me.

"I'm not hungry," I mumbled.

"Samantha, please." The smile faded instantly. "Just eat. I don't need this right now."

"What?" My head jerked up.

"Don't you snap at me. Just eat." She returned the

cartoony smile to her face and the dinner resumed in near silence. I had never wanted to be anywhere else so badly as I did at that moment.

When I finally escaped, I went to my room and sat slumped over my desk. I knew that there was plenty of work that I should be doing but I couldn't bring myself to do any of it.

I thought about Dad, lying in bed, probably watching some show or other to distract himself. Neither he nor Mum would admit it, but he was clearly not himself lately. This wasn't the first time he had missed dinner. I couldn't blame him either. He had lost so many friends lately; it would've taken a toll on anyone.

I thought of Mum, clearly exhausted and just wanting happiness from me. I wasn't sure I could ever give that to her.

***

It happened on a Thursday, sometime after that. I tried to ignore how I was feeling and to snap myself out of it. I was just being stupid. I had no reason to be feeling this way, no right to be this unhappy. I should've been able to get through that night, like all the other times before, but this was different. The current was too strong this time.

I tried to ignore the urge as I sat slumped on the floor, attempting to force myself to just put on the CD, like I had promised. I tried to remind myself that this moment would pass, just like it had every other time, but this one was longer and stronger than ever before.

I knew that he would never forgive me, but I hoped at least he would understand. I hoped Michael would remember what it felt like that day, holding that rope in his hand. Surely, he'd remember the thoughts that floated through his head, screaming at him to end it all even though that made no sense, even though that would only make things worse and would have destroyed his mother, leaving her to drown in even more grief. I hoped he'd remember how that voice took over everything until it was all he could hear ... until I found him and managed to bring him back from the brink.

My whole body and mind felt empty and numb. I could imagine a hand reaching out towards me, about to take control, and I was powerless to stop it. My body didn't feel like my own as I watched my feet step over towards the desk, my hand pulling open the desk drawer.

It lay there before me as always, rusted in bloodstains but as sharp as ever. I picked up the blade and the voice in my head grew louder than ever before.

I was tired, so very tired. I hated waiting; waiting and waiting for things to get better or to change. It seemed I was stuck like this with no choice but to suffer in endless monotony.

I thought of my parents downstairs, watching their

usual programs on TV. I thought of my brother in his bedroom, studying for a major exam in his chemistry course. I thought of Michael suffering at the hands of his mother but still always putting her before himself and protecting her.

I was one more burden that they didn't need. A little less negativity in their lives would help them all.

The blade dragged itself across my skin, and blood quickly began to seep out. The familiar rush of pain and relief began to flow over me, but this time, it wasn't enough.

I dug the blade in deeper, unflinching at the pain of it. I cut it in over and over again; horizontally, diagonally and vertically. I lowered myself to the ground as the blood seeped out of me, stronger than it ever had before. I watched it flowing as the seconds ticked by into minutes. The pain rushed through me with overwhelming relief as I fell to the floor. I watched the blood seeping out of my veins onto the carpet and thought belatedly that I should've covered it over first.

As the blood flowed out, my body grew weak and my head became fuzzy; my vision blurring. A noise sounded in the distance. It was my phone ringing. I had left it on my bed. It rung unceasingly, and I willed it to stop, for the caller to let me go. This was it. I was done. I suddenly felt the dull *thud*, *thud* of footsteps on the landing. I knew they were Dad's, his irregular footfall distinguishable by the limp on account of his prosthetic leg. He was now in the bathroom, mere feet from me.

I suddenly remembered a time, many years ago now, when he came home after a particularly long and difficult stint serving in the Lebanon. He was honourably discharged, having been caught up in a blast that cost him his leg. I remembered Mum's tears as she heard the news over the phone. "He's alive, he's fine," she said, over and over again. I wondered if she was trying to reassure us or to reassure herself as she wiped away her tears.

"I wouldn't be here without you," I recalled Dad's words to me, "You mean the world to me. Don't you ever forget that." I remembered how he had looked, going over his old photographs of all his lost friends. I remembered his heartache for Sean, his devastation that the war he had left behind was continuing to kill his friends. I could hear him crying through the walls when he thought no one could hear. I was going to do it to him, again.

I thought about Mum in all her bubbliness. I wanted to say sorry; sorry I could never be the happy girl she wanted. She'd come home every day from work having looked after children, to then looking after Dad and endlessly worrying about him. Through the thin walls, I could hear her words of reassurance that everything would be alright. I wished she would say those words to me. She never seemed to quiver - she was always there - an unrelenting force of support.

I remembered my brother's words, "I'm always right here, whatever it is." I thought of how Gerard held my hand through everything when we were younger and promised it would be okay, I would be okay, Dad was okay and so was Nan; she was in a better place now and out of pain.

Her smiling face floated before me; the face I thought I had forgotten. My heart swelled at the memory of her. *Come back*, I pleaded, *Come back*.

"You can come see me whenever you like, you're a big girl now," her voice echoed in my mind, "Just not like this, not now, my little dragon."

Her face suddenly morphed into Michael's as my heart rate steadily increased, and my vision blurred into near nothingness.

"You promised," he said, "You promised you'd stay with me."

"I'm so sorry," I said. My mind was racing, panicking. I pictured his mother - her hand striking his face, her fist slamming into his stomach, him falling over, bleeding, with no one to step in and save him. I saw the threatening noose dangling before me, and Michael hanging there, on the day when I wasn't there, the day I didn't venture out into the cold rain, the day I didn't happen upon him in the graveyard. The day I didn't save him.

I was making a mistake. He needed me. I needed to save him, to make sure he was safe.

I tried to will my body to move, but I could barely see now. My heart beat faster in an attempt to stay alive. The blood flowing from my arm had stained the carpet in a dramatic pool of red. I had to stop it. I wanted to take it back, to pull the blood back into my body, to make it stop. Please make it stop! I couldn't die, not now; he needed me.

A scream was the last thing I heard.

24.

I was a child again, my life stretched out before me. Nan was there in her glowing warmth, bustling about, making me sweet treats to eat.

Gerard was positioned in front of the television, playing a game on his new PlayStation 2 console. I watched over his shoulder as the small pixelated character seamlessly dodged enemies and obstacles repeatedly, until suddenly he was facing a monster unlike any other. The character failed and died. It wasn't listening to Gerard's commands and he almost threw the controller through the TV screen in frustration. Nan scolded him, telling him to control his temper or she'd switch the game off again.

He'd try his best to remain calm, but I could see it boiling up inside him as the monster defeated his character once more. I couldn't help but laugh.

The room was filled with a warm glow, almost ethereal ... or surreal. My vision began to increasingly defocus until a brilliant white light overtook my vision. I tried to hang on. I tried to call out to them; to Nan. I wanted to stay there forever.

Then, they were gone and the room had transformed. I was standing in a house I didn't recognise. I heard noises gathering around me; the sound of people, lots of them.

I walked down the stairs laid out in front of me, gripping onto the banister with each step.

I followed the murmur of voices towards a room further back in the house. On my way, I glanced up at the walls surrounding me and noticed a number of photographs featuring the faces of two young girls. There were so many photographs of them all the way along the hallway. The first few showed the girls as young children captured separately, as if completely unaware of each other; entirely different. Steadily, they grew older as I moved along the wall until eventually they reached their teenage years, when suddenly the photographs morphed together so the girls shared the same frame. Another few photographs passed; one depicting a bespectacled girl hugging her friend closely. Then, just as suddenly, the girls were separated again into separate frames as though purposefully looking away from each other.

A strange feeling had begun to sliver down my spine as I looked at the pictures more closely. Suddenly, the realisation dawned on me that I did know this house after all and I knew those girls too.

I left the line of photographs behind and continued

211

down the rest of the elongated hallway, following the steady rise of voices. I tried to make out the words and to recognise the speakers, but it was all just an incomprehensible cacophony in my head.

Finally, I reached the room where all these people had gathered and suddenly silence fell as they acknowledged my presence. I stood on the threshold, failing to recognise a single face before me, although they seemed to know me. I felt something warm trickling down my left arm. I glanced at the floor and noticed splotches of red gathering on the wooden floorboards beneath me.

I awaited their laughter, their judgment, but they just kept staring silently as the blood fell from my arm. I was frozen in place, my mind completely blank. They wouldn't stop staring. Eventually, someone broke through the crowd, pulling me away and back into the hallway. The noise of the gathered voices rose again in my absence.

"What are you doing?" she asked. It was the bespectacled girl in the photograph. How had I forgotten her?

"Rachel?" I said. I wanted to simultaneously hug and punch her, but I stood still instead. My eyes begun to betray me as tears overflowed and fell down my cheeks. She was looking at me with pity in her eyes.

"Look at the state of you," she said, looking me up and down with barely disguised disgust, "I mean, I know you're just a dramatic attention seeker, but this is taking it to the next level." She laughed.

I glanced down at the marks littered across my arms and realised she was right; that after all this time, she'd been perfectly right. I was nothing more than a pathetic attention seeking nobody.

Her laughter continued to reverberate through my ears, sure to rupture them at any moment. Her magnified eyes were glaring right into me, stripping me bare for all to see. Suddenly, the chatter surrounding me transformed into echoed, boisterous laughter.

I started to run. I didn't know where I was going, but I ran towards what I hoped was the front door. I pulled it open, the doorknob stiff in my shaking hand, and was met with another brilliant white light. The laughter finally faded into silence.

Familiar walls built themselves around me. I looked down at myself, noticing that my clothes had now changed and there was no sign of blood or scratches on my skin.

A couch with accompanying armchairs manifested itself before me, followed by occupants eagerly watching the television in front of them. I walked towards them slowly, cautiously. The silence surrounding me felt eerie and wrong. They were my parents, of course they were. And this was our living room.

I tried to speak, but no sound would come. I tried

to call out to them, but the words caught in my throat. Despite the action playing out on the TV, there wasn't a sound to be heard. I waved my hand in front of their faces, trying to catch their attention, but it was as if I wasn't there. Their eyes were fixed on the screen in front of them, unblinking.

I tried to touch them - I even hit them - but there wasn't even a flicker in response. Growing frantic now, I left the room and found my brother standing in the kitchen, a plate of toast in his hand. I tried to shout at him, but still only silence remained. He stood stock still, unblinking, frozen in time. I tried everything; punching, kicking and shoving, but it was all useless.

I ran around the house in a panic, trying to find some sort of answer as to what was going on. Everything had frozen with every clock having stopped ticking. I ran towards the room that I knew was mine and found her lying there.

She looked just like me, only worse. She lay lifeless on the floor, her hair covering her face, damp with sweat and clinging to her skin. Her arms lay stretched out on either side of her, covered in violent wounds. The beige carpet had grown dark as it absorbed the blood that had been seeping out of her but that, too, was frozen in time.

I lowered myself to the ground and started crawling towards the girl. I reached my hand out towards her and uncovered her face. Of course I already

214

knew who she was, yet the revelation still came as a shock. Her face was mine. She was me and I was her.

I screamed silent screams.

Again, the world seemed to extinguish into nothingness. Suddenly, my screams broke through the silence, startling me as the sound hit my ears.

I was surrounded by seemingly unending darkness. I waited for something to happen, anything to happen, and just then I heard the faintest noise in the distance. I narrowed my eyes until a shape of some kind became distinguishable. I quickly jumped up and walked towards it, the emptiness that was surrounding me growing claustrophobic.

Even with his back turned towards me I realised who it was and broke into a run. I ran and ran, wondering if the distance between us would ever lessen. Eventually I caught up with him, flinging my arms around him as I did so, and found his embracing warmth the same as it always had been.

I felt the tears flowing and did nothing to hold them back. This was all I wanted, all I needed.

I could feel the hesitation emanating from him. I pulled back, taking in Michael's face as if for the first time. His usual smile was nowhere to be found.

"What's wrong?" I asked. The words hung in the air as he responded with silence. Instead, he turned to look up above us. I hadn't even noticed it until now.

A noose was suspended in the air, attached to

nothing in the abyss above. "What is this?" I asked.

"You promised me," he said.

"I promised you?"

"You promised you'd stay. You promised you'd stay with me," he said. I looked back up at the threatening noose above us and remembered that night once again that I had somehow forgotten. I promised I would stay with him, I promised I would help him.

"But I'm still here," I said. I was growing more confused by the minute.

What was going on?

Where were we?

There was literally nothing around or near us, the darkness seeming to stretch on indefinitely.

"You left me," he said. His lip started to quiver and I felt my heart break.

"I didn't leave, I didn't!" I pleaded.

Somehow, bruises started to appear one by one on his face, discolouring his skin. A wound opened up on his forehead and started trickling blood down his face.

I found myself backing away from him as he began to weep. He shouted, "You left me!" over and over again, growing more hysterical with each outburst. I didn't know what to do or say. I was frozen in place again.

The noose above us began to lower, coming closer and closer. I begged him to stop. "I'm sorry, I didn't mean it. I didn't mean to," I said, again and again between his outbursts, but he seemed inconsolable as if he had been put on some endless loop with no pause button.

The noose continued to lower. It seemed to have a life of its own as it came level with Michael's head and wrapped itself around his neck. I started screaming again, begging him to stop, begging for this to stop.

I couldn't bare it. I couldn't look as the noose pulled him upward.

My vision began to blur once more as the world around me disintegrated. A ringing noise began to surround me. A steady *beep*, *beep*, *beep* began to pulsate through me as I closed my eyes once more.

25.

I tried to prise my eyes open, but they were sewn shut. They felt so desperately heavy, as if there was no life left in them. In fact, every part of me felt so heavy.

What had happened?

Slowly, the ringing noise began to subside as other sounds became distinguishable, some voices among them.

Suddenly, I didn't want to open my eyes anymore. I didn't want to see them; the faces that belonged to the voices. I wanted to just go back to sleep, but the memory of Michael hanging above me was burned into the back of my eyelids. I couldn't go back there.

But what if this was just another dream?

I had to open my eyes. I needed to know for sure if I had made it out alive ... or if I had ... died.

Memories of what had happened slowly began to come back to me ... and then arrived all at once. My eyes shot open with the realisation of it all. I had died - I had done it - I had killed myself. I had cut too deeply and too much. I had bled out onto the floor and ruined the carpet.

The scream - someone had screamed. Through the haze of my dying memory, I couldn't remember who it was, or even recall if it had been a male or a female voice.

My vision began to clear and a plain, beige ceiling came into focus above me. The beeping noise continued, faster than before, in sync with my heartbeat. The sound of running footsteps caused me to sit up a little just as she came bounding towards me.

"Oh, thank God, thank God," Mum said hurriedly, putting down a cup of coffee on the bedside table on my right before wrapping her arms around me. She started crying into my shoulder; I felt the vibration of it wracking through me. She planted kisses all over my face and my eyes began to swell with tears; there was no way I could hold them back. I pulled my heavy arms up to hug her. They were wrapped in layers of gauze, so stiff and tight that I could barely move them. We stayed like that for a while, just crying into each other's embrace. I didn't think she would cry so much or at least not for me.

I blinked my eyes open and over her shoulder saw Dad standing there, shedding his own tears as he clutched onto his walking stick. I could see he was trying to control himself as we made eye contact. He tried to force a smile, but it fell almost instantly.

I never knew that heartbreak was a physical thing

until that moment. I thought for sure I would die right there from the sheer pain of it all. I felt so sorry, so indescribably sorry, and I knew that I should've apologised. I should've grovelled and begged for their forgiveness, but words wouldn't come. I hoped my tears were enough to convey my regret.

Eventually, Mum released me to look straight into my eyes. Her face was blotchy as her tears continued to fall. She wiped them away hastily and silently kissed me on the forehead.

I braced myself for the reprimand, but instead they said nothing. Dad approached me on the other side of the bed and bent down to wrap me in his arms. He held me for a long moment, more fiercely than he ever had before. He kissed me gently on the cheek before letting me go.

Numerous moments passed in silence as Mum and Dad sat either side of me. They were smiling at me but not with happiness, or at least not entirely.

I wondered if I should break the silence. I owed them an apology; I knew that much, but how do you apologise for something like that? Sorry I bled out on the floor, sorry I ruined the carpet, sorry for scaring you and making you scream, for making you cry. Sorry, sorry, sorry.

"I'm so sorry." I tried to keep my voice from breaking. "I'm so sorry ... for everything."

Mum took my hand in hers and despite her smile,

looked as though she might cry again. I knew that smile; the one given to children after they did something wrong; the smile that meant, "it's not your fault", the smile laden with a sigh. Her smile was meant solely to comfort *me*.

"You have nothing to be sorry about," Mum said, trying her best to keep her voice steady.

"We're the ones who should be sorry," Dad chipped in. He was usually much better at controlling his emotions in front of others, in not ever letting anything show, but even he seemed to be struggling. It was almost like a scene in a soap opera with everyone deliberately over-acting.

"What?" I said, confused, "What do you mean you're the ones who should be sorry?" I thought that it was a very strange thing for him to say. It didn't make any sense. I had done it. I made that choice. This was my fault, not theirs.

"We should've known," Dad replied. He glanced over towards Mum as if sharing a thought, as if asking for her approval for what he was about to say. She nodded. "It breaks our hearts to think you couldn't come to us about this, about what was going on, about how you were feeling.

"I tried to let you know that you could always come to me," he took a break to breathe deeply. "At least, I meant to. But if you didn't feel that … what does that make us? What kind of parents does that make us?

221

We failed you."

I heard the muffled sounds of Mum crying into her right hand as her grip tightened around mine. His words swum in my head. I couldn't comprehend it. They had somehow managed to spin this into something that *they* had perpetrated; that this was inherently their fault simply because they weren't able to stop it.

I had never thought about it like that before. The look in their eyes and on their faces became clear to me, unmasked and laid bare for all to see: it was disappointment, but not disappointment in me - disappointment in themselves.

"It's not your fault," I said meekly. The words came out as little more than a whisper.

I could see the collection of questions gathering in their minds, desperate to burst out. I could see that they were putting on a brave face. It was like they had been told to hold their questions for a while until I, the hapless child, was strong enough, or willing enough, to answer them. I thought that time would never come, that I would never be strong enough to face their doubt, or willing enough to confront their confusion and disbelief.

"I know you want to know why," I said, addressing the main question I felt they were most desperate to ask. A simultaneous glance passed between them.

I waited in silence as they debated wordlessly with one another. I could almost see the exchange of dialogue

222

through the looks on their faces. Mum's face said, "C'mon please, I need to ask, I need to know where I went wrong." Dad's face said, "We should wait. She needs to recover first. We shouldn't give her any further stress."

After a couple of minutes, they seemed to reach a consensus and turned back to me. Dad spoke first, "Sammy, we don't need to talk about it right now. You just need to rest."

I didn't want to rest. My spirit felt completely restless. I wanted to jump up from the bed and embrace the impossibility of still being alive. I could remember it as clear as day. I remembered the moment when my numb mind ordered my arms to pick up that blade for the first time in weeks. I remembered the heavy weight of my hands as I drove the blade across my skin and the stark contrast of the bright red of the blood against the pale white of my skin. I remembered the intensifying physical pain with each cut, as each wound merged with the other. I remembered the blood pooling on the ground, being absorbed by the carpet, and how sorry I was to be leaving such a mess behind. I remembered the feeling of my heartbeat in my chest, beating faster and faster in its attempt to keep me alive. And I remembered my vision steadily fading.

Then I remembered the images that had flooded my head, playing out as clearly as a movie right there before my mind's eye. I remembered the flashing wave of doubt, the realisation that I was making a grave mistake.

I had never been a religious person, never believing in any higher power, although the idea was a nice one. I had never found reason to believe that some ethereal presence was looking down upon me, watching my every move and forever on the lookout for a moment of intervention. But now I wondered if something had answered my call for help. I wondered if all the effort I spent trying to get back up, all the silent pleas I made to revert my mistake and all the desolation in my heart had surged out of me and somehow, somewhere ... someone or something had heard me.

I recalled that scream again. I would surely never forget it; the scream that came just as my vision failed and I started to slip away, the scream that surely belonged to one of them, finding me at that exact moment - the moment before it was too late.

An image flashed before my mind's eye. I was back there again, in that other world where everything had been frozen, where no one would respond, and where I found myself looking down upon my own dead body. That had been a dream to me, a nightmare even, but they had seen it too ... only for them it was real.

A tugging sensation pulled at my heart as the gravity of what I had done fell upon me. I had never meant for them to see that; to see me at my absolute worst.

"Once you feel a little better," Mum said, interrupting my train of thought, "Then we can talk properly." She plastered another one of those smiles on her face and I wanted to tell her that it was okay, that she didn't need to pretend, not in front of me, not anymore. No more pretending.

***

I wished they would've just let me go home. I felt fine, better than I had been for quite a while, in fact. My parents avidly showered me in affection; Mum bought a big bouquet even though I didn't care much for flowers. "To brighten up the room," she said. She probably thought they would make me feel a little happier, and at least looking at them reminded me of her and of how much she truly cared for me. Their colours were extremely vibrant and beautiful, and I felt a longing for my sketchbook so that I could capture their form within its pages.

My arms were still numb, heavy and wrapped up in layers of gauze. Every now and again, I would move them in such a way that they would respond with a shot of pain that went through my body. When one of the nurses came in to re-dress the bandages, I saw the violent marks etched into my skin. I felt disconnected from the sight like I couldn't remember doing it. Surely, I hadn't done that to myself?

But I had. They told me that the wounds had been substantially deep and that my body had struggled to clot and heal them in time. I had been lucky, they said.

I dared not to ask anyone if they knew where Michael was or if they had heard from him. I didn't want to know. For a moment, I wondered if he even knew or if anyone had been able to contact him. Maybe he didn't know yet and I felt a flicker of hope that I could simply keep it hidden from him.

That hope didn't last long.

"Oh, of course he knows," Mum told me, "We know you two have been getting close lately ..."

"That's one way to put it," Gerard chimed in. He let out a giddy laugh like a child embarrassed by the thought of a crush. Gerard hadn't really spoken much to me since he first came to see me. He would smile sympathetically at me every once in a while, and on the occasions when we were left alone in a room he'd try his best to talk about something - anything - other than what had happened. I wondered if he was simply following the doctor's orders to "let me rest" or if it was truly too much for him to contemplate.

All the same, I appreciated him and his attempts at humour to lighten the situation however slightly. Most of all, I appreciated his reassurance that nothing had changed between us whatsoever.

"I got his number from your phone," Mum continued, returning me to the topic at hand. "Hope you don't mind. I thought he should know." She had noticed my reaction and that maybe I hadn't wanted him to be told at all. "I thought you'd want him to know, right?"

"Yeah, of course," I said. She gave me that smile that said she knew I was lying, but she'd accept it as truth anyway.

Still, he didn't come, and I worried that this was it - I had ruined everything in my stupid impulsiveness.

26.

I felt like the world had completely changed, and it terrified me. Suddenly I had this profound insight into a world where I didn't exist.

I didn't think that it would do this to them; that it would shatter them so completely as I caught Mum crying into Dad's shoulder outside of my room. I heard them repeatedly blaming themselves and asking what it was they did wrong to make their own child feel so completely unloved. I wanted to tell them that wasn't it at all. I just wanted it to end. I wanted - *needed* - it to stop, but I didn't know that by doing so, I'd be leaving further pain in my wake.

I waited for him to come. I wanted him to be here. I thought he, of all people, would understand my motives. He would understand the selflessness involved in such feelings; in just wanting to lessen the burden I've placed upon others. I thought he would understand what it was to be convinced that no other option existed. Still, he had yet to appear.

"I talked to the school today," Mum said, on my

second day in hospital. I just wanted to go home and pretend none of this had ever happened, but the doctors wanted to make sure I was strong enough first. I could feel them watching me with each step and breath I took.

A shiver went through my body like lightning as I envisioned my classmates finding out about what had happened. What would they say? *Oh, what a selfish bitch. Attention seeking drama queen. Worthless piece of shit.* I could hear it as clear as day. I couldn't possibly go back; I could never bear to hear that. My school life had always been so quiet and inconsequential that I could never face those looks of pity and judgment.

Mum must have seen the look on my face. "Oh, don't worry, I was only talking to the principal. No one else will know. You're just off sick." She patted me sympathetically on the hand.

"Thanks for saving me the embarrassment," I said, with just a touch of sarcasm. I really wished she hadn't said anything at all as I felt sure my absence would have gone unnoticed.

Mum looked dumbfounded at me, the fake smile fading from her face. "Embarrassment?"

"What exactly did you say?" I followed up with but my question was met with silence. She looked away, her eyes darting around the room. She didn't need to answer me. "You told them? Why would you do that?" Dad stared over at her; he had no part in it apparently. I was stunned to think she could be so inconsiderate.

"Only the principal," she claimed, but he was hardly going to keep it to himself. He would tell the other teachers and they would start to whisper, to discuss and conspire about it. Then a student would overhear, and it would spread like wildfire across the school and I would surely never be able to show my face again.

"You don't need to feel ashamed," Dad chimed in, attempting to break the tension as Mum was still speechless, "This was just a little accident. You didn't mean to do it, right? There's no shame in it."

"An accident?" I said. Is that what they really believed? I wanted to believe that too, that it was something that was completely out of my control and completely unintended. I only wanted to harm, not kill myself, but then I felt like I couldn't stop and, more importantly, I hadn't wanted to. I had *chosen* to do it. This was no accident.

The tension in the room instantly multiplied. Now it was Dad's turn to look ashamed. They still would never speak about it frankly with me. They would dance around the topic, like it was some sort of bomb that would explode at the slightest touch.

"Well, this looks cosy." A fourth voice entered. My heart fluttered, wondering if he had finally decided to arrive, but it was just Gerard. "Am I interrupting something?" he asked.

"No, nothing, we were just talking," Dad said.

"I was just telling Samantha," Mum said, shooting

me a warning glance, "That the school has been informed that she'll be out for a few days. They needed to know because it's a very important time right now in the middle of her exams and I was worried it might affect things."

"Did you tell them ... what happened?" Gerard asked, his eyebrows furrowing. I wanted to hug him. He understood, he knew what I was feeling. Mum shrugged her shoulders as if to say, "So what if I did?"

"I mean, not explicitly, but they know she's in hospital and I thought ... if they knew, they could maybe hold some classes or workshops to educate people about this kind of thing; what to look out for and maybe ... if people hear about this ... I thought, maybe ..." Her resolve seemed to be faltering with each word. "I thought it might stop this from happening to someone else, is all. I mean, how could no one have noticed?" she whispered with a mix of frustration and anger. "How did no one notice?"

Gerard glanced at me and offered me a sympathetic smile. "Because she didn't want to be noticed."

"Well, thanks," I said, sarcastically.

He laughed. "I didn't mean it like that. I meant ..." He pulled up another chair to join us beside the bed. "This has been going on for a while, right?" I glanced over at my parents to gauge their expressions. They were looking at Gerard with some kind of wonderment.

231

"You've been feeling like this for a while, right?" I could barely respond, so I just nodded. "So, she's been hiding it." He spoke to them more than to me now. "Not wanting to worry or annoy anyone, I'd imagine." He spoke so frankly, as if it was the simplest thing in the world and not a big deal at all.

"How do you know that?" Mum said softly, evidently stunned.

"Because everyone feels like that, on some level, sometimes. You think about sharing your problems, but you don't want to add to the problems of others," he shrugged, as if it was incredibly obvious.

Silence fell again for a moment as Gerard's words sunk in. "Honey," Mum's attention turned back to me, "If that's how you've been feeling, you don't need to hide it from us. You can tell us anything, you know that. We are here for you, always, okay? No matter what."

"Don't start crying again," I urged her.

She laughed at my insistence. "I'm sorry, I've been crying a lot but, what do you expect? My little girl didn't think she could come to me."

"It wasn't like that," I said, feeling my own emotions betraying me as a tear slid down my cheek, "I was just afraid."

"Afraid of what?" she asked. I didn't know what to say. The truth was, I feared her reaction, her judgment and in turn perhaps that did equate to my not trusting her or anyone.

"Of what you'd say."

"Honey ..." she trailed off, gripping my hand again. She stood up and leaned over to wrap me into a hug. From over her shoulder, I saw a shape forming in the doorway.

Our eyes locked as he remained unmoving, watching the scene before him. Gerard followed my gaze and turned to see Michael standing in the doorway. The sudden attention must have scared him as he hastily left without saying a word.

Mum let me go and returned back to her seat.

"That was him, right?" Gerard asked. "Why'd he run off?"

"Your guess is as good as mine," I said nonchalantly. My heart had dropped right into my stomach. I couldn't read his face in that moment; I didn't know what he was thinking but he looked almost ... scared.

"I'll go and get him," Gerard said, springing up out of the chair and exiting the room. I wanted to stop him. They had never even met before and this wasn't exactly how I envisioned introducing him to my family, but Gerard was gone before I could form the words in my mind.

"Don't worry about him," Mum said, "I imagine you gave him a bit of a scare." She tried to laugh it off. Is that all it was? Had I just scared him?

I forced a smile and pretended I wasn't that

bothered. After what was surely the longest five minutes or so, Dad made an excuse to leave the room, ushering Mum to come with him. She seemed confused at his sudden urgency until she glanced at the door. Dad motioned for her to move further out of the room. "Let's just give them a minute," he said, offering her his outstretched hand.

Michael was standing just outside the door, still seemingly apprehensive about crossing the threshold. I suddenly didn't want them to leave us alone, but I watched as they passed him on their way out. He offered them a weak smile but still seemed unable to step forwards. I waited agonisingly for him to enter, thinking he'd surely change his mind again.

Eventually, after debating with himself countless times, he slowly stepped into the room. I offered a muffled, "Hello," in greeting, wanting more than anything to curl up into a ball and hide. I searched his face to discern how he was feeling. He looked afraid, sad and angry all at once.

He walked over to me cautiously, trying not to make direct eye contact, and carefully placed a shaking hand on top of mine, avoiding the bandages strapped around my arms. The silence fell heavily between us as his bottom lip began to quiver. I didn't know what to do.

"Where've you been?" I couldn't help but ask. The question had plagued my mind frequently. I had been there two days already and he hadn't appeared, until now.

Was it wrong to expect him to visit me once he found out what had happened? Was it wrong of me to want that support?

"I'm sorry," he said softly. I had to strain a little to hear him. "I wanted to come sooner, I did." He looked up at me solemnly and my heart broke at the sight of the pain glistening in his eyes; it tore right through me and I felt myself shattering like glass. Now, I was the one crying.

He came forwards, wrapped his arms around me and we cried into each other because there was nothing else to say right then.

27.

After a while, we both started to proclaim apologies, although he didn't need to. This was all my fault, after all. Our embrace tightened and tightened, to the point that it almost hurt, but I didn't care.

"I'm sorry," he said for the umpteenth time, "It sounds so stupid now, but I was ..."

"Scared," I finished for him. Mum was right, I had scared him. I thought about how it must have felt to receive a call like that, to be told that someone you were close to had almost died and was now lying pitifully in a hospital. I wondered if she had been explicit in telling him too, showcasing my idiocy and weakness. Even if she didn't, the state of my arms would give it all away.

"I guess." He clearly wasn't sure what to say next and I thought it best not to push him. Our embrace ended as he pulled away and stood up from the bed. I could almost see the words flashing across his face as he tried to form sentences, pitting one option against another. Eventually, he continued, "Sam ..." His eyes lingered on mine for the longest time. He visibly tensed with the incoming question, the one on everyone's lips. "Why?"

I had been anticipating that question ever since my eyes fluttered open and I discovered that I had been granted a second chance at life. I expected it, waited for it, and now there it was. It's funny, the weight of that simple word.

"I don't know." That was the truth; I didn't know. There was nothing or no one to blame.

"You don't know?" he repeated. I knew that wasn't the answer he was expecting and most certainly not the one he wanted, but it was all I had.

"I don't know why I did it. I don't know why it happened." I was ready to break down in tears again any second now. He looked at me with clear disbelief in his eyes.

"But why? ... you didn't ... you promised ..." He took deep breaths between each phrase in an attempt to keep his voice steady. He started pacing back and forth in front of me. "You promised ... you'd come to me ... call me ... if you ever ... felt like that." He glared at me piercingly, demanding some sort of reasoning.

"It's not ... it wasn't like that." I tried to find the words to explain. His deep breaths were growing quicker as he continued to pace. I wished he'd stop doing that. "Are you angry with me?" I asked, although his body language was answer enough.

"Angry?" he said with a hint of laughter. "I'm not ... I'm not angry." He seemed to be saying it more to himself than to me.

"Michael, don't lie to me," I said, "I know that it was ... a stupid thing to do." He continued to pace at the foot of my bed. I was growing increasingly more agitated with each step he took. "Will you please stop?" He persisted in pacing. "Stop and look at me."

Eventually, my words reached him. He stood still. "Why would you do this to me?" he almost whispered.

"What?" I said.

"Everything we've been through, Sam." He finally turned to face me, his glistening eyes boring right into mine. "Everything we've said. Everything *you* said. How could you just ... forget?" His chest continued to rise and fall heavily. I could see him trying to control his emotions, but his anger and frustration were pouring out of him now.

"Of course I didn't forget," I said, thinking back on where we'd come from. How could I?

"Did you not stop to think for just one minute ... about me? About what this would do to me?" he said, attempting to keep his voice quiet while his emotions betrayed him. I felt like he was interrogating me as if I had done this deliberately to scar him. He repeated the questions, demanding an answer, but I found myself speechless.

Eventually, the words forced themselves out, "Are you serious? You were all I thought about, all I ever thought about - you and my family. All I ever thought about was how much better off everyone would be without me. I didn't want to be a burden anymore. I wanted to stop bringing everyone down with my cloud of negativity. I just wanted it to stop ... and I thought ... I thought you, of all people ... might understand." The words flew out of me in a hurry and pooled at my feet. I wanted to take them back as soon as I had said them. They didn't feel real. They felt like someone else had said them; those were someone else's thoughts, someone else's feelings. Yet, at the same time, I knew they were mine.

He stood speechless for a long while as I waited for him to respond. His anger seemed to subside, replaced by sorrow. "But didn't you think ... about that night," he walked up close to me again and sat down in the chair beside my bed before taking my hand in his. "That night we met, the night you pulled me back from the edge and saved me? You told me, as a complete stranger, that you cared about me and wanted me to live. Imagine if that happened now; what would you say, how much would you care?" His words were sinking in. "Can you just imagine," he gulped down his hesitation. "If you had ... died. What would I have done? Those words, that night, would suddenly have meant nothing. I would've-"

"Don't say it," I interrupted him, anticipating the conclusion.

"I would've died, Sam," he said as he clutched my

hand in his. "You have been the one thing truly keeping me going through all of this. If I lost you ..." He shrugged as if to say the sentence didn't need completing.

A wave of guilt suddenly overtook me as I remembered those last moments before my vision faded. "I tried to stop. You have to believe me. I realised it was a mistake and I tried to stop but I couldn't, it was too late. I never wanted to hurt you."

"I know. I'm sorry, I know. I just couldn't help but feel ... angry. You're right though, I should've been able to understand. I do understand. I know what it's like to feel like that, to feel that desperate for it to just ... stop."

"I didn't even mean to," I said, "Just, all of a sudden, something took over and I couldn't think straight. It was almost like I couldn't see anymore, like I wasn't in control anymore. You have every right to be pissed at me."

"I'm not pissed at you," he said. I wondered if even he believed that. "I was just confused ... and sad. I have always been there for you and I always will be, you know that."

"I know. I'm so sorry." The tears had begun to flow again. He found a space for himself on the bed so he could get up next to me and I allowed myself to lean into him.

***

I could feel their eyes piercing into me as I left the hospital, their words of judgment loud yet silent at the same time. They all knew, I was sure of it. I had no secrets anymore. I walked down the unending path of shame as I thanked the doctors for saving me from the brink of death after having deliberately crossed it.

They offered kind smiles whilst their words of acknowledgment were tinged with notes of pity. I couldn't get out of there fast enough. I couldn't wait to feel the sun on my skin, the wind pulling through my hair and the sheer absence of imposing walls. Its brilliance hit me like a tonne of bricks.

I started laughing at myself. This was the best I had felt in so long ... like I was suddenly ... alive, and it had taken almost dying to feel like it.

At home, every time Mum looked at me, she seemed ready to burst into tears and kept bringing me into hugs without saying a word. She started cooking my favourite meals more often, and bought me new clothes and presents. I told her I didn't need anything, but for days afterwards I'd find a new package placed on my bed.

The first day I came home, I went straight up to my room, refusing any offer of dinner despite my parents' protestations. I was exhausted and really needed to rest after the bustling sounds that had surrounded me at the hospital. I just wanted to embrace nothingness for a while.

I paused before the doorway, suddenly unable to move. The door was the same as it always had been, with etches in its woodwork from my childhood. But now it was shrouded in an aura of darkness.

I held my breath and pushed myself through the doorway. I moved quickly towards the bed, realising belatedly that something was different.

Something soft and fluffy lay beneath my feet, caressing my shoe-less toes. I glanced down to find a rather large, colourful rug on the floor. I almost called out to my parents to ask what this was for, but I realised soon enough and stopped myself.

The memory of it flooded before my eyes as I bent down and flipped back the edge of the rug. I expected to see it, but at the same time wished I didn't have to. The stain glared at me knowingly, seeping into my skin. The patch of carpet was a much darker shade of beige now, despite it having been vigorously cleaned by someone. I could smell the stench of overpowering bleach still emanating from it. I could visualise the blood as clearly as if it was still there, pouring out of my veins. I felt raw with the image of my mother struggling on her hands and knees, desperately trying to remove it. I wondered how long she had spent trying to clean it before giving up, instead covering it with a colourful rug in the hope of hiding it from me.

"Thank you for the rug," I said, returning

downstairs a while later. It was a beautiful rug after all, and I should be grateful that I didn't have to look at the ghost of my mistake every day. Mum gave me another tearful hug without another word.

But with the extra affection came less privacy and alone time, something I was very much accustomed to. For weeks, they wouldn't let me keep my bedroom door closed and would quickly open it if they found it so. Despite what I had done, I didn't think I deserved to lose the right to my solitude.

Gerard tried to be more open with me and we talked more than we ever had before. He'd call in to see me each day after college and make awkward small talk. We had breakfast together a lot more too, which I found strange because I knew that most days his classes didn't start until the afternoon. Yet there he was, at seven a.m. each day. It would seem I was being monitored.

I was terrified to return to school after what happened. I didn't expect the principal to keep my situation quiet for long, if at all. I walked the same route to school at the usual time, and dragged myself through the corridors, heavily anticipating the knowing glares of everyone I passed.

However, no one seemed to notice, or at least no more so than usual. Maybe word hadn't gotten out after all and my secret was still safe.

As the day progressed, I realised I was wrong. I should've noticed it sooner. They were trying hard,

243

almost too hard, not to look at me with pity and judgment. So instead, they elected not to look at me at all. I'd catch their eye by chance, and it'd be but a flicker before they'd turn away, yet I could see it in their eyes that they knew my secret.

"Don't look so worried," Michael said. At least he seemed to be the same as always, although he had become even more affectionate. I honestly thought I had ruined everything between us and what we had. I apologised almost every day for what I had done, for breaking my promise and for almost leaving him. He told me it was okay, but for a long time I couldn't believe him.

He started texting me more often too, even into the late hours of the night or during class. I'd sneakily pull the phone out of my pocket under the desk, careful to remain hidden:

You are beautiful.

> You're not even in
> my   class.   You
> can't even see me.

I don't need to.

It was enough to make me smile for the rest of the day.

"I feel like everyone's staring at me," I said during

lunch one day, as he told me again to stop looking so worried, as if it was that simple.

"Nobody's staring at you." I knew he was just saying that to make me feel better, but he knew as well as I that people were, at the very least, looking at me.

"They think I'm some sort of freak. They're too scared to say anything to me. Like I'll snap or something."

"You're not a freak," Mark sputtered in between bites of his sandwich. Of course, he and Cian knew. Michael confessed that he had told them (although the night in the graveyard was still a secret) back when he had felt too confused and too conflicted to see me. He said he needed someone to talk sense into him. They offered to come with him to make it 'easier' but he wanted to come alone in the end as he knew he'd be an emotional mess.

I didn't really care that they hadn't visited me in hospital on their own. In a sense, they were still more Michael's friends than mine, but at least they didn't look at me any differently. I appreciated that more than anything.

They never directly addressed it with me, instead choosing to offer simple smiles in greeting when I returned. It was like nothing had happened. They seemed to skate around the topic, and in all honesty I was glad they did. I felt I had talked about it more than enough by that stage.

"I mean, I'll be honest," Mark continued, swallowing the previous few bites quickly, "Most of the school has heard and well ... it's a curious thing, you know? Almost ... a fascination."

"What are you on about?" Michael said, almost scolding him for saying such a thing.

"It might sound harsh but it's true," he paused to take another bite of food, swallowing it quickly. "You ever wonder how those true crime shows are so popular? How come no one's disgusted knowing those things actually happened? They're not. They're intrigued, interested, curious ... they want to make sense of it, they want to know why."

"I hardly think that's the same thing." Michael chuckled.

"Maybe not exactly, but more or less. All I'm trying to say is, they're not looking at you because they think you're a freak or something, they're looking at you because they're curious, is all. They just wanna understand." Mark finished, shrugging his shoulders to signify that he had made his point.

28.

Funnily enough, after feeling so desperate for so long for things to change, I just wanted things to go back to how they were, but I knew they never would. The 'incident' hung over our family like a ghost; one that was always there no matter how much we ignored it, sending a perpetual chill down our collective spines. It didn't take long for the whispers to spread well beyond the school. Those glances followed me everywhere – to the faces of my neighbours, my parents' friends, the local businesspeople and complete strangers. It's just curiosity, I tried to remind myself, just as Mark had said. It was the preferable belief but still, I could feel their emanating pity. I felt as if I had been put out on display as an abnormality, one of God's mistakes for people to gawk at and say, *thank goodness I'm not like that.*

I was tired of hiding, tired of pretending to smile when I wanted to cry and tired of making small talk when I just wanted to sleep for days.

Every day, Michael would send me messages of reassurances and would listen endlessly to the tirade going on in my head. He seemed never to falter or to grow frustrated, but I felt certain that it was a façade, that he was hiding his true feelings for fear of upsetting me and pushing the crazy girl too far. It was only a matter of time before he, too, would realise that I was too dramatic and he'd be much happier without my negativity dragging him down.

I'd mention these worries to him and he'd quickly scold me, telling me I was being ridiculous. Still, the thoughts would remain firm in my mind, like trees in a forest. I started to talk even less than I used to, to hide the true thoughts in my mind. I knew most of them were irrational and repetitive, and I knew how he would respond to them, as he had done so already. So I kept silent, and tried to pretend that everything was alright.

But he'd always see right through me. He'd extract it out of me every time and offer me the same feelings of reassurance and comfort. I tried to search his face for feelings of frustration or a sign of annoyance but it was never there. All I ever found was warmth, support and what I dared to hope was a feeling of ... love.

The blade was long gone. I somehow expected it to still be in the drawer when I pulled it open, which I did when the desperation got the better of me. I searched through my room on the off chance that I had the sense of mind to fling it somewhere before I started to fall but no, it was gone.

A few weeks later, I finally convinced my parents to allow me to close my door again. I was relieved to have a sense of my treasured privacy back, and to be able to let go and release my emotions for a little while, away from prying eyes. The tears came hard and fast and I thought they would never stop. I wanted them to stop … and I knew one way to make them.

I glanced down at my arms, the marks of every mistake glaring up at me. They had healed over now into everlasting scars. I yearned for that feeling more and more as I counted them. I traced my fingers over the bumpy wounds and as my desperation grew, I dug my nails into my skin and started to scratch furiously. The pain washed over my mind and the tears stopped.

There was no blood but the pain was enough. The red marks glared up at me, telling me that I was no better. How was I so stupid to think that I was better when nothing had changed?

***

It wasn't long before my parents sent me to see a doctor. I wanted to pretend that it didn't matter, that it was just a one-off incident, but they saw right through it. I had nothing to hide behind anymore. I explained to the doctor in as few words as possible how I was feeling. She asked me why I did it – why I had chosen to take my own life. I told her that I didn't 'choose' to. A choice implies alternative options but at the time there were none. She gave me a sideways glance.

After a couple of weeks, I was told I had an appointment with a local psychologist. The word sounded in my ears with an unending vibration. It was confirmation that I had indeed lost all sense of myself. I had considered going to see one many times before, but I couldn't bear the thought of being told that I truly had lost my mind and that there was nothing they could do for me; that I would just have to live with it.

Dad drove me to my first appointment (and all the others too, in fact). We didn't say much on the way there. I tried again to tell him I didn't need to go, that it was just a stupid little incident and it would never happen again. He didn't even bother arguing with me, instead letting the silence between us speak for him.

On the way to the psychologist's office, we drove past the nursing home; the place people went to die. The memory of Nan flooded before my mind's eye and I wondered what she would think of me now and of where they were taking me. I had heard that people of her generation didn't even think that mental illness was a real thing; they thought that things like depression were just elongated bad moods to be snapped out of and that you just had to move on. I tried to recall the memory of her smile and her laugh, but all I could think about was how fragile she had become in the end; forced to live to death.

Eventually, we pulled up at a short building situated on the outer limits of the town. It was strangely out of the way, as though hidden, for which I was grateful.

Dad parked the car near the door. I watched him glance over the building and wondered what he was thinking. I unbuckled my seatbelt and started to get out.

He stopped me just before I opened the car door. "Hey, Sammy," he said, "You know I love you, right?"

"Yeah, I know. I love you too, Dad."

"You're such a strong, brave girl," he shook his head, correcting himself, "A strong *woman*."

I chuckled. "Thanks?"

"I'm not kidding. I am so proud of you. You have no reason to be ashamed. I honestly think it takes great courage to ask for help, and sometimes ... even more to accept it." He stared off into the distance. I was lost for words.

"Dad ..." I should've said something, I knew that. This was an opening.

"Oh, don't you start worrying about me now too, kiddo. I'll be all right. Now hurry up, you'll be late." He ushered me out of the car.

A knot suddenly began forming in my stomach. A long, red-bricked building stood before me. From the outside, it looked to be little more than an extended bungalow and was beautifully framed by an assortment of flowers. A number of cars were parked outside,

251

showing that the place was pretty popular. I began to feel a little better, knowing I wasn't going to be the only one taking the walk of shame down the corridor.

Dad said he'd call back in about an hour to collect me, but as I entered the main door, I glanced back over my shoulder and could see the car was still there, the engine now turned off. Dad reclined his seat slightly to lean back and closed his eyes.

"Hi, may I help you?" The receptionist in the lobby asked, smiling at me from behind her glasses. She seemed perky - almost too much to be genuine, I thought. Her blond hair was tied into a ponytail, with some loose strands framing her face nicely. I guessed she was in her thirties.

"I ... I have an appointment with Dr. Murphy," I said, almost forgetting the name my parents had given me.

She began to type information on the computer in front of her. "Ah, Miss Ward, is it? Dr. Murphy's just down this hallway, last door on the right." She beamed at me again with that smile which surely had to be fake. No one could be that cheerful, least not in a place like this.

I followed her directions and began walking down the lengthy corridor towards the doctor's office. I tried to see into the other rooms as I passed by but most of them were closed, unwilling to give up their secrets to me. I read the name plaques on each door until I found the one labelled 'Dr. Murphy.'

I hesitated, unsure whether to knock or just enter. I glanced up at the clock above and realised I was still a few minutes early. There were some chairs lined up against the wall outside the office so I decided to sit down and wait, assuming I would be called in when it was time.

An elderly man sat opposite me, clutching a walking frame with wrinkled hands that shook ever so slightly. I could feel him looking at me as I tried my best not to make eye contact. I wanted to pretend that I was invisible, but he caught my attention eventually and offered me a sympathetic smile.

"You're far too young to be in here," he said in his croaky voice. I didn't know what to say to that, so I just said nothing, smiling back meekly in response. I waited in silence for the door to open.

***

When I finally went into the doctor's room, it wasn't at all what I had expected. I had anticipated the infamous couch placed before a medic's desk or chair. I had imagined a bored middle-aged man asking a list of questions about the intimate details of my childhood. I imagined watching the hands on the clock sounding a *tick, tock, tick, tock* while he scribbled down my answers, analysing my every word. I had envisaged dull, brown walls that seemed to close in upon me more and more with each passing second until I could barely breathe.

However, it wasn't like that at all.

A young woman, no older than thirty, opened her door a minute after my appointment time and welcomed me into her room. She held a strikingly strong resemblance to the receptionist, and I thought for a moment that she was the same person. Doctor Murphy's face appeared a lot kinder though - rounder and softer. Her slightly plump figure added to her aura of comfort and understanding. Her eyes seemed to hold memories of every story that she had ever been told and I trusted her instantly. I felt hers were wise eyes, understanding in their experience.

"Come on in," she said, holding the door open for me. I glanced back over my shoulder to catch the eye of the old man, and he smiled, waving a hand briefly in goodbye.

"It's Samantha, isn't it?" She said, welcoming me into the office.

"Sam." I said succinctly, not really liking the full version of my name.

"Sam. My name is Doctor Jessica Murphy. I'm so glad you decided to visit me and I'm looking forward to getting to know you. Now, how're you doing today?"

"I'm fine," I said automatically. I glanced around me and realised that my expectations were entirely wrong. The walls were a warm shade of yellow which made the room look larger than it actually was. The windows were open wide to let air in while still being shrouded by blinds to provide privacy. The aroma of various flower bouquets filled the air. The room felt alive and comforting, as if the walls were wrapping their metaphorical arms around me.

"That's good to hear," she said. She walked over to her desk, and offered me a seat in a chair in front of it. As we sat down, facing each other, the knot in my stomach began to form with renewed vigour until I thought I would be sick.

"No need to be so worried," she said, evidently analysing the look on my face. "We'll make it short today for your first time. I just want to get to know you a little bit and then we can make a plan. Does that sound okay?" She smiled gently at me. I felt readily exposed, sitting there in front of this complete stranger with nothing but air between us. I thought she could surely see right into the depths of my soul.

I nodded silently; I didn't have a choice to do anything but. I hoped she already knew why I was here as I didn't want to go through it all again with yet another stranger.

"Before we continue, I want to give you something," she said. She got up from her chair and went to the cabinet standing in the corner. She pulled some sort of document out of one of the drawers before turning back to me.

"Now, this is just a bit of a questionnaire. I want you to answer this as honestly as possible. I'm sure you've done stuff like this in school before." She held out the small bundle of stapled pages and waited. Feeling hesitant, I forced my hand up to take them. A number of statements were printed on each page, with a series of dots and numbers beside each one. "All I want you to do is read through each statement carefully and rate how much you agree or disagree with it. These," she said, pointing towards the numbers beside each statement, "indicate how much you agree or disagree. Circle five if you definitely agree, zero if you absolutely don't, and so on. Does that make sense?" I nodded in response. It seemed fairly simple. "Now, I ask you not to think about your answers too much. Go with your initial reaction, even if you're unsure."

I nodded again and agreed to fill it in. She invited me to sit by the desk and handed me a pen. She excused herself from the room, telling me she'd be back in about ten minutes to give me some privacy. I thanked her genuinely for that as I didn't want to feel her eyes peering over my shoulder.

I glanced down at the papers before me, the words swimming before my eyes. I forced myself to focus as the doctor shut the office door behind her. I flicked through the pages and saw there were at least thirty statements for me to go through, maybe more. The first statement read, "I feel happy most of the time." My hand instinctively moved to circle the number 1 printed beside it.

I paused. How easy would it be to just lie? Were these few pages really supposed to analyse me? Was this questionnaire their method of finding out how well, or indeed how ill, my mind was? Was this how they decided whether I needed help or not?

I thought maybe I should exaggerate every answer by only circling the fives and the zeros. I thought if I agreed more with the happier statements – basically lie – then they would diagnose me stable and send me on my way. Whereas if I agreed more with the less-happy statements, such as the fifth statement which read, "I frequently think about harming myself," then I might be considered a danger to myself and locked up in some mental institution.

You're such a brave, strong girl. Dad's words resounded in my mind. *I honestly think it takes great courage to ask for help, and sometimes ... even more to accept it.* So, I convinced myself to be honest, for his sake and for Mum's - for everyone's. As I read over each statement, I found myself leaning towards either extreme of the scoring system, straying from the mid-point to ensure my thoughts were clear.

I went through the rest of the pages, pausing on statements such as, "I don't think anyone would miss me," "My family would be better off without me," and,

"I look forward to my future." They seemed almost endless but eventually I made it to the end of the last page, just as the door to the office opened and the doctor returned.

"Are we finished?" she said. I didn't want to give them to her; I wanted to keep their content a secret, but I knew I didn't have a choice. I handed them to her, feeling great uncertainty as I did so. "Thank you, Samantha. I'll look over this later, okay? Now, why don't you tell me a bit about yourself."

I felt like a weight had just been lifted off my shoulders because she hadn't asked me to talk about *it*. It seemed odd to sit there with a complete stranger - a stranger who was supposed to help me with whatever was wrong - and just make small talk.

"Do you have many friends, Samantha? At school, or wherever," she asked after some time. I guess the casual conversations couldn't last long, especially with my limited responses.

"Um, a couple, I guess." I thought of Michael, of Mark and Cian too, although I still didn't know if they were *my* friends. Then Rachel's face flashed before my mind's eye but I wanted to bat the air to get rid of the image. She didn't exist anymore.

"Tell me about them. Who are they?"

"Well, there's Michael. And his friends."

"Oh? Who's he? Have you been friends long?" I started to regret having mentioned him.

"About six or seven months, I guess." I tried to count back how long it had been since fate threw us together. It felt so long ago now, another lifetime.

She laughed. "I think you're blushing. Is he more than a friend, perhaps?" Oh, God.

"M-Maybe ... I guess ..." Why was I so nervous?

"That's all right. And how are things with you two?"

"They're fine. Perfect. He's been the best thing to happen to me in so long."

"That's really sweet. Did you meet in school?" My heart froze in my chest. I wasn't a good liar, not verbally at least. Yes, we had gone to the same school for a few years but had somehow never crossed paths until that night in the graveyard. I thought for a moment ... I couldn't tell her about that, of course I couldn't. I was still sworn to secrecy, no matter how confidential this meeting was.

I swallowed my hesitation. "Yeah ... in school."

Luckily, she didn't question me any further. "Do you think you can talk to him - trust him - when you need someone?" she asked.

"Of course. He's one of the few people in my life who's never made me feel like crap or turned me away."

She paused for such a long moment that I thought I had said something wrong. "What do you mean by that?"

"What?" I suddenly couldn't remember my own

259

words.

"You mean to say that he's the only one you trust?"

Yes, that was the truth, but it sounded bad. "Um ... what ... I mean ..." I stumbled.

"You think that if you talk to people, about how you're feeling, or whatever it is, that they'll turn you away - fob you off and ignore you?"

"Think? ... I know." My words were barely more than a whisper, but she had heard them.

"I'm sorry you feel that way, but I assure you that isn't the case. Unfortunately, there will always be some people who don't understand, but you are surrounded by people who love you and will try. You need to have faith in that; in knowing that your family and friends love you even if they struggle to understand or struggle to help you."

I wasn't sure if I could believe her words, but I couldn't argue with them either. I had seen the disappointment in my parents' eyes, the upset I caused when I let the darkness win. I would likely always fear their rejection, no matter how many reassurances I received from them. The nightmares continued and the worries never ceased. I had to consciously choose to ignore those worries and fears in the hope that one day I would stop having them.

29.

Everything I had been feeling, everything that had happened, was summed up in just one single word - depression. The GP gave me a prescription for some pills that would hopefully help, and told me I had to continue seeing Dr. Murphy every week for a few months in order to 'get better'.

I held the pills in my hand. They looked like little pieces of pink plastic imprinted with a small, almost illegible, number on each to denote the dosage. It felt strange to think that this tiny thing was designed to help me disperse the darkness in my mind.

I longed for it to do so. I wondered how much of its power relied on my belief, but I didn't care; fake or not, I would take the chance.

Mum seemed almost afraid to talk about it. She bought the pills and seemed to hesitate when handing them to me.

"To think someone your age needs to take things like that," she said as she watched me swallow them for the first time. It seemed a lot of people were quick to compare my condition to my age as if they couldn't possibly correlate.

Should my youth have protected me? Should it have allowed me to maintain a positive perspective, no matter what?

At what age would this be somehow understandable?

"Are they helping you?" Mum asked a few weeks later, just as the medicine slipped down my throat again. I wondered if she thought I might not take them without her supervision, but I wanted them to help me as much as she did.

"I guess," I said, although not really sure myself. The doctor told me that it'd be a while before I saw any improvement and I tried to remind Mum of this, but still she questioned me. "They're not miracle drugs, you know."

"I know. It's just ... I've been reading up about it. A lot of people say they don't do anything at all for them, so do let me know if you don't ... notice any difference so we can tell the doctor. There's no point in taking them if they're not helping."

I understood her worries. I was worried too. I had heard those same stories, of people being prescribed all kinds of drugs only to feel no different at all, but I wanted to *believe* that they would do something for me.

Dad wasn't nearly as bad as Mum. Every time I saw her, I'd see the same look of disappointment,

disappointment in herself, imprinted on her face. I could see a hint of it in Dad's too but he was a lot better at hiding it.

Dad never really talked to me about what I had done. Maybe he was afraid to mention it? Maybe he didn't know how to, or just knew I didn't want him to. I wondered if he was angry with me, like how I sensed he was angry at his friend, Sean, when he died.

He drove me to each psychologist's appointment without saying anything of much significance, instead resorting to small talk to break the tension. I was extremely glad of it as he was treating me just the same as before - mostly, at least.

I stayed in the living room to watch TV with him one night after being practically pulled out of my room by my parents who didn't want me spending every night alone anymore. Dad stretched out his legs on the coffee table in front of him and let out a notable sound of pain. I knew that he was terribly self-conscious about his leg even though we all knew about it and had seen it plenty of times.

"You can take it off if you like," I said, knowing that the pressure from the prosthetic was likely aggravating his stump.

"No, no, it's all right." The lie was obvious on his face. I knew how much he hated it.

"Seriously, I can tell it's hurting you. Take it off, I don't mind. It might've grossed me out once, but I've got used to it now."

He laughed. "If you're sure." With another grunt of pain, he brought his leg back down and detached the prosthetic, tossing it aside with perhaps too much vigour as it fell to the ground with a loud *clang*. He let out a heavy sigh. "That is soooo much better. That bloody thing is a menace sometimes."

"Well, if it bothers you, don't feel you have to wear it for our sakes."

"That's nice of you to say, Sam," he said, "I don't think I'll ever not be self-conscious about it though. It's a nasty thing to look at."

I was barely ten years old when Dad came home from the Lebanon (or "the Leb" as he sometimes called it), having lost most of his left leg in a bomb blast. The sight of the stump terrified me; it was like something out of a *Goosebumps* episode. He was very careful around me after that and always made sure that it was covered up whenever I was present. Eventually, my disgust and horror subsided into curiosity, and I struggled to keep my eyes off it whenever we were together. I was fascinated by the idea of a fake leg and the notion of replacing broken or missing body parts with mechanical ones. If only the same could be done for the mind.

"It's your war wound," I said, quite literally. "It shows you've been in battle ... and survived. You shouldn't be ashamed of that." I couldn't imagine what it must've been like to fight on a real-life battlefield. He had told me that the role of the Irish Army was a neutral one, and he and his comrades had been sent to aid the innocent and help the wounded on both sides of the conflict. However, every once in a while, their men got caught in the crossfire and limbs and lives were lost.

He smiled smugly at me. "You know what, you're right." He began to relax a lot more and focused on the TV movie which showed Bruce Willis hard at work saving Christmas from Severus Snape. We watched the film in silence for a few minutes, but I wasn't all that interested in it and was beginning to plot my escape for the night. Then Dad interrupted my train of thought, "You know, we all have to fight battles in our lives, some more literally than others ..." I knew he was referring to himself and his experiences, but also to mine. "Sometimes, we don't come out unscathed, but that's okay." He looked me squarely in the eye and I knew he was trying to talk to me - really *talk* to me. "Like you said, scars are nothing to be ashamed of. They are a testament of our strength, our determination and perseverance. They are proof that we are warriors and if we can get through this, we can get through anything." He took a swig from the glass in his hand, clearly satisfied with his little speech.

I glanced down at the marks on my arms, now sufficiently healed to be exposed. For the longest time, I had viewed them as evidence of my weakness, my failure and my stupidity, but now I could see them as something else: proof of my survival and my strength. The thought made me smile.

***

I held my phone in my hand and thought about texting him, or even calling him. It felt like hours were slipping by in the grip of my indecision. I wanted to tell Michael everything about how I was feeling and about all the thoughts running through my head, even though I had told him many times before. He had promised time and again that he'd always be there for me, ready and waiting if I ever wanted to talk, no matter what.

Surely, it must get tiring and annoying though, to hear the same old tirade repeatedly and then have to deliver the same reassurances every time? He had enough of his own problems to deal with and I didn't want to add to his list.

We were as bad as each other. I should've seen it. I should have *known*. He spent so long worrying about me and comforting me whilst he was still fighting his own battles. He was still struggling and he was still lying about it.

Whenever we spent time together, I'd catch a look in his eye for just a moment that exposed the chink in his armour. I'd ask him repeatedly if he was okay and unflinchingly, he'd respond, "Of course, I'm fine," and would offer me that smile I had fallen in love with.

I'd try to push him to be honest sometimes because I could see he wasn't fine. He knew I wasn't oblivious to his lies but still, he'd refuse to talk about it or admit it even on the days when his skin betrayed him. One day, he arrived at school and walked up to the usual spot where myself, Cian and Mark were seated. A silence fell as he approached us, his battered appearance even more alarming that day. I glanced at the others to gauge their reaction and wondered if they would say something. He had told me before that they didn't know; he never dared to talk to them about it. However, watching their reactions now told me that they knew.

I thought for sure that one of them would say something. I even expected a funny remark but instead the silence continued as he sat down beside me, groaning as he did so.

"Are you all right?" I asked. This question was becoming a standard greeting.

"I'm fine, fine," he said, repeating it as if to reassure himself too.

"Sure, sure," I mocked. It was obvious that he was anything but fine, but he was never one to complain.

"Why are you lying?" I asked him later on when we were alone. I had hoped he'd be more honest with me now.

"Lying about what?" He'd feign innocence to appear ignorant of the truth. He was stuffing books into his bag from his locker and was avidly avoiding eye contact because he knew it would give him away.

"Don't do that. You know what I mean," I said. His silent response confirmed it. "You're not fine."

He slammed the locker door shut and finished zipping up his bag quickly, the books stuffed inside uncomfortably. He threw the bag over his shoulder and stormed away. I followed him without a word. I didn't understand why he was getting angry with me. I wanted to help and to be there for him, just as he had been for me. I recalled his reaction in the hospital that day and his sense of betrayal. He chastised me for breaking my promise, yet now he seemed to be doing the same.

We walked in silence until we exited the school. I was eager to re-start the conversation but as I met the eyes of many students on our way out - all of whom were glaring at the fresh bruises painted across his face – I decided to stay quiet until we were away from eavesdroppers and their judgmental faces.

As we left the school gate, he seemed adamant to remain silent. I knew if I let him, he would go home without another word and pretend everything was okay. He would kiss me goodbye, say he'd see me tomorrow and I'd be left wondering what I had let him go home to.

"Talk to me," I said, with a hint of urgency in my voice.

"Sorry," he said, as if snapping himself out of a reverie, "Got lost in a train of thought. What's up?" he asked as if I hadn't spoken to him at all.

"What happened? Tell me." The smile vanished from his face as he realised I wasn't going to just give up; not anymore.

"There's nothing to tell, it's fine."

"It's clearly not fine, Michael. Look at you." He stopped suddenly, bringing me to a halt beside him. He glanced around to make sure we were alone and that no one could hear our words or stare at him.

"What do you want me to say?" he asked. I sensed his anger and frustration again but couldn't understand why he was angry with *me*. "It doesn't matter. What happened, happened, and that's that," he said matter-of-factly.

"Why are you getting angry with me?" I asked, feeling perplexed and somewhat hurt, "I just want to help you, that's all."

"I'm not-" he broke off, took a deep breath and brushed his hand against my face. The warmth of his skin soothed me instantly but still, my concern for him grew. "I'm not angry with you. I'm sorry."

"What happened?" I asked again.

He let his hand fall to his side. "I think it's pretty obvious what happened." He tried to laugh but it came out as little more than a heightened breath. "She just ... lost it - again." He shrugged his shoulders as if it was no big deal. In my mind's eye, I could see her standing before him, the alcohol in her system overriding her

269

senses. I saw her hand raised, lashing out against his face. I saw him crumple helpless to the floor, not wanting to hit her back because it wasn't her fault, after all. I heard him try to reason with her but her fist would continue to slam into his face, into his chest, into his sides until she had exhausted herself.

I felt tears of hopelessness welling up in my eyes. I could sense his pain, even though he was trying so hard to keep it from me. It broke my heart to think that someone was hurting him like that and I could do nothing about it.

"We have to do something," I said, almost pleadingly, "Why didn't you tell me about this? You said she stopped. You said she was getting better."

"She was. I mean, I thought she was."

"You didn't tell me." I hoped the hurt was showing on my face. I was trying my best to hold my tears back.

"I know. You didn't need to know. You have enough going on already without that - without me."

"What?" Suddenly, the tears stood frozen in my eyes as I tried to calculate the meaning behind his words. "What do you mean?"

"Even if I did tell you, there's nothing you could've done so I would've just ... added to your list of problems. I would've made things even harder for you when you're doing so well; when you need to focus on getting better."

"Are you serious?" I said. I saw the glimmer of tears building up in his eyes now as he spoke.

"In fact, I hate even telling you this now. You don't need to worry about it, okay? This is my problem and I'll deal with it."

I had a sense that he was going to leave it there. "You can't do that. Don't ever do that."

"What?" he asked, clearly confused.

"How do you think that makes me feel? You want me to be honest with you, you want me to come to you whenever I'm ... struggling ... but then you won't come to me because you don't want to burden me? Don't you hear what you're saying? What if I'm adding to *your* list of problems?" I threw his words back at him, tears causing my voice to crack as I finished talking.

He laughed - not a full laugh but a laugh, nonetheless. I didn't think this was the time for laughing.

"Fate must be playing a joke," he said, giving me his first genuine smile of the day.

"What do you mean?" I asked. He raised his hand towards my face again and I felt the moisture on my cheek as he wiped away a falling tear.

"I'm afraid of adding to your problems, you're afraid of adding to mine. So, nobody says anything. Still, we need each other."

I sighed with relief. "Good," I chuckled, "'cos it sounded like you were gonna leave me there."

271

"What? Don't be ridiculous," he said as he pulled his arms around me and brought me in close. "I am going nowhere."

"But don't lie to me," I said, "I don't want you saying things are fine when they're not." He pulled away from the embrace and held my face in his hands, allowing our foreheads to touch. "Maybe if we share our list of problems, it won't be so bad."

He laughed again and kissed me firmly on the lips. "I promise."

30.

The exams were looming upon us. The end of the year had arrived and suddenly the dreaded Leaving Certificate examinations commenced. We had been warned about them for so long; the end result of our school careers that was sure to shape the rest of our lives and determine whether or not we'd achieve our dreams. It all seemed rather pointless to me. I knew in the deepest recesses of my heart that I wanted nothing more than to draw and paint for the rest of my life. The idea of making a livelihood out of my passion seemed wonderful. So why would I need to know about trigonometry?

It seemed ridiculous for a college to determine my ability based on my aptitude for subjects I would never use again. However, the portfolio was also hugely important, maybe even more so. If you did well enough with the portfolio, it wouldn't matter if you failed an exam or two. In the end, grades and a strong body of work would seal my fate.

The Crawford College in Cork had always seemed

the obvious place for me to go. I would daydream about walking through the doors with my over-sized portfolio folder slung over my shoulder. I dreamed about stepping into the interview room and expressing my desire for art and for my right to be there. They would beam up at me and welcome me with open arms. I'd spend each day surrounded in art, being taught by true masters to whom I could never measure up.

I wanted to hold on to that vision and believe in it wholeheartedly. My stomach was beginning to churn at the thought of the impending assessment.

I mentioned the assessment to Dr. Murphy as the date drew nearer. The pit in my stomach grew with each passing day but I tried to ignore it, instead attempting to hold on to that ray of hope.

"Are you prepared?" she asked me. I had gathered every piece of art I had created over the years, even unearthing old sketchbooks to go with the portfolio. I had gathered my 'secret' drawings - the ones I never wanted anyone to see and now barely even remembered doing. I flicked through each one, almost amazed at their content, their expression and their message. I hesitated to include them in the portfolio for I knew that they spoke of the torment in my mind, they screamed it, proclaimed it, made it obvious that I had fallen far down. However, I also considered them among some of my best work; they were raw and unbiased, uninfluenced and thus original.

274

I decided to show Dr. Murphy to get someone's opinion on them. She already knew about my craziness and the darkness surrounding my depression, and so I felt no shame in showing them to her. I couldn't show them to my parents or even to Michael for fear of how they'd react.

"I don't know if I should include these," I said, pulling the stack of pages out from my bag which were stored safely in my sketchbook to keep them from getting damaged. "I thought, maybe, you could look at them and tell me what you think."

"Oh, well, I'm no art critic," she joked. I liked the fact that she used humour with me sometimes and that she tried to create an informal atmosphere when we talked. After a while, I began to see her as a friend as well as a psychologist.

"Well, that's not what I'm worried about really," I confessed, "I mean, I think they're good, they're just ... personal." I felt that word best described my conflict. She nodded as if she understood.

"Well, I'll try my best," she said and held out her hand to take the drawings.

I handed them over shakily, telling myself repeatedly that it didn't matter if they altered what she thought about me. At the same time, I also knew that if she couldn't bear to look at them, I could never show them to anyone else, much less a prolific college's examiner. This was a test and one I needed to perform well in.

I waited impatiently as she went through each drawing. I watched her face eagerly to try to gauge her reaction and guess what she was thinking. She was very good at keeping a neutral expression, her poker face strong, as was to be expected in her line of work.

I waited and watched as she glanced over the last image. I thought I saw her shoulders tense at one point, but the movement was too subtle to be sure.

She placed the images down on the desk beside her and turned to face me. She put a smile back on her face and I wondered how forced it was. "These are very interesting images. You certainly have a very great talent, Samantha," she said, as perkily as ever.

"T-thank you," I said.

"This image in particular," she motioned towards the one that lay on top of the pile, "It's really quite impressive. The emotion you clearly put into this is just flowing off of it." I glanced down at the image on the desk. I knew this one well, even though I had drawn it so long ago. It was probably one of my favourites too. The image showed a person gripping their head, screaming silently whilst their mind sprayed off, piece by piece into the distance. "I don't know why you were so hesitant. These show that you are very talented and creative, and can invoke such strong feelings through your art.

"Why are you so worried about these?"

"I guess I thought ..." I searched for the words for a moment. "I thought they might be ... weird. I thought maybe they'd see these images and think ... that I'm insane or something." I tried to laugh it off, but she was regarding me very seriously.

"You know some of the greatest artists of our time had their own demons, and some may argue that those demons are what made them great. These are images that only you can see, that only you can create. Sure, some people may feel uncomfortable when looking at them, but what is the purpose of art if not to make people feel things?

"You have been through quite a lot in your short life and I am certain that you have so much to say. You just need to be a little less afraid, a little less concerned about what others may say in response. If those examiners are able to look at these images think, "*Wow*," and then not be able to stop thinking about them for days afterwards, then you have done your job as an artist.

"Art is there to make people think, and you have some perfect examples on your hands here."

Her words gave me a new sense of clarity and I felt that I had no choice but to submit them. I included them alongside other less emotive pieces of work in an attempt to soften their potential impact – that was assuming they would create one of course.

I allowed myself to feel confident as I dragged my

277

large portfolio to the city and brought it through those giant doors of the college. I stuck a sticker with my name and designated number on my portfolio of work and watched it disappear behind closed doors. I was told to return a few hours later to collect it.

***

Dad came with me that day and tried his best to distract me from my anxieties. We roamed around some of the shops in the city that I rarely got to see, just to waste time. We drank coffee in a quaint, vintage-style café whilst my mind envisioned the many different scenarios of the examiners analysing my work and reacting to it. I imagined shocked faces of awe intermixed with guffawed reactions of dismay. I imagined them slamming the folder shut after just one picture, deciding it wouldn't even be worth their time to see them all. I saw them laughing as they flicked through, wondering why anyone had bothered telling me to try.

`Try not to worry so much`

Michael texted me while I nervously waited. I told him everything I was thinking and everything I was imagining.

`That's just your`

```
self-doubt
taking over but
trust me,
it's wrong. You're
incredible.
```

I wanted to believe it, or at least pretend to believe it, but I couldn't stop imagining what the examiners were thinking, what they were saying, and I was beginning to feel hopeless. I just knew it wasn't good.

I returned a few hours later – the intervening hours seeming to have dragged on for an eternity - to pick up the portfolio. There were a bundle of identical folders stacked in the entrance hall of the college, each one filled with so much work, passion and hope. It occurred to me then how many others had similar dreams to me and that I wasn't the only one depending on this place.

I plucked my folder out of the pile and stood waiting for a moment. Surely there was more to it than this? I watched other hopeful students collect their folders and leave through the front doors. The aura of failure was emanating up through me, directly from the pages within my large folder.

I pulled the folders strap over my shoulder and began to leave. My dad asked someone when I'd get the results (I didn't even think to) and they said within a couple of weeks which was quite a while before my exam results would be released. The knot in my stomach had somehow morphed into a complete abyss.

31.

The Leaving Certificate exams came and went in a hurry. For so long, it had been this far-off event that had always been out of reach, but now it was here and had become a reality. My hand cramped as it laboured through page after page of the English examination paper. For some reason, the teacher had proclaimed that at least six pages were expected for the questions offering the most marks. There was no way I could write that much in under two hours, let alone do it several times over. I'd be lucky if the entire exam amounted to six pages.

I wrote about the trials of Billy Elliot and how he overcame gender and cultural stereotypes to become the greatest of dancers. It was a story I had come to love, and I tried to show that in my answers as I rambled on about 'cultural context' even though I barely knew what that meant.

I wrote line after line of Shakespeare, again wondering why it was so important that I needed to know these quotes which would be gone from my head as soon as I left the examination hall. I repeated every memorised phrase and meaning that I had crammed into my head over the past few weeks and hoped that my answers were at least comprehensible.

I struggled through the rest of the exams the best I could. I poured out all of the useless information in my head in the hope it would be enough to pass, as the ticking clock above warned me of my doom. After two weeks of constant examinations, the final paper was finally taken from my hands.

It took a while for the reality to set in that this was it; the day that I had spent so long waiting for, yearning for. I expected to feel ecstatic and overjoyed beyond words. Instead, I felt ... nothing.

As I strode through the hallway on that final day with Michael's hand in mine, I thought to myself that I would never be here again. I watched groups of students as they cried into one another's shoulder with a mixture of joy and sadness. I glanced over the open lockers in the hallways, their secrets now exposed for all to see. My eyes trailed past each closed classroom door, glimpsing the rooms beyond and still, I felt nothing.

I waited for the happiness to hit me. I had been looking forward to this moment for so long, when I'd walk through those doors as a secondary school student one last time. This was the change that I had been waiting for for so long. So why did I feel nothing at all?

"Are you all right?" Michael asked as we neared

the front door.

"It feels weird," I said simply.

"Weird? What's weird?" he said, pulling me to a stop outside.

"This is it. We're done."

His eyebrows perked up dramatically and he seemed to be holding his breath all of a sudden. It took me a second to realise what I'd said.

"I mean school. School. We're done with school."

He let out his breath slowly, "Don't DO that to me." We started laughing. "I guess it is weird. It's been a heck of a long time coming." He pulled me in close as we gazed up at the gates. "Gonna miss it?"

"No way." Perhaps the nothingness I was feeling was, in fact, numbness from the shock that this day had finally arrived. I felt a smile spread across my face as we started walking away from the building, leaving it in our dust.

"You're coming out tonight, right?" Michael asked me after a moment of silence.

"Out? Tonight? Why?" I said.

"I told you, right?" he said. Apparently my confusion was evident on my face as he quickly followed up, "Maybe, I didn't? Probably not, oops. There's a gig tonight. Well, sort of."

"A gig?" I repeated, wondering where this was going.

"Sort of. It's an open mic, someone organised it

just for us students to celebrate the end of term. And well ... Mark not-so-subtly signed my name up for it." He laughed nervously.

"You're gonna perform?" I said, thinking back to the one and only time I had seen him perform properly. I needed to hear and see him perform again.

He shrugged his shoulders as if he was unsure. "I guess so."

"Well, that's great. Of course I'll come," I assured him. How could I not?

"Great! Thank you." He pulled me in for a kiss that I wanted to last forever. "It's gonna be a special one, I promise you."

***

I had never really been to any proper 'gigs' before other than a Westlife concert when I was younger, but I wouldn't count that as a gig. The open mic event was in a local pub and I felt quite nervous about it. Whenever my family had dragged me out to some gathering at a pub in the past, I had never enjoyed it. The noise would be like a cacophony in my head so I'd give up trying to talk in the end and sit silently, hearing everything yet nothing at the same time.

I tried to tell myself that tonight wouldn't be like that. I pulled a hairbrush through my mess of hair and looked for something decent to wear. I didn't want to dress up (I didn't own anything very fancy anyway) but I tried to make a bit more effort with my appearance than usual.

Mum took my hand and placed some money on my palm just as I was about to leave the house. She was almost too pleased that I was going out to a pub like a 'normal' person. I told her it was just a school thing, practically everyone from my year would be there, it wasn't a big deal - but the beaming smile remained on her face.

I made my way to the pub with a spring in my step. I hadn't felt this good in so long. I felt like it was finally happening; that things were finally changing for the better. This was just the start of my new life.

I braced myself at the entrance of the pub, taking a deep breath and protectively drawing my arms across my chest. I wished I had asked Mark or Cian to meet me here, since Michael of course couldn't. I told myself that I was being stupid, so I tried to shake off my nerves and released my arms. I pulled open the door and prepared for the forthcoming ambush. I anticipated having to shout immediately to even get a foot in the door, but the entranceway was surprisingly clear. The pub wasn't as crowded as I feared, but there were still a decent amount of people milling about.

Michael had told me the open mic session would start around eight p.m. I glanced at the clock on the wall and realised I was quite early, as usual.

Anxiously, I stepped inside and tried not to meet the eye of the bartender as he had already started to shoot glances at me. My throat was quickly running dry and I yearned for a Coke but thought I should find a familiar face first.

In the distance, a pair of hands began flailing in the air. It was Cian, waving frantically at me. Mark was sat opposite him and as he turned around to face me, he started waving too. My heart leapt in my chest as the anxiety of being alone eased and I happily approached them. I sat down beside Mark and tried to see if I could find Michael anywhere.

"Michael's not here, he's off getting ready." Mark answered my unspoken question. He was wearing his long hair loose for once which fell halfway down his back. I had never seen him without his ponytail before. He looked almost unrecognisable.

"I never knew your hair was that long," I said. It looked incredibly silky smooth and I had to resist the urge to reach out and stroke it.

"Oh, it feels so good," he said, comically flicking it back like he was in a shampoo advertisement. "Huh, I guess you've never seen me like this. They demand I tie it up in school."

"Really? Why?"

"'Cos I'm a dude," Mark said. Cian laughed in response. "You think I'm joking but I'm serious! It feels so good to be free." He meant this literally as he seamlessly pulled his fingers through his long hair, not a single tangle in sight.

"It looks better this way too," I noted, hoping he wouldn't take that badly.

"Oh, so much better," he agreed with joy.

Suddenly, I felt a warmth surround me as a pair of arms wrapped around me. "Hi," he said into my ear, turning to kiss me on the cheek fiercely. Cian made a gagging motion in response. "He's just jealous," Michael said, jumping down to sit beside Cian. He ruffled his hair, much to Cian's disgruntlement as he quickly smoothed it back down again. His blonde hair had grown a lot longer recently too.

"You disgust me," Cian said with a glare and a grimace. He suddenly looked like a Disney villain.

"So, what's the plan?" Mark piped in, "When's the maestro on?"

Michael laughed. "About another hour. There are a few people before me."

"How long do you get?" I asked, wondering if we were only going to get one quick song.

"About fifteen minutes," he responded with an air of nervousness, "So that's about three songs, maybe four."

"What're you playing? Still haven't told us," Cian asked, taking a gulp of his drink.

"And I'm not going to. It's a surprise," Michael said, flicking Cian on the nose.

"Boooooooring," Mark mocked and we all laughed.

We waited patiently for the first performer to take the stage. The crew for the night seemed to be taking an exceedingly long time setting everything up. The man on the stage repeatedly said, "One, two, one, two," into the mic, but he wasn't satisfied so kept shouting at the person at the sound desk who was stationed a long way from the stage. They really should've used walkie-talkies to make life easier for them both.

After what felt like an eternity later, the first person took to the stage and set up a keyboard. He introduced himself as James and I searched my mind in recognition. I think I had seen him around in the school but didn't share any classes with him, so didn't know him. I found it strange to think that I could be in the same building with someone for six years but never meet them and get acquainted.

I watched as his fingers danced across the keys, eliciting melodic notes that seemed to float in the air. His first couple of songs were a bit melancholic yet exceedingly beautiful as his angelic voice overlaid the lyrics. I found tears welling up in my eyes and wondered if this was the kind of celebration that was intended.

The pub was silent as he played and I knew that he, like Michael, had real talent as he brought everyone to tears.

Fifteen minutes elapsed and James took a bow,

gracefully embracing the crowd's applause. He quickly stowed away his keyboard and jumped off the stage happily.

"Thank God for that," Cian said. He shook himself dramatically, ridding himself of whatever James had done.

"You didn't like it?" Michael asked him.

"I almost fell asleep," Cian yawned exaggeratedly, to further emphasise his boredom.

"He was really good," Michael commented. "You don't know real talent."

"Yeah, but I know who to go to if I need a good lullaby," Cian joked.

"Well, he was good all right," Mark jumped in, "Those songs, though, those lyrics, kind of a downer. Thought we were having a party?"

Michael shrugged his shoulders. "Now that, I have to agree with."

After another few minutes, a second person took to the stage with a guitar in hand. It was a girl this time named Lydia, whose set was a lot more upbeat. She played a lot of songs that I had heard on the radio, even one from the 80s. Even though it was just Lydia and her guitar, she managed to get people in the crowd dancing and the atmosphere of the place immediately picked up. The onlookers seemed genuinely disheartened when she left the stage.

"Aw, it was just getting started," Cian said, adding

to the disappointment and encores from the crowd.

"Hey, it's almost my turn," Michael said. His leg was shaking beneath the table, making the whole floor seem to quake. I could see the sweat building up on his brow. "I'm glad I'm not following her, though. I hope the next guy sucks."

"Shut up, you'll do great," I said, hoping my words were enough to give him a little boost of confidence.

He smiled back at me and said, "Thank you."

I had never seen him as nervous as this and didn't really know what to do to make it better or to make him feel more at ease.

"Do you get stage fright?" I wondered aloud.

"No, not really, but, you know, I haven't properly performed before. Not on my own, not like this," he said, glancing around. The crowd had been steadily growing since the start of the night and the pub was properly packed now.

"Whoa, it got busy fast," Mark commented, turning around to take in the growing crowd.

"Just my luck," Michael sighed.

"Hey, we'll come up to the stage and you can just focus on us, ignore everyone else? If that helps," I suggested.

"Unless you'd rather ignore us too," Mark added.

"No, I think that might help actually. Thanks, Sam." I felt glad that I could help him, even in some small way. I hoped that maybe three familiar faces up front would be enough to stem the anxiety caused by the dozens of unfamiliar ones.

Thankfully, it seemed Michael's wish was granted as the person now performing on stage was nowhere near as good as the people before him. "He probably did this for a dare," Cian concluded as the performer failed to keep his voice in tune. He had simply put on a backing track and attempted to play the guitar along with it, but it felt horribly disjointed. He looked so happy to be up there though, having the time of his life and his energy began to spread through the crowd and kept things alive as he performed some terrible karaoke.

"Trust me, you're better than that," Mark whispered across to Michael as the performer finally left the stage. "Anyone's better than that."

"I'll take that as a compliment." Michael laughed. He did seem to be a bit calmer now, even at the expense of someone else being deemed terrible. "I guess I better go."

"Good luck. You'll do great," I said, hoping he'd believe my words. He kissed me fiercely right there in front of everyone, much to the others' embarrassment.

He left the three of us sitting at the table and went up towards the stage to prepare himself. A minute later, Cian led the three of us towards the front of the stage, shouting, "Number one fans here!" to get through the crowd. I was glad for his gusto; I wouldn't have been able to push through on my own, I would've just stayed at the back. A number of people cast us menacing glares as we pushed past them, but I tried not to care.

Finally, we made our way towards the front of the crowd and got a spot at the foot of the stage. It looked so much bigger and so much more intimidating from here. Someone came onto the stage and placed a stool beside the microphone before hastily running off again. The crowd around me seemed to be growing even more now and I tried to ignore the people pressing into my back. The noise had grown a lot, too, in just a few minutes and I could barely make out what Cian and Mark were saying beside me, so I just focused on the stage and waited.

After what felt like the longest ten minutes, I finally found Michael's face again in the shadows at the back of the stage as he crept slowly into the light. He seemed like the coming of an ethereal angel as the lights on the stage lit up his features, his shadow casting long and sharp along the wooden floor. He held a guitar in his hand which seemed to have been with him for years which the numerous stickers and scratches littering its surface suggested. He would tell me later how it had once belonged to his dad so he wouldn't ever give it away. It was precious to him and he believed that its age offered a more unique sound, one of wisdom and experience.

He positioned himself on the stool beside the

microphone and made one last check to ensure the guitar was perfectly tuned. He looked almost lonely up there on his own, but he also looked like he was in his element. This was exactly where he belonged.

Satisfied that the guitar was ready, he finally looked up towards the crowd and I managed to catch his eye. I mouthed more encouragement and wishes of luck to him and even stupidly gave him the thumbs up which seemed to make him laugh. Hopefully, that was a good sign.

"Hello," he said into the microphone. His voice shot out around the room and seemed to reverberate in my eardrums, "I'm Michael." The nervousness in his voice was obvious as he fiddled with the strings on the guitar. "I have a few songs I'd like to perform tonight. Some I've written, some I haven't." He shrugged like it was no big deal.

He worked his way through the first song with calm and ease. As his fingers plucked and strummed the strings, a feeling of familiarity washed over me. He was playing *Iris*, the song from the CD he gave me, the one that stood out above all the others. He had my complete attention. Suddenly no one else was there, he was all I could see, all I could hear and all I could feel. He played it perfectly and seemed to be singing the words right at me with intense passion and meaning. I knew he felt it too. That song was ours.

I wasn't the only one that knew the song, of

293

course. As the chorus soared, the crowd began to sing along, not one voice silent, so that his was almost drowned out. I wanted to tell them all to shut up, but then again, the chorus of pained words was something not to be silenced. "Good idea to choose a popular one," Cian said into my ear as the song finished. I didn't want it to end.

He played a couple of songs after that, covers of other well-known songs perhaps considered a bit more light-hearted than the first. The crowd even began to clap along with the beat at times and I found myself beaming up at him, watching him play effortlessly with joy written across his face as the crowd echoed the melody.

"Thank you," he said after finishing another song. His time was almost up now, I knew. "You guys are great. Thank you. Now, for this last one-" The crowd audibly booed, causing him to laugh modestly. "This is a special one. One I've been working on for a long time and it means a lot to me." He looked me right in the eye as he said, "I wrote it for someone I know, about them even; a person who has really changed my life."

"*Blech*," Cian mockingly shouted.

"Shut up," Michael said back, laughingly. "I wanted to write something to show them how I feel and how much they mean to me. Needless to say, we've both been through a lot and well, I'll let the song do the rest of the talking. This is *Hold On*." He never directly said it was for me, not wanting to share our story with everyone because it was ours and ours alone but still, I knew.

The melody swam over me as I listened. I wanted to crawl up and listen even closer. The notes playing through the guitar were gentle yet determined. They spoke of fear and excitement at the same time.

The guitar's introduction eased as he brought in the lyrics:

In a world so dark
You just gotta
Let the light in

Can't you see me
I'm standing right here
Just let me in

My heart ached as I heard the meaning behind his words. The repeated chorus was simple yet powerful, his voice seeming to ache as he pleaded:

Just hold on
Hold on for me

His face showed his expression even more as he sung, as his voice grew almost hoarse with the passion behind his words and I thought I would break right there

295

and then.

My mind floated back to that night, to that night when I had given up, to that night when the darkness had overtaken me. I knew I had hurt him; I knew he felt like my mistake had betrayed him. But now his words were telling me that it's okay, he understood what it's like to feel that way but to hold on anyway ... for him.

> *Don't you know the dead*
> *The dead can't feel*
> *So please just stay*
> *You will be healed*

As he sung out the chorus one last time, the air in the place had frozen as everyone listened in silence, captivated by his words. I couldn't move as our eyes locked. Suddenly, the sound of applause shattered through the air, but still I remained unmoving.

The crowd began to disperse slightly as Michael made his way off the stage. "Are you all right?" Cian asked beside me when I was finally able to hear through the ringing in my ears.

"I'm fine, yeah," I said, shaking myself a little as if to wake up.

"That was quite powerful, all right," Cian said, no doubt taking in my reaction. That was one way to put it.

Without another word, I pulled away from the crowd, leaving Mark and Cian and made my way towards the back of the stage. I found Michael within moments. He looked a bit surprised to see me. I walked straight towards him without stopping and wrapped my arms around his neck.

As he returned the embrace, I whispered, "I'm so sorry," into his ear.

"What?" He seemed genuinely confused. I couldn't hold the tears back anymore as I begun to tremble in his arms. "No, no," he said, as if suddenly understanding what I had concluded. "That is not what I meant. I didn't mean to ... guilt you or whatever, if that's what you think?" He wiped the tear sliding down my face. "I just, I know it's tough and I just wanted ... to give you something ... a lot more meaningful than someone else's words. My own." He kissed me and pulled me back in for an embrace that I hoped would never end.

"I love you, you know ... in case it wasn't obvious," he joked.

A laugh mingled with my tears. "I love you, too."

32.

We stayed for the remaining acts in the pub, but I didn't much care to listen to any of them. None of them mattered as none of them could've possibly compared to Michael's performance. Eventually, time was called and we were ushered out of the pub. Michael and I left together, hand in hand, and split off from Mark and Cian. I clung desperately to each passing minute, willing the time to slow down.

Despite my wish, time continued to go too fast. Night had fallen heavily upon us and the streetlamps were barely bright enough to light the way. We walked aimlessly and talked about nothing. It was cold as usual, so I pulled my coat even tighter around myself to fend off the wind.

There was not a single other person in sight which gave the place an eerie feel. Everywhere was shutting down for the night and the lights in passing houses were steadily being flicked off.

"We'll get out of this place someday, right?" Michael asked. "You and me." He let go of my hand and wrapped his arm around my shoulder. I felt his warmth emanating through my clothes as I looked up at him. His eyes seemed to be filled with a worldly wonder, perhaps dreaming of far off places where nothing but happiness existed.

"Of course," I said. I yearned, more than anything, to get out of this town someday too; to live in a bustling city where there was never a dull day. Those days still felt so far away. "Where do you want to go?"

"Anywhere, really," he said, truly meaning it. "Anywhere but here. Sometimes this town makes me feel ... trapped. Like I have no choice but to just wait."

"I know what you mean," I said. I knew that feeling all too well. "I hate feeling like I just have to go with the flow, that there's nothing I can do. I want to be happy now, not later."

"You're not happy?" He sounded offended.

"No, no, I am. I am happy. I'm so happy with you ... but ... it's weird. It's like I still want more. I know that sounds so selfish, but I just feel like there should be more ... than this."

"We'll find it someday. We'll find the place we belong, where we were always meant to be. Someday – someday soon." I felt the yearning in his heart echoing mine. A buzzing sound interrupted my train of thought. I realised it was a phone ringing and instinctively reached for the one lying in my pocket, but it lay motionless in my hand.

"Sorry, that's me," he said, pulling away rather reluctantly. I knew immediately who it was calling him. His face dropped as he read the name lit up on the screen.

"Don't answer it," I said, without thinking. I knew I had no right to interfere, it wasn't really my business, as he often reminded me. She would usually call him at some point whenever we spent time together. In my mind, I had already predicted the conversation to its conclusion. My heart grew heavy. I didn't want tonight to be ruined.

He smiled apologetically at me as he answered the phone, stepping a few feet away. I allowed him his privacy, but couldn't help overhear his side of the conversation, "I can't ... I'll be home later ... later, I promise ... You can't ... what?"

I waited impatiently as I watched his shoulders grow increasingly more tense with agitation. I tried to keep my anger and growing sadness in check as I anticipated the outcome.

He hung up the phone and returned to me. "I'm sorry," he said. His expression told me the rest.

"You have to leave?" I finished for him.

"I'm sorry," he repeated, "I wish I didn't have to."

"You don't," I said, wishing that would be enough to make him stay.

"Sam, don't be upset. I have to go."

"Why? The more you go, the more she'll know

you'll come," I said, trying to keep the anger out of my voice. I worried I had already overstepped as tears threatened to fall down my face. "Don't go."

He sighed, as if some part of him agreed with me. "It's complicated, Sam," he said a bit more sternly, "I really am so sorry, but I have to go."

I tried again to make him stay, but I knew I would only annoy him more if I pushed too hard. There was nothing I could do. I tried to tell myself that it wasn't his fault. Maybe she was in trouble? He always said it was never her fault either, that she was unwell and didn't really mean any of it, but that could never excuse it. Nothing could excuse the fear I felt as he walked away, wondering where the next batch of bruises would appear upon his skin.

I felt completely powerless as I dragged myself home, the elation of the open mic event completely lost. I tried to steady my racing heart, telling myself that he would be okay, I'd see him again soon and things would be different soon, especially once we got to college.

Once I was finally home, I passed by the living room where my parents were watching TV. I got through the usual questions of how the night was whilst avoiding the ending. I exaggerated my tiredness and headed towards my room.

"You're home early," Gerard said, making me jump as he exited the bathroom. "Have a good night?"

"Yeah, it was fine," I said. Gerard looked at me

questioningly. I quickly corrected myself, "It was great, actually. Sorry, I'm really tired." Real tiredness was actually beginning to hit me now.

"Heh, yeah, you look it," he laughed, "Hope you had fun." He began walking past me towards his own bedroom, and for a brief moment I considered telling him everything, just to get it off my chest. He paused as he was about to close his door and asked, "You sure you're okay? You two have a fight or something?"

I held back the truth. "No, it's fine. He just had to head home early. That's all."

"Ah," he said as if he understood. "That happens. Well, you know where I am if you wanna talk."

"I know," I said. He said that a lot nowadays, ever since ... then. I pondered the idea as he closed the door and I continued into my room. I wanted to tell him. I wanted to tell someone.

I was sworn to secrecy, but did that really matter anymore?

Maybe I needed to betray my promise in order to help Michael, but I couldn't bear the thought of him hating me. I lay down on my bed fully clothed as my mind began to reel with possibilities. My eyes grew heavier and I allowed the drowsiness to overtake me.

A loud, irritating sound roused me suddenly. I moaned loudly, turning over onto my side. As I woke up fully, I realised the noise was my phone ringing. I immediately picked it up, thinking of Michael.

"Hello?" I asked, trying to push my drowsiness aside.

"S-Sam?" He spoke so quietly I barely heard it, but it was loud enough to cause me to sit up, suddenly alert.

"Michael?" The phone was too close to his mouth as I could hear each one of his staggered breaths. "What's wrong?" I asked as a shiver began to creep up my spine.

"I'm so sorry," he continued to whisper. His breath stopped as a simultaneous bang echoed through the phone line. That noise reverberated right through me and I was instantly terrified.

"What's going on? What was that?" I asked even though I already knew.

"I don't know what to do. I don't know what to do." He repeated himself several times, his voice getting increasingly shakier at every utterance and I felt my heart crumble within my chest. "She won't listen. She won't listen."

"You need to get out of there. Right now." It sounded like he was whimpering and in my mind I pictured him curled up in the corner of his room like a frightened child. I yearned to leap through the phone line to protect him.

"I can't," he whispered, almost inaudibly. I wanted to ask why, but then I thought he had likely already tried. "I'm trapped." I could hear more crashing and banging in the background, his voice like that of a terrified child powerless against a giant monster.

"You have to call the guards," I told him. That was the only logical thing to do now.

"No, no, I can't." I expected that response as we had talked about it before. The Gardai were always out of the question. Despite her crimes, he never wanted her to get arrested, to be taken away, to be punished for something that wasn't her fault. I wondered if he still thought that now as he quivered alone in his room. "I need you."

I didn't know what he expected me to be able to do but I said, "Okay, I'm coming. Just stay right there. Stay away from her."

"Okay," he agreed in little more than a whisper. As I reluctantly hung up the phone, I started to dial 999, but then hesitated. He had told me not to but I felt now, more than ever, that I *had* to. My hands were shaking as I held the phone, my thumb poised over the dial button. My heart was hammering against my ribcage and I tried to keep my breathing steady. I couldn't think straight and I didn't know what to do.

Suddenly, I found myself cancelling the call and running out of my room, straight into Gerard's without even bothering to knock.

He turned around at his desk, startled at my unexpected presence. He quickly paused the game he was playing. "Sam? What's up?"

304

My body began to shake uncontrollably as the tears gushed from my eyes. Gerard jumped up from his chair and wrapped his arms around me until I managed to calm myself down enough to talk.

"What's wrong?" he asked, his tone increasingly concerned, "What's happened?"

"I need a lift to Michael's."

He checked the time on his phone. "What, now?" I hadn't even realised it was after one a.m. "Right now? Tell me what happened, why are you so upset?" He pleaded with me, his hand resting on my arm as a means of comfort, but the gesture gave me little.

"There's no time. I need to go. He's in trouble," I said, shaking off his hand and rushing to the stairs.

"What do you mean he's in trouble?"

"Please! I'll explain on the way, we need to go."

33.

After I had explained everything to him, Gerard hesitantly agreed to drive me to Michael's house. "Jesus," he said, after I had told him about the ongoing abuse and the terrifying phone call tonight, "When you came into me, I thought you two had broken up or something but this ... was the last thing I would've guessed."

We were driving through the streets quickly, but still not quick enough for me. I sat, restless, in the passenger seat, my legs jerking up and down in agitation as I watched the town's buildings pass by.

I had never been inside Michael's house before but had passed by it with him, so I was confident that I could find it.

"He doesn't want to involve the guards," I said, explaining why the obvious plan hadn't been implemented. "He doesn't want to just lock her away or whatever."

"But now he's scared for his life," Gerard surmised.

"It sure sounded like it," I said. That phone call continued to re-play in my head, on repeat. "It's just up here," I said as we turned into an estate towards the edge of town.

Although Michael's house sat in the middle of a row of identical properties, I had no doubt that I would recognise it. It was almost like it was surrounded by an aura that was pulling me towards it. I pointed it out to Gerard as we drew near.

"You're not going in," Gerard said, as he parked the car outside the house.

"What? Of course I'm going in."

"Not if there's someone in there as violent as you say there is."

"I have to go in there. I have to help him." There was no way he was going to make me sit this one out. I couldn't just wait patiently in the car like a good little girl while someone I loved might be hurt.

He sighed, knowing I'd follow him. "Fine. But stay behind me and walk slowly."

As we made our way through the front garden, I paid extra attention to the sounds around me, waiting to hear any shouting or loud noises like the ones I had heard on the phone, but there was nothing except the sound of the night in the air.

"The door's open," Gerard said quietly, as we reached the doorstep.

"What?" I stepped around him to see more clearly

and sure enough, the front door had been left open - not wide open - but enough to welcome intruders. The house was eerily quiet, and a chill ran down my spine.

"Maybe he forgot to close it," I said, hoping Michael had somehow escaped and ran away.

Gerard knocked gently on the door, just loud enough to be heard. "Hello?" he said into the hallway, as he eased the door open slowly. I tried to ignore the hammering of my heart as I listened for anything unusual - any sound at all – but there was just silence.

Gerard carefully stepped into the hallway and I followed closely behind. He picked up an umbrella which was standing against the wall.

"What are you doing?" I asked.

"Just in case," he said. I doubted an umbrella would do much in the way of offering a defence, but it was better than nothing.

We crept along the hallway and peered into the kitchen and living room. The rooms had been decimated, as if a hurricane had swept through, leaving barely anything but the walls and furniture intact. Plates lay shattered across the kitchen tiles and shards of glass from broken picture frames littered the living room floor like destroyed memories.

"He might still be upstairs," I said, assuming he had called me from the safety of his bedroom. Gerard nodded in agreement as he regarded the destruction of the house.

The stairs creaked under the weight of our feet as we made our way up. "Michael?" I called out. I tried to remain calm as nothing but silence answered me.

Splitting up, we searched each of the rooms in turn. The first one I entered was one which appeared to be his mother's bedroom. I wanted to leave immediately, but the collection of photographs strewn on the bed caught my attention. I moved towards them for a closer look. It was like looking into a stranger's past. One of the pictures showed a bride and groom, posing outside some church doors, looking completely overjoyed. I presumed they were Michael's parents. In another photograph, the same two people looked very happy as the woman cradled her pregnancy bump. A third picture had captured Michael with his dad who was holding a guitar as if trying to teach his son how to play. Tears started to well up in my eyes. Looking over those photographs made me think that maybe Michael was right, maybe his mother had never come to terms with the death of her beloved husband.

I left the room quickly, the feeling of trepidation growing ever stronger.

Finally, I made my way to the last room at the end of the hallway and as soon as I entered it, I knew it was his. His guitar stood propped against the side of his bed and his walls were adorned with posters of his favourite musicians. I called out his name repeatedly, thinking he could be cowering somewhere out of sight, too shaken to move or speak.

"Sam, no one's here," Gerard said, following me into Michael's room.

Quickly, I pulled my phone out of my pocket and dialled Michael's number. It was worth a shot, I thought. A ringing sound echoed through the room and my heart skipped a beat.

I followed the sound and realised that it was coming from the large built-in wardrobe. I lowered the phone from my ear as I lay a shaking hand on the wardrobe door handle and pulled it wide open. I fell to my knees as I spotted the distinct light of a phone screen illuminating the space.

My heart plummeted as I realised this was where he had been hiding when he called me earlier, terrified.

I picked up his phone and ended the call.

***

I felt almost too weak to stand as we left the house still no closer to finding Michael. He had trusted me, relied on me, but I hadn't arrived fast enough. I had failed.

I sat on top of the garden wall while Gerard pulled out his phone and began to dial a number. "We've gotta report this, Sam, okay? That was not a good scene in there. If he's missing and she's unstable, we've gotta call it."

I knew he was right - of course I did. I would have

to forget my promise if it meant saving his life. "I know." I listened to Gerard as he explained to the operator what had happened. As he leaned against the car, something stirred in my memory; I remembered that day at school when I had seen his mother, standing beside a red, beaten-up old car, howling at Michael. I jumped down from the wall and looked around the area. The car wasn't there.

"The car," I said softly.

"What?" Gerard turned to me, still on the phone.

"The car's gone." Michael's motorbike was still there but the red car was gone. "Her car. It's gone."

"We think she might have taken him in her car, it's missing too," Gerard said into the phone, relaying my observation. "Sam, what kind of car, do you know?"

I had no idea about the different car models. "Red, small and old," was the best description I could offer.

"We're not sure," he was speaking into the phone again, "Just small, red, a bit old-looking."

I wondered what good such a vague description would do as it was far from unique. It was useless and I had failed him again.

"Sam," Gerard said, now off the phone and grabbing me by the shoulders as I paced around restlessly. "They'll find him. I promise you. C'mon." As he guided me back towards the car, I thought my shaking legs would give way at any minute.

I didn't want to leave. I wanted to stay there and

wait for him, even though I knew that was pointless. I couldn't bear the thought of returning home though without knowing what had happened.

After driving for a few minutes, Gerard broke the silence, "All right, here's what we'll do. Instead of going straight home, we'll drive around for a while, see if we can spot the car, ask anyone who may be around if they've seen it. The guards will be doing that too, but we'll help speed it up."

I tried to express my gratitude, but could barely say a word because of the effort it was taking just to control my emotions. We drove aimlessly around the town, repeatedly circling back around the same number of streets and praying for some sort of clue, but we spotted nothing out of the ordinary. As the feeling of fear multiplied by the second, my hopes diminished just as quickly.

We couldn't find many people walking around at this time of night and the few who were around were completely unable to help us. It was hopeless, no one was paying attention.

"Hey, sorry," Gerard said, pulling over to the kerb beside an elderly couple, "Any chance you saw a small, red, old-looking car pass this way? My friend left quite upset and I just wanna make sure she's okay, but can't get in touch." He had fabricated that story each time. I wondered if anyone believed it.

I anticipated the same, "No, sorry," response we'd

received so far, but instead the man said, "Yeah, feckin' hell, she just went speeding past here with a right face on 'er."

The woman chimed in, "Yes, right up that way, straight out of town. There was someone else in the car too - asleep, I think."

"Oh God. Thank you so much," Gerard said, "Sorry to have bothered you." We quickly sped off.

"They saw it?" I asked, not wanting to raise my hopes.

"Yeah. She left town." He started accelerating in the hope of catching up with her, although she had a head start on us. I allowed myself to feel a glimmer of hope again. At least she had been seen.

The woman's words repeated in my head. "She said he was asleep."

"Hmm?" Gerard said, his eyes fixed on the road.

"That woman - she said there was someone else in the car but they were asleep. Why would he be asleep?" The fear rose up within me again.

"She might have seen wrong. He'll be fine, Sam."

I tried to hang onto those words as we made our way out of town. As the time ticked by, I realised that I recognised this particular patch of road and found my eyes glancing leftwards as I remembered our usual spot; the place where Michael had taken me many times when he'd wanted to get away from it all. At the highest point of the cliff, where we shared our first kiss, shone two bright, rectangular lights.

"Ger." I didn't want to believe my eyes; it couldn't be. He didn't seem to hear me and was almost past the spot completely. "Ger, stop!"

"What?" My sudden loud voice startled him as he quickly put his foot on the brake. The seatbelt pulled against me as the car lurched to a stop.

"Up there. The cliff." My heart was pounding faster than ever before. I looked again to make sure I wasn't mistaken or hallucinating.

I waited for Gerard's reaction to confirm he was seeing it too. The light from the moon was reflecting off of the car's unmistakable red roof.

"Holy shit. No way. What the *fuck* is she doing up there? We can't drive up there!"

I was out of the car before he could say anymore.

314

34.

My legs moved faster than they had ever moved before. I could feel the adrenaline rushing through my veins as I focused on the car in the distance, just barely visible thanks to the glowing headlights.

It was like the type of dream where you're endlessly running but can't seem to get anywhere, no matter how fast you run. I urged my feet to move faster, but it felt like I would never make it. I could hear Gerard running behind me and it wasn't long before he had caught up. He grabbed me by the arm, forcing me to stop.

"Let go of me!" I shouted at him. I needed to get to that car and get him out. I had to save him.

"Samantha, you need to be careful!" he said sternly. Gerard rarely used my full name, causing him to sound more serious than I had ever heard him. "You can't just run up there. They're way too close to the edge."

The car was still so far away from us. I could just about make out the outline of the edge of the cliff,

315

kissing the car's front wheels. My heart quickened within my chest.

"That's exactly why I have to get there." I tried not to yell.

I shrugged off Gerard's grip and ran towards the car again. "Samantha!" he yelled after me. I got a good bit closer to the car, but Gerard caught me once again.

"It's too dangerous. We need to call for help."

I knew he was right. My heart was urging my legs to keep going, but my head knew I could make it worse. I felt Gerard grip my arm, pleading with me.

Right then, I saw Michael's face pressed up against the window on the passenger's side. He looked like he was asleep, just as that woman had said. Even from this distance, I could see his face was bloody and beaten.

"Michael!" The scream escaped from my lungs as I pulled myself from Gerard's grip. My heart pounded against my ribcage as the roar of the engine reverberated in the air. The car began to reverse slightly back down the hill. Maybe she had changed her mind?

Suddenly, the car stopped again. I ran with all my might until I reached it. I had made it at last. I tried to pull open the passenger door, Michael still leaning against it, but it wouldn't budge because of course, she had locked it. I looked in through the window and saw her sitting there, her eyes gazing forwards, completely ignoring me.

I knocked softly on the window, trying not to startle her. I tried to remain calm as I pleaded, "Open the door," but my shaking voice made my anxiety obvious. I repeated the command over and over, getting louder with each knock. But still, Michael didn't move and neither did she.

After a while, as my laboured breath made it difficult to speak, I stopped shouting and instead just stood watching her. Slowly, she turned her head to face me. I wanted to scream at her, to demand answers, but the face that looked back at me was an empty one, devoid of any expression. There was no one there to reason with anymore.

She faced forwards again and turned the key in the ignition. I started to shout again, banging harshly on the glass, pulling so hard on the door handle that my hands hurt. But I was powerless.

The car began to move towards the edge of the cliff and I gripped the door handle, as if my strength alone could hold it back. Gerard ran up behind me and wrapped his arms around me, pulling my hand away from the car. I screamed myself hoarse as the car gained speed, unstoppable as it raced towards the precipice.

I watched in horror as the car flew over the edge and disappeared into the abyss below. The sound of the car hitting the water broke me as it echoed in the wind.

I tore myself from Gerard's grip and ran up towards the edge, as if I still had a chance of stopping it.

He caught me again before I could get that far.

"Sam!" Gerard screamed at me. He picked me up in his arms like I was a child and brought me away from the edge again. He placed me firmly on the ground and held me still. "Sam, listen to me!"

I could barely hear him over the sound of my sobbing, over the sound of my world imploding. He held my face in his hands and looked directly into my eyes, trying to get me to focus on him. "You need to stay right here. Do you hear me? Right here!" I didn't have the strength to move, even if I wanted to. "You need to stay here and call for help. Do you hear me, Sam?"

I wanted to say, "of course I hear you, I'm not stupid," but every time I tried to speak, I just cried instead. Nodding was all I could do.

Reluctantly, he let me go and hurried away. I didn't know where he was going; I didn't want him to leave me. As I sat, motionless, I saw his blurry silhouette through the fogginess of my tears until he ran down the other side of the hill and out of view. *The beach*, I remembered. Of course. I had forgotten about the path leading to the water in my grief. Maybe there was still a chance. Maybe we could still save Michael.

I pulled the phone out of my pocket and dialled 999 with shaking hands. I relayed what I could, trying to push through my panicking nerves. I tried to tell them where we were although I didn't really know - "The road out of town," wasn't much for them to go on. I felt completely hopeless and started to panic, thoughts flowing through my mind telling me I couldn't do this, that I would fail yet again when it literally mattered the most. Looking out ahead of me, I saw the headlights of Gerard's car. I quickly described it to the woman on the phone.

She promised she would pass on the message to the people who had already gone out in response to our last call. Gerard still wasn't back, so I forced my aching body off the ground and followed the same path he had taken. It took me a couple of minutes to drag my shaking legs down to the shore. On the edge of the water, in danger of being washed away, was Gerard's jacket. Even though it was soaking wet, I picked it up and held it close to me.

I couldn't believe he had actually jumped in. Fear and panic began to grip me again as my eyes frantically searched the surface of the water, begging for some sort of sign - any sign – that he was all right. I couldn't lose them both; I just couldn't.

I fell to my knees on the soft earth and howled out their names. It felt like an eternity as I waited to see some sign of life.

How could he stay down there so long?

I tried to get myself to move. I wanted to jump in after them, and even though my swimming skills were limited, I needed to try. But I couldn't move - the ground was holding me in place - so instead, I wept and waited.

Finally, a sound broke through the air. Something was moving in the water. I couldn't make it out at first and I thought maybe my hope was causing me to hallucinate. After a long minute, my heart rate began to quickly escalate as I saw Gerard, and he wasn't alone.

"Gerard!" I screamed with all my might. Without thinking, I abandoned the jacket and started walking into the water towards him. Gerard had Michael's arm draped around his shoulders. His face kept dipping into the water with the motion of Gerard's strokes; he still wasn't awake.

I felt too stunned to move so I just stood there, knee-deep in water, waiting for them to reach me. Gerard barely looked at me as he kept his eyes trained on the shore. He pushed himself forwards for the last stretch before he was able to stand. Then, as if he was weightless, he lifted Michael up into his arms and waded the rest of the way through the water with him.

He laid Michael down on the ground, just as the sirens sounded. My legs were shaking as I rushed over to them. Michael wasn't moving and his skin was grey and lifeless. My mind was completely blank as I just stood there, watching helplessly.

"Ger ..." I said. Gerard placed his hands over Michael's chest, rhythmically pressing down again and again, counting under his breath. He paused the compression and pinched Michael's nostrils closed with one hand while he breathed air into his lungs.

I crumpled at the sight, falling to my knees beside them. Gerard was trying to resuscitate him ... because he had died. I gripped Michael's frozen hand, limp and unresponsive in mine. "Please ... Please don't do this to me," I said, as if this was all his fault.

Gerard continued administering CPR for what felt like the longest time ever. I could hear running footsteps in the distance; the paramedics were on their way. Gerard bent down to give Michael more air and recoiled suddenly as Michael's body convulsed. I jolted back, too, in response to the unexpected movement.

Gerard quickly turned Michael onto his side to allow the water to escape his lungs and allow him to breathe. Relief broke through my numbness as the sound of his tortured breathing confirmed he was alive. Gerard held him in place as the paramedics swarmed around us. Tears were flowing ceaselessly down my face as I gripped his hand even tighter.

A hand gripped my shoulder. "Miss?" A stranger's voice. I focused my attention on Michael's face, desperate to make sure he was okay. His eyes flickered open for just a moment, catching mine.

"Miss?" The stranger spoke again. "Miss, you need to step away. We'll look after him, but you need to step away."

I didn't want to leave him, not for a minute, even though I knew I had to. The paramedics were the only ones who could help him right now.

I reluctantly let go of his hand as one of the crew pulled me away. They wrapped a blanket around my shoulders and moved me off to the side. I searched around to find Gerard and saw a medic attending to him too, but he was avidly pushing them away. I ran over to him, ignoring the medics around me.

I wrapped my arms around Gerard's neck and held him closely. "Are you okay?" I asked through my tears.

"I'm fine, this guy's making a fuss," he joked, much to the paramedic's disdain, "Are *you* okay?"

"No." I laughed nervously and released my hold on him. I glanced over towards Michael to watch them lift him onto a stretcher, an oxygen mask strapped to his face. "Thank you so much," I said.

Gerard pulled me in tighter and whispered, "Don't thank me yet."

"What?" Michael was breathing now, he was going to be okay, wasn't he?

Gerard paused and sighed deeply. "I tried. I tried to get her out too. I don't know what it was, her belt was stuck or something, it just wouldn't give. And it looked like, like she had just … surrendered to it."

"Surrendered?" I asked, perplexed. I realised that I hadn't even thought about his mother and for a moment I felt awful for forgetting about her even though she was the one who had caused this in the first place …

"Never mind, I shouldn't bother you with it."

"No, I want to know what you mean."

"It'll only upset you."

"I think I'm already beyond upset, thanks." I tried to joke but the tears threatened to break again and I struggled to hold them back.

"Well, it looked to me that once they hit the water, she gave in. She didn't fight it. She accepted that this was it and just quickly drowned. I tried to get her out, but couldn't. I tried and tried but ..."

I looked up at Gerard and saw tears glistening in his eyes. His lip quivered and he pinched the bridge of his nose in an attempt to stop his tears. I didn't know what to say. I didn't even know how to feel. I wouldn't have wished that experience on anyone, let alone my brilliant, brave brother. I had never seen Gerard so upset before, not even at Nan's funeral, which seemed like a lifetime ago now.

"It's not your fault. You saved him. You did the best you could." I tried to offer him what little comfort I could.

"I know. This just isn't how I imagined spending my night." He laughed nervously.

We watched in silence as the paramedics brought Michael back up the hill and into the waiting ambulance. Another medic tried to help Gerard up to follow suit. He kept refusing, claiming he was fine and didn't need to go, but the paramedic wasn't having it. I told him to go with them, I needed to be sure that they were both alright.

I rode with them in the ambulance and tried to steady my racing heart, and tried to believe that everything was going to be okay.

324

35.

I watched the hands on the clock tick hour after hour as I sat in the waiting room, staring blankly at the bare wall in front of me. They had taken Gerard away, just to make sure he was okay after the ordeal. I was left alone, forced to wait while they carried out their tests.

I felt the weight of the world crushing down upon my shoulders as I tried to ignore the glares of everyone else within the waiting room. I tried to distract myself by reading the multitude of posters on the wall; reminders for cancer screenings and warnings about smoking. I read each poster word for word, without a single one registering among the cacophony of thoughts in my mind. Even the tiny TV perched in the corner of the room couldn't help me forget my worries.

The ticking of the clock continued, each second feeling more hopeless than the last. After watching the hour hand revolve a third time, I decided that I had had enough of waiting.

Ignoring the faces of the others in the room, I stood up and walked determinedly towards the door, but

I didn't get very far.

"Miss Ward?" A young doctor with unkempt hair asked, stepping in through the door to the waiting room and halting me in my tracks.

"Yes?" I responded.

"This way," he said, leaving the room without waiting for a response. I hurried after him as he walked quickly down the corridor.

Eventually, after turning several corners, he stopped outside a room and turned to face me. He waited with a look of impatience as I caught up with him.

"Your brother's inside," he said, motioning towards the open door beside us. I glanced inside and saw Gerard sitting in an armchair. "He's all right. He might feel a bit cold for a while but physically speaking, there are no problems. You may go in."

He started to walk back down the corridor. "What about Michael?" I said, stopping him before he went too far, "Where is he?"

"Michael ...?" he asked, clearly not knowing who I was referring to.

"Gallagher. We came in with him."

This didn't appear to mean much to the doctor. "I am not sure, Miss. I'll look into it." He glanced at his watch as if determining whether he had enough time to do so, before scurrying away.

I ran into the room and wrapped my arms around my brother.

"Hey!" he said, "I'm all right, I'm fine." I held onto him for as long as I could.

"You could've died," I cried into him, "I could've lost you."

"I know." He hugged me back fiercely. At least his strength was back. He let me go and rubbed away the tears from my face. "But I couldn't just sit back and do nothing. If I had, if we had just waited for the paramedics to jump in instead ..." The words hung in the air and of course, I knew he was right, but I never would have asked it of him; I never would have dared trade one for the other. Had Gerard not done what he had, had he not been so brave, Michael wouldn't have been rescued.

"I'll owe you for the rest of my life." I didn't know how I could ever begin repaying him though.

He laughed it off, hugging me tighter for a moment. "Everything's going to be okay."

In my mind, the image of the car plunging forwards off the cliff re-played over and over as if on a loop, until I wanted to tear my eyes out. I blinked persistently in a bid to remove the images; the image of Michael's face in the car window moments before he fell to his doom would surely be seared into my mind forever. I thought of his mother beside him and felt myself boiling with an impossible rage.

"His mother ..." I left the sentence hang. I already knew, I didn't need to ask.

"Yeah. I did try, like I said, but she was gone."

"Will they be able to ... get her out?" Did Michael even know yet? I yearned, more than ever, to go to him, to make sure he was okay. I didn't know if he was even awake yet. Someone would have to break the news that she was no longer here. Even in my hatred of her, even in remembering how afraid he was when he called me, I still knew how devastated he'd be. He couldn't save her - he didn't save her. I hoped he'd at least be able to say goodbye.

"Well, they'll get someone to pull the car up and retrieve her body if that's what you mean, yeah."

"So, he can say goodbye." Silence hung between us for a while as my mind whirled. I wondered what would come next; what all of this would mean and how things would change.

There was nothing we could do but wait.

***

A while later, I was finally allowed to see him. "Be careful, he's still quite weak. Also, maybe don't talk about the incident just yet until he's ready," the nurse cautioned as I stood at the door to his room. I could feel my heart hammering against my chest as if it knew that he was close by.

I nodded hastily, urging her to leave. There were six occupied beds in the room, his being furthest from

328

the door, closest to the window. I walked past the nurse and hurried towards him. My breath quickened as I reached the bed. I had to hold myself back, my emotions threatening to overtake me, as he blinked up at me with one swollen eye. A laceration on his forehead had received stitches and his left arm was wrapped in a cast.

I was frozen at the foot of the bed, suddenly unsure about getting closer; suddenly cautioning myself against my desire to wrap myself around him. I didn't want to cause him any pain in his condition.

"Sam," he croaked, his voice barely audible.

A river of tears broke free and began flowing down my face as I carefully wrapped my arms around him.

A sense of *déjà vu* trickled down my spine as he wrapped his unbroken arm around me and held me as tightly as he could. We shook against each other, crying from both relief and sadness.

I pulled back from him steadily and carefully kissed his lips. He recoiled a little in pain.

"I'm sorry," I said, jumping away from him. I didn't want to cause him anymore pain.

"It's okay ... I'm okay," he spoke in a low voice.

I sat down on the chair beside the bed, unsure of what to do or say. What did people do in these situations? I knew I shouldn't talk about what happened, not yet anyway, but what else could I have said to someone who had almost died?

"I thought I had lost you. I was so scared." It was pretty obvious to say such a thing but those were the only words flowing through my mind. I had almost lost him. The image of him lying on the ground by the shore, limp and lifeless, magnified itself in my mind until it was all I could see.

"Me too," he said with a weak, forced smile. I wondered if he knew he had died, even for that brief moment; if he'd felt himself slipping away. I still remembered how it had felt for me - the all-consuming darkness, the complete and utter nothingness. I remembered waking up in a daze, not knowing where I was and not fully understanding what had happened.

"How do you feel?"

"Not so great," he joked, "I've been better." I reached over and grabbed his hand, holding it gently and stroking his skin beneath my thumb.

"Sam." I could hear a sense of trepidation in his voice. I knew what was coming. "Where is she?"

I looked up at him and saw the tears filling his eyes. He must've already known. He must've seen her as the car plunged forwards, he must've seen her face as he struggled to free himself in the water. He already knew, really, but still, he just wanted to be told she was all right.

I wanted to tell him that more than anything. His lip began to quiver as my hesitation answered for me. "Sam ..." His voice was pleading, begging me to correct him, begging me to say everything was all right.

"I'm so sorry," I whispered as my own resurgence of tears caused my voice to break. I moved onto the bed, squeezing myself in beside him and put my arm around him.

"No ... n-n-no ..." He cried into my chest as I held him, wishing I could do something to make it better, but there was nothing I could do. There was nothing for him but this pain. I held him as his body quaked with his growing grief as he finally began to accept what had happened.

36.

With a broken arm, extremely bruised ribs and lungs from the near-drowning, Michael remained in hospital for another few days. There were so many questions I wanted to ask but I remembered the nurse's caution and held back. Right now, Michael needed to focus on his recovery.

Despite everything she had done and how much she had hurt him, I could still see the marks of grief on his face. His utter devastation broke my heart into pieces. I felt completely helpless.

Mark and Cian came over to visit a number of times. I wondered how much they knew about what had happened. They knew it was a car accident, and that his mum had died, but I wondered if they knew it wasn't technically an accident.

They joked around a lot with Michael when I was there, acting as though nothing major had just happened. Or, at least, that's how it was when I was with them. I gave them time to be alone, to allow him the opportunity to open up to them, hoping he felt free enough to do so now, but he still never really did.

"Why won't you tell them?" I asked him after they had left.

"They don't need to know."

"They're your best friends, they should know. They care about you, they can help."

"There's nothing they can do now, Sam. The last thing I want is to sully her memory. It doesn't matter how it happened - it just happened."

There was nothing I could do to sway his decision. He didn't want to talk about it.

"What's going to happen?" he asked me the day before he was discharged from hospital. We had been sitting in silence for a while, watching a show on the TV in the hospital room which I'm sure neither of us actually cared about.

"What do you mean?" I said.

"What am I going to do? Where am I going to go?" I didn't know what to say. I hadn't even paused to ask that before. Where was he going to live? He couldn't just go home and be alone in that house.

"You must have someone. A relative, someone you can stay with. An aunt, an uncle?" I realised I knew nothing about his extended family as the conversation had never come up before.

"Well, sure, of course I have relatives, but I haven't seen anyone in years. They're not a part of my life." He gazed off into the distance, as if looking into another world.

"Is there any way you could reach out to them?" He looked at me blankly and didn't answer. "Well, if your mum had sisters or brothers, there must be some way to find them, they have to know what happened, at least."

"She only had the one - Marie. She used to come around a lot when I was younger, they must've been close then, but I don't think ... I haven't seen her since Dad."

"Do you want to find her?" I asked, not really sure how to proceed. He nodded slowly after a moment which I took as an agreement.

"You know, you can always stay with us. At least for now." He laughed at the suggestion. "Or with Mark, or Cian. Maybe."

His laughter died off as he considered. "Would you actually be okay with that? That wouldn't be weird?"

Thinking about it, of course it seemed a bit weird to be offering him to move in with me but what other option was there? Besides, his arm was still in a cast, held up by a sling. I wanted to help him and to look after him for as long as I could.

"Not at all. We're family now," I said.

***

My parents were eager to help and welcomed him into the spare bedroom once he left the hospital. Even if he wasn't staying for too long, I wanted to give him some comfort and help him adjust to his new life.

"Everything's going to be all right, I promise you," I said to him repeatedly, but I don't think he ever believed me. I wondered if I would see him smile genuinely ever again.

"You were right," he said as we lay together during a stolen moment. "You were always right. I should've done something. Really done something. I could've saved her." He'd repeat those words, and I'd repeat my reassurances.

"You said it yourself - she was sick. You did what you could." Sometimes, I felt like I was lying to him. I didn't believe those words, and I hated myself for it. Part of me was still mad, at her, at him, at myself. I should've told someone, I should've made it happen even if he ended up hating me for it. I reminded myself that none of that mattered anymore. "This is not your fault."

He sighed and thanked me for my words, although I doubted he believed them.

It was another few days before we finally received the call. News of what had happened had begun to spread throughout the country. I had to turn off the radio and TV hurriedly a number of times as different stations caught up on its reports. He didn't need to hear it; the worst event of his life dictated so blandly, so matter-of-

335

factly, as if it was just something that happened every day.

His aunt eventually managed to contact Michael. She was stepping in to take over the funeral arrangements which took Michael by surprise. He had only just begun to consider making them. He was angered at first, to have someone who was practically a stranger act like they were the most important person in his mother's life, yet I was just glad there was someone there to take the pressure off him. He didn't put up a fight for long.

They chatted over the phone for half an hour or so. He said she sounded quite nice, and genuine in her offer to help. They arranged to meet in a local café the next day but as he wasn't comfortable meeting her alone, I went with him.

"I don't even know her," he said. We found a table in the back of the café and ordered some tea. I could see his eyes searching through the recesses of his memory for some recollection of her. "I can't even remember what she looks like. I think she was at Dad's funeral but that was so long ago. I don't think I've seen any family since then."

He had told me that had been the start of it all, what had first sparked his mother's decline. She had blocked everyone out, refusing to see anyone.

"All this time, she just let your mum pull away? Who does that?" I could see he was torn, but there was nothing I could do or say to make it any better, so I let him vent. "She could've made an effort to find me if Mum was so unresponsive." He stirred the spoon in his cup, contemplatively. "It's a wonder she called at all, I suppose," he said after a minute or two.

"You're family," I said matter-of-factly. It had taken me a long time to learn the true meaning of that word. "I don't know what happened between them and neither do you really, but at the end of the day, you're still family, and family comes together at times like these."

"We're practically strangers," he said, looking towards the wall and away from me.

"Well, maybe it's time to fix that?"

I was met with silence for another minute before he huffed and replied, "Don't you realise what this means?" He turned back to me with a sudden fierce look in his eyes. "Don't you know what's going to happen?"

"What do you mean?" I asked, unsure where his train of thought was leading. The cup of tea sitting on the table in front of me was starting to go cold now.

"She'll come in, claim we're family and demand that I leave with her. She'll demand to be able to ... look after me or whatever. Don't you see? That is what I've always feared, except now someone's going to take me away from *you*."

It's not as though I hadn't thought about it, of course I had. I knew he couldn't just live at my house no matter how much we wanted that. She was still his aunt, no matter what had happened between her and his mother. Surely she'd want to help him? "No one can take you away, Michael," I tried to steady my voice and remain calm. "No one can make you leave; you're eighteen now. Sure, she might suggest you live with her and maybe you should, but no one can *make* you. This is your choice." He seemed dumbfounded; his frustration suddenly knocked out of him as if he had forgotten the depth of his freedom. "I don't want to lose you and I don't want you to go away. You're the best thing that's ever happened to me … but maybe this is exactly what you need - to start a new life," I said meekly. I didn't expect him to stay for me and I would never ask that of him, even if it was my greatest desire.

"I'm not going anywhere," he said.

At that moment, the bell hanging above the café door tinkled its announcement of a new customer. A woman with striking blonde hair entered. She wore a beige duffel coat and had a thick scarf wrapped around her neck. There was no questioning who she was - she looked just like Michael's mother only younger and far healthier than she had been.

She strode over to us determinedly, clearly recognising Michael. He leant back slightly in his chair, suddenly hesitant about the meeting, but there was no turning back now.

"Michael," she said with an cheerful tone, "How

are you?" She already knew, of course, but made it a part of her customary greeting nonetheless. "It has been far too long." She seemed teary-eyed as she added, "You've grown so much."

"Time does that to a person." His old, sarcastic humour defused some of the tension in the room.

She laughed. "I guess it does." An awkward silence quickly began to build, and I wondered if it was my turn to say something.

"This is Sam," he introduced me.

"Marie." She held out her hand to shake mine. She sat down beside Michael, the tension between them now almost palpable.

After another exceedingly long silence, she finally said, "Look, I know this is really awkward, but I just have to say, Michael ..."

I glanced at him to gauge his reaction and sensed he was urging her to stop speaking. "... I am so sorry," she continued, "If I had known ... if I had had any idea what was going on ... I would've been there straight away, you have to know that. I really hope you don't hate me."

"I don't hate you," he replied, slightly surprised by his own admission.

She smiled. "I suppose you barely remember me, really. When did I last see you? Was it..." she trailed off for a moment, looking into the distance for the lost memory.

"The funeral," Michael helped her. She clasped his arm and gasped. "Dad's funeral."

"Oh no, really? Was it?" She was completely deflated by the realisation that it had been almost six years since they last met. "I am truly so sorry. Anna, she ... I knew she took it hard, of course I did. She loved Robert so, so much. What happened was devastating." As if sensing Michael's reaction, she quickly added, "Oh, of course, for you too – it was so awful." Stating the obvious seemed to be her thing. "I tried to keep in touch and help her, but she just kept pushing me away. Any time I called over, she'd pretend she wasn't there; whenever I phoned, she wouldn't pick up. It got to the point where I just couldn't reach her anymore. She locked me and everyone else out, and completely locked herself in.

"I-I had no idea ..." She raised her hand towards the wound on Michael's head. He recoiled slightly and she quickly pulled her hand back. Tears filled her eyes. "I never in a million years thought she would ever hurt you. She was such a gentle soul and such a good person ... before what happened destroyed her."

"She destroyed herself." I couldn't believe he had just said that. He had always been so careful never to blame her, insisting it was never her fault. "I was grieving too. I was just as traumatised, yet all she knew was her own pain; she couldn't see mine."

My heart broke all over again. I wanted to reach

340

out and hold him; remind him it was going to be okay. I hoped he was finally starting to believe that none of this had been his fault.

"Oh, sweetie ..." She hugged him awkwardly and I suddenly felt like I shouldn't be there.

I waited uncomfortably until their embrace ended. She took a tissue out of her handbag and dabbed her eyes with it, being careful not to smudge her make-up. "Well, as you know," she started, "The removal is tonight and the funeral is on Friday. Are you coming?"

"Of course I'm coming," Michael quickly responded, obviously insulted.

"Okay, okay - I just thought if it's too painful, if you just want to come to the funeral, that's all right. Don't push yourself."

I was steadily warming to this woman. Her warmth felt genuine and she seemed to be truly lovely. I didn't want to disrespect Anna's memory by wishing that Marie had been his mother instead, but I felt it all the same.

"I'll be there. For her," Michael agreed.

"You're welcome to come too, Samantha." She smiled at me.

"Of course. For you," I said, turning to Michael.

"Good. Now let me buy you kids some breakfast."

Epilogue

The funeral was beautiful and intimate as Michael only had a few extended family members. Marie was accompanied by her husband and their two young children. They showed Michael great kindness and understanding, offering him support throughout the day.

Michael barely knew any of the people in attendance at his mother's funeral. He pointed out the few people he *did* recognise to me, which included distant relatives from both sides of his family. Most of our teachers from school were also there to pay their respects and offer support.

Michael wondered how many of the others were here on Marie's invitation. Many of them had also likely heard about the incident on the news and had chosen to attend for neighbourly support.

We were sitting with his immediate family at the front of the church, whilst Mark and Cian were seated in the row behind. "I'm here for you, man, no matter what," Cian said, placing a hand of support on Michael's shoulder. Michael would eventually tell them what had really happened, but not now, not yet.

Michael remained silent throughout most of the ceremony which began with the priest reading the customary sermons to offer some hope and comfort. I doubted that his assurance of Anna now being with God offered Michael any comfort. Even the thought of her being re-united with Robert wouldn't ease the pain.

I held Michael's hand and tried to silently offer him comfort and support. In his other hand he held a piece of paper with all the words he needed to say. His eyes were brimming with tears.

"You don't have to do it, you know," I said, watching his worried expression as he looked at the paper in his hand. "If it's too much for you, people will understand." I paused for a moment. *"She'll* understand."

He took a deep breath, "No, I have to. I'll be fine." After a while, the priest invited him forwards and the congregation in the church steadily fell silent. As he neared the altar, I wanted to go up with him and hold onto him, to give him support. I could see his hands shaking as he unfurled the paper once again and prepared to read from it.

He sniffled and cleared his throat before beginning. "First, I just wanna say ... thank you all for coming. It would've meant a lot to Mum." He paused for another moment to steady himself. I watched as he read over what he had prepared, but then he re-folded the sheet as if to dismiss it. "But really, she died a long time ago," his words began to reverberate through the church, "I loved her so much, she knew that, everyone knew that, and no matter how bad things got, I still loved her. But the mother I had growing up, died six years ago. Dad was suddenly taken from us in an accident too soon and she couldn't deal with it. Most of her died that day, along with him, and what remained was a broken woman trying her best to survive.

"In the end, things got pretty bad, as some of you know, but I don't want to talk about that. I don't want that to be our lasting memory of her. The darkness won, it swallowed her whole, but I won't let it overshadow her memory.

"My mum was kind, loving and incredibly funny. She'd make the best dinners that would warm me right down to my core. She helped out a lot in the primary school and always had loads of cookies prepared. She was the sunlight on a stormy day and always pushed me to be my best. Her love was never-ending and her smile, well, completely infectious. She only wanted the best for me, and she tried so hard. I couldn't ..." he broke off, clearly struggling to continue. The priest began to walk over to him, but Michael waved him away. "Sorry. I just ... wanna say that ... I'm sorry. I'm so sorry, Mum. I should've ... done something to help you but I-I was too scared." His voice was beginning to break, and the tears were flowing down my cheeks in time with his. I had to

344

stop myself from running up to him. "I hope ... I hope you're with Dad now, and that you're happy again, at long last. I'm so sorry." His hand covered his mouth to stifle the cries and suddenly Marie was there beside him, with her arm wrapped around him. I watched in stunned silence as he lent into her and allowed her to help him sit back down beside me. I knew there was nothing I could do or say, so I let him cry as I held him tightly.

We watched in complete silence as her coffin was lowered into the ground. I held Michael's hand while the priest recited the same prayer over and over as part of the rosary. The few people assembled by the graveside responded by reciting the next section of the prayer, but Michael's lips didn't move.

The headstone already in place at the top of the plot had the name of Michael's father, Robert Gallagher, inscribed in the marble. His coffin was just about visible, six feet further down and for an achingly long minute, they lowered Anna's coffin on top. Marie started to hand out flowers to the bystanders, after firstly placing one solemnly in Michael's hand, holding it for a moment longer in silent support.

They let him go first. He let go of my hand to step towards the grave, and stood almost too close to the edge. The wind pushed against him and I suddenly worried he'd fall in. He murmured something before raising his arm, allowing the flower to float down and land on her coffin.

Sometimes the tragedy isn't the greatest heartache; rather, it's learning how to adjust to life afterwards when your life is suddenly turned upside down until you barely recognise it anymore. Michael would mourn her forever, that much was unquestionable, but I hoped, at least, that someday he would be able to forgive himself and forgive her too.

***

He decided he would live with his aunt for now. It would be best, all things considered. It had been a bit strange being in the same house together all the time, but I still wanted him to stay. I wanted to look after him and make him happy, but he longed to get away from it all - from the town and the memories. Marie offered him a fresh start. Plus, she lived a lot closer to Cork City, just on the outskirts in fact, which would make going to college a lot easier.

Michael was accepted to study music at University College Cork, which was no surprise. He talked about it as though it didn't matter, that it was just the next step, but I could tell that he was overjoyed to be going there.

A couple of weeks after the funeral, as life returned to normal, a letter arrived through the door. Mum came into my room early in the morning to wake me up. It was rare that a letter arrived with my name on it, so there was no question as to what the envelope contained. I weighed it steadily in my hand, wary of its contents. I didn't want to read it.

"Open it!" Mum encouraged, clapping her hands together.

I took a deep breath, certain that I didn't even need to open it. I could almost feel the rejection emanating out of it. I opened the folded piece of paper slowly as Mum waited impatiently.

The Crawford logo on the header of the page left no remaining doubt. This was it, the moment of truth.

My eyes scanned down the page, looking for that one word, "regret", but I couldn't find it. Scarcely allowing myself to believe it, I read back over the page, slower this time.

"Dear Ms. Ward," the letter began. Beneath my name, as if some sort of mirage, was the word, "Congratulations!

"Thank you for your interest in Crawford College of Art and Design. The examining board has awarded your portfolio of work with 540/600 points. Official offers will be posted after Leaving Certificate results are announced.

"Thank you again for considering Crawford.

"We look forward to welcoming you!"

I read it three times over, as Mum grew more and more impatient. Tears began to well up in my eyes. I looked up at her, unable to speak.

Looking downhearted, she said, "What's it say?"

Without a word, I handed her the letter.

She let out a sound of excitement as she read it, clapping her left hand to her face. "You got in! You did it!" She pulled me up from the bed, wrapping her arms around me. "I am so, so proud of you, honey!"

It took another while for the news to really sink in. I was going to Crawford. It was happening.

***

Dad said I inspired him: *It takes great courage to ask for help, and sometimes ... even more to accept it.* He kept telling me how brave I was and said he wanted to be brave, too. "I'm tired of being scared," he told me, "I want to just enjoy life again." I tried my best to let him know that I was proud of him too. He started having professional therapy and, for a while, he cried even more than usual. Then he joined a therapy group for veterans and made some new friends. I couldn't have been happier for him.

I continued to see Dr. Murphy for another year and took my medication on a strict schedule. I told her everything about what had happened; how I had watched as Michael plummeted off the cliff that night. I shared my terror and hopelessness, which seemed to linger for weeks thereafter, and I shared my anger before it could consume me. I was angry at her, angry at him

348

and angry at myself. Dr. Murphy never once asked me to try to ignore that anger or rationalise it. Rather, she helped me learn how to accept it - to accept everything - that I was feeling, "Acknowledge it, accept it, only then can you move on." I laid myself bare until nothing remained anymore. I felt free.

The demons would still sometimes darken my door, continuing to tempt and tease me. The memory of the blade across my skin haunted me every day and I still sometimes craved its touch - that sense of relief and distraction. However, I didn't need that anymore. I didn't need to escape, I didn't need my fantastical worlds in childhood drawings, and I didn't need to sing songs with Mary Poppins anymore.

Michael started seeing his own psychologist, finally releasing all those pent-up feelings he had kept stored within himself. He'd tell me how freeing it felt to let it all out now that no severe consequence was possible, but he still wanted to protect his mother and still refused to call her abusive. "That makes her sound like a monster," he said. He hated how his psychologist kept using that word. "A monster is something without feeling, without control. She was sick, she couldn't help it, not really."

"Michael ..."

"... I know," he said, leaving the thought to hang in the air. She could've helped it, he knew that well, but instead, the monster inside had killed her. Sometimes, the demons win.

Time continued on, the world continued to revolve and the sun set and rose each day, but everything had changed. We promised each other that no matter what, we would be there for one another and that no secret would lie between us. We would stand strong and proud together and fight our demons, hand in hand.

Acknowledgements

I can't believe I get to write an acknowledgments section for my debut novel. It still doesn't feel quite real (will it ever?!)

I wrote the first (terrible) version of this story when I was fifteen. Back then, it was largely therapeutic. I believed in it then, too, but it became too difficult when trying to recover from depression and self-harm and then I ultimately lost faith in it.

It returned to me years later, completely changed with blistering hindsight and I knew in my core that I had to write it, as scary as it was to put my every troubled thought on the page.

I have so many people to thank. First and foremost, the man to whom I've dedicated this book, Ross Lane. I thank you from the bottom of my heart for your unending support – both in writing and in life. The demons still visit me sometimes, but you're always there to help me fight them off. All the times I thought this book wasn't any good, or no one would care to read it, you encouraged me to push through my doubt and instilled in me a new kind of confidence.

And all those times you made me sit down and *get to work*; thanks for that, too! In case it wasn't obvious, I love you.

Next, a huge thank you to my parents. I hope reading this wasn't too difficult. I hope you know that I love you so much. You have always been unconditionally supportive of me and my ambitions. When I was a kid, I started practicing typing by copying a book and that is my earliest memory of being encouraged to write my own stories, by Dad. You both supported me so much when I was younger, and ever since. Thank you!

To Heather, for being the one to finally step in way back when and put me on my journey of recovery. I am eternally grateful for you.

To Ben, for all the nights spent shooting zombies, for keeping me company at my loneliest, for just being the best.

To Jake, who doesn't even read books, but maybe this one? Thanks for being there, goofball.

A big, major thank you to my friends and beta readers who were truly instrumental in the formation of this book; Ross (again), Brian O'Sullivan, Ciaran Hyland, Róisín O'Mahoney and Catherine Friend. Your feedback, suggestions and encouragement really helped make this novel possible. Thank you!

An extra shout out to Brian and the wonderful Rosie Allott for your amazing friendship and support.

For being there to discuss ideas with me, or to just cheer me on, and for showing me what real friends are; thank you.

Thank you, of course, to everyone at Cranthorpe Millner! You made this happen. To Kirsty for believing in this story and giving it a chance, thank you.

To my editors, Rhiannon and Michelle for your immense knowledge and keen eyes, thank you, thank you, thank you! You spotted so many issues I completely missed. Your guidance and suggestions truly helped to make this book something that I could really be proud of.

To Sian for always being there to answer my questions, no matter how silly. It meant a lot to this rookie author to have someone they could go to.

To Shannon and the marketing team at Cranthorpe Millner, thank you for your advice and guidance and your boundless efforts in making this book a success.

Many thanks to [] for the stunning cover! I practically cried the first time I saw it; it could not have been more perfect. Thank you for leading your talent to my novel.

I also want to thank some people who may never read this book; John Green and Stephen Chbosky. As I said before, I almost gave up on this story and I honestly would not have returned to it without your

353

work and its influence upon me. I can only hope to see my book on a shelf alongside one of yours someday. Thank you.

Last, but not least, thanks to you, reader, for picking up this book and reading to the very last page. Thanks for giving this little story a chance, for giving me a chance. It means more than you will ever know.

If you enjoyed this book, please share it with your friends, if you feel moved to do so. It is my greatest dream that this novel makes an impact and gets people talking about mental health. If it makes a difference in even just one person's life, then mission accomplished!

Thank you for reading!
And remember …
Don't let the demons win.

If you need help, please reach out:

<u>Ireland</u>

SAMARITANS

24/7 listening service for anyone in distress.
Helpline: <u>116 123</u>
<u>www.samaritans.org</u>

PIETA HOUSE

Provides free counselling to those with suicidal
ideation, those engaging in self-harm, and those
bereaved by suicide.
Helpline: <u>1800</u> 247 247
Text: 51444
Web: <u>www.pieta.ie</u>

CHILDLINE

24/7 helpline for children and young people in distress.
Helpline: <u>1800 66 66 66</u>

Text: 50101
www.childline.ie

AWARE

Provides information and support around depression
and anxiety.
Helpline: <u>1800</u> 80 48 48 (10am – 10pm)
Web: www.aware.ie

SPUN OUT

Promoting general healthy living and wellbeing in Irish
youth.
Helpline: <u>01 6753554</u> (10am – 6pm)
Text: 50808 or 0861800280
Web: www.spunout.ie

GROW

GROW helps people who have suffered, or are
suffering, from mental health problems & has a
national network of over 120 weekly peer support
groups.

Helpline: <u>1890 474 474</u>
Web: <u>www.grow.ie</u>

JIGSAW

Jigsaw Ireland is designed to ensure every person
between 16 and 25 has someone to talk to.
Webchat: <u>www.jigsaw.ie/</u>

<u>UK</u>

SAMARITANS

24/7 listening service for anyone in distress.
Helpline: <u>116 123</u>
Web: <u>www.samaritans.org</u>

NATIONAL SUICIDE PREVENTION HELPLINE UK

Offers a supportive listening service to anyone with
thoughts of suicide
Helpline: <u>0800 689 5652</u> (24/7)

CAMPAIGN AGAINST LIVING MISERABLY (CALM)

A listening service for anyone who's struggling and needs someone to talk to
Helpline: 0800 58 58 58 (5pm-midnight)
Webchat: https://www.thecalmzone.net/help/webchat/

THE MIX

Support service for those under 25
Helpline: 0808 808 4994 (3pm-midnight)
Web: https://www.themix.org.uk/

PAPYRUS HOPELINEUK

For those under 35 who're struggling with suicidal feelings, or concerned about a young person who might be struggling
Helpline: 0800 068 4141 (10am-10pm weekdays, 2pm-10pm weekends)
Text: 07786 209 697
Web: https://www.papyrus-uk.org/